AN EYE
FOR AN EYE

**Center Point
Large Print**

Also by Irene Hannon
and available from Center Point Large Print

Against All Odds

**This Large Print Book carries the
Seal of Approval of N.A.V.H.**

2 HEROES OF QUANTICO

AN EYE
FOR AN EYE

IRENE HANNON

CENTER POINT PUBLISHING
THORNDIKE, MAINE

This Center Point Large Print edition
is published in the year 2009 by arrangement with
Revell, a division of Baker Publishing Group.

The text of this Large Print edition is unabridged.
In other aspects, this book may vary
from the original edition.
Printed in the United States of America.
Set in 16-point Times New Roman type.

ISBN: 978-1-60285-617-2

Library of Congress Cataloging-in-Publication Data

Hannon, Irene.
  An eye for an eye / Irene Hannon.
    p. cm.
  ISBN 978-1-60285-617-2 (library binding : alk. paper)
  1. United States. Federal Bureau of Investigation--Officials and employees--Fiction.
  2. Large type books. I. Title.

PS3558.A4793E94 2009b
813'.54--dc22

2009027267

To my father, James Hannon,
who always wanted me to write a mystery.

I hope suspense counts, Dad . . .
Because this series is for you!

His quarry was late.

Very late.

Shading his eyes, the man scanned the deserted jogging path and shifted the rifle cradled in his arms. He couldn't linger much longer without risking detection. In the past couple of hours he'd already seen a few too many runners and dog walkers, despite the oppressive August heat. But no one had yet ventured anywhere near his concealed position in the woods at the edge of the park.

After studying his quarry's habits, he'd chosen the time and place with care. And he'd walked through the exercise dozens of times in his mind. Park behind the First Congregational Church, unoccupied on this sultry St. Louis Saturday. Leave the car at the far end of the isolated parking lot, next to the woods that separated church property from the park. Cut through the dense thicket. Wait for his target. Take his shot. Return to the car, slide the rifle back inside the weed-eater box on the back seat. Drive home. Dispose of the gun.

He stroked the sleek steel barrel, the taste of regret sharp on his tongue. He hated the thought of destroying his favorite hunting rifle. But hanging on to it once this job was finished would be too dangerous. His only consolation was that it would end its life doing God's work.

Shifting his position, he lifted his arm and wiped the sweat from his forehead with the sleeve of his dark green shirt. Then he turned to scan the empty church parking lot barely visible through the shrubby undergrowth beneath the trees. He hadn't sought out a house of God as his staging area, but it was fitting. For he was here to follow a directive from the Good Book. To claim an eye for an eye.

And if his quarry didn't show today . . . he'd find another time to carry out his mission.

Ten minutes later, as he was about to scrap his plans and head back to his car, his patience was rewarded. A surge of adrenaline shot through him as his target appeared in the distance. He wiped his damp palms on his slacks. Closed his eyes.

Jesus, guide my aim as I do your work.

Exchanging his cotton gloves for a pair in snug-fitting latex, he lifted the rifle. Fitted the stock against his shoulder. Pinned the figure in his crosshairs.

And waited.

There was no need to rush. He could do the job at 150 yards, but why not wait until a hundred? The closer the target, the better the odds he could finish this in one shot.

Either way, in three minutes, max, the score would be settled. Justice would be done.

Timing and patience were everything—whether hunting animals or people.

• • •

Warmth rose in shimmering waves from the asphalt jogging path, the humidity already stifling at eight o'clock in the morning. A trickle of sweat headed south between Mark Sanders's shoulder blades, while another tracked down his temple. Without breaking rhythm or slowing his pace, he tilted his head and lifted his arm to wipe the sleeve of his T-shirt across his forehead. The heat was bad, but he'd endured far hotter conditions. A sweltering St. Louis August was no worse than Afghanistan or Iraq or Colombia. And it was far safer.

Safety, however, was a relative term. And he never took it for granted.

Scrutinizing the terrain as he ran, he remained alert for anything out of the ordinary. That drill—an on-the-job necessity—had become a habit in his personal life as well. But the peaceful suburban park gave him little cause for concern. The place was deserted, the typical Saturday crowd sleeping in, lingering over a second cup of coffee or hibernating in air-conditioning.

Forty-five minutes ago, as he'd downed a quick glass of juice, Mark had been tempted to follow their lead. Now he was glad he hadn't. Despite the heat, it felt good to run. To be *able* to run. Three months ago, when the bullet had ripped through his leg, he hadn't been sure he'd ever use his jogging shoes again. But thanks to a great surgeon and intensive rehab, he was well on the road to a full recovery. And his short-term assignment to the understaffed St. Louis office, which had liberated him from the torture of temporary desk duty, had been a godsend. In another month, he should be physically ready to rejoin his team in Quantico.

As for mental readiness—that was another question.

Images from the final, fateful moments in the quick shop invaded his consciousness with the ruthless tenacity of an insidious cancer, twisting his gut into a tight, painful knot. As the familiar bleakness settled over him, Mark knew he had to find a way to stop rehashing a past he couldn't change. To stop second-guessing himself, wondering if there was anything he could have done to prevent the tragedy. The testimony of his partner and witnesses had confirmed he'd followed protocol. The security video had backed that up. Despite the media scrutiny and public outcry, the review board had cleared him of wrongdoing.

Yet nothing changed the bottom line.

He bore full responsibility for the death of an innocent teen.

The bullet had come from his gun.

As a result, for the first time in his twelve years with the FBI, he felt like one of the bad guys instead of one of the good guys.

Until he got past that, Mark knew he couldn't

10

rejoin the Hostage Rescue Team. He respected his colleagues too much to put them at risk. They were among the most highly trained and best-equipped tactical personnel in the world, and they didn't need an operator in their midst whose confidence was anything less than rock solid. The life-and-death situations they dealt with required instant decisions, and Mark wasn't certain he could deliver on that. Not yet, anyway. And neither was the counselor he'd been required to talk with after the shooting.

In the interim, he'd figured the job in St. Louis would be quiet enough—relative to his usual duties—to give him a chance to regain his perspective. He'd been here six weeks; he had four to go. By then, he should be ready to go back to Quantico. Physically and mentally.

At least he hoped so.

At the moment, however, he needed a distraction from his unsettling thoughts. And the attractive woman who'd appeared in the distance provided one as she strode toward him.

Mark slowed a bit, forcibly compartmentalizing his morose musings as he enjoyed the smooth, easy grace of her stride, the long length of leg showing beneath her hot pink running shorts, the wide expanse of golden skin displayed above her white tank top. Despite the heat, she was walking at a good clip, her blonde hair pulled back into a ponytail, a becoming flush on her cheeks.

Not a bad view for a Saturday morning.

He tried to tame the appreciative grin that tugged at his lips, glad his reflective sunglasses hid his eyes. If he wasn't careful, she'd catch him ogling her.

As the distance separating them narrowed, Mark shifted his attention to her face. And reduced his speed again. She looked familiar. He was sure he'd seen her before. But where?

And then it registered.

Emily Lawson.

Two decades had elapsed since their parting, but he'd studied enough age-enhanced images to get a feel for how people looked after the passage of years. And in truth, her appearance wasn't that much different, once you got past the cosmetic changes. Her once-long hair had been cropped to shoulder length, and her angular adolescent build had softened into an appealing womanliness, but her features were the same. Stunning green eyes, classic high cheekbones, firm chin, and supple, expressive lips.

His gaze lingered on her lips.

A guy didn't forget his first kiss.

He stopped as she prepared to pass him, his restrained grin broadening into a smile.

"Excuse me, ma'am, but I believe we've met. Emily Lawson, right?"

The woman's step faltered as she shot him a startled glance. Easing away from him, she rubbed her palms on her shorts. "I'm sorry, but I don't think I know you."

If Mark had had any doubts about the woman's identity, they vanished as soon as she spoke. Her distinctive voice, rich and smooth as warm honey, hadn't changed one iota.

His smile still in place, Mark removed his sunglasses. "I suppose time hasn't been as kind to me as it has been to you. You've hardly changed in twenty years. But I could never forget the first girl I kissed."

Emily's mouth dropped open. "Mark Sanders?"

"Guilty."

"I don't believe this!" Her posture relaxed, and her lips tipped up into a delighted smile as she propped her hands on her hips. "What in the world are you doing here?"

Frowning in irritation, the man lowered the rifle a few inches and surveyed the scene. Intent on keeping his quarry in his crosshairs, he hadn't noticed the second person approaching. Now the two of them were engaged in an animated conversation.

At least no one else was in this section of the park yet, he confirmed with a quick scan. He'd prefer to do this with no witnesses, but it didn't much matter if his target had a companion. He'd be long gone before the police arrived.

Hurting an innocent person, however, wouldn't be right. He needed to wait for a clean line of sight.

A slight shift in their positions was all it would take, and that could happen at any moment.

Fitting the stock snug against his shoulder, he once more aligned his quarry in his scope.

"I'm on temporary assignment in St. Louis." Mark folded his arms across his chest and smiled as he answered Emily's question. "I'll be here for another four weeks."

"Where's home?"

"My mailing address is Quantico, Virginia. But I don't spend much time there."

"Quantico." She tilted her head and gave him a speculative look. "Let me guess. FBI."

He arched an eyebrow. "Not bad."

"Deductive reasoning." Grinning, she ticked off the clues on her fingers. "A, you were very interested in law in high school, and law enforcement is a practical application of that. B, you always liked to be in the middle of the action. C, Quantico's claim to fame is FBI headquarters. And D . . . you always were one of the good guys."

At her last comment, his smile seemed to dim a few watts, she noted. Curious.

"I appreciate the vote of confidence. What about you? How did you end up in St. Louis? And what are you doing these days?"

"I got my PhD here, and since I liked the city, I stayed and opened a practice. I'm a clinical psychologist."

"I seem to recall that even as a teenager you enjoyed trying to figure out what made people tick." His tone was teasing, but his expression told her he was impressed. "I suppose I'd better be careful what I say. I wouldn't want to reveal any classified information."

She gave him a skeptical look. "I have a feeling my interrogation skills would pale in comparison to your ability to deflect questions. There's probably a whole course in verbal judo for FBI agents."

He chuckled. "Why don't we put that to the test? I don't know about you, but I've had it with the heat. How about sharing a cold drink somewhere and catching up?"

Emily regarded the man beside her, intrigued by the invitation. And tempted. The lanky seventeen-year-old she remembered had matured into a virile man with a powerful presence. At six-foot plus, he was an imposing figure, with long, muscular legs, broad shoulders, calendar-quality abs and pecs, and biceps to die for. The subtle character lines in his face were new, as were the subtle glints of silver in the dark brown hair at his temples. But the tiny dimple in his cheek when he grinned, the strong jawline, the ever-so-slight crook in his nose—all of those nuances were the same. As were the deep-brown eyes and that quirk in his lips when he smiled. Sweet memories of their long-ago summertime romance in Tennessee stirred, tugging at her heart.

No doubt about it. Her quiet Saturday had just gotten a whole lot more interesting.

"I could be persuaded. I've been fantasizing about a double chocolate chip frappuccino for the past few minutes. But I can't go anywhere like this." She looked down at her limp attire. "I need to be hosed down first. Or better yet, take a cold shower."

"I could use a cold shower myself." His lips lifted into a lazy smile as he gave her a slow, appreciative perusal.

Emily felt the flush on her cheeks deepen. "Mark Sanders! Are you flirting with me?"

"I plead the fifth. But just to cover my back, is there a husband I should be concerned about?" His gaze flicked to her ringless left hand.

Her smile faded, and with it her lighthearted mood. "Not anymore. I lost him five years ago, less than six months after we were married. Grant was a firefighter. He died in the line of duty."

He let out a slow breath. "I'm sorry."

"So am I. He was a good man." She swallowed and summoned up her smile again. "How about you, Mark? Do you have a wife back in Quantico?"

"No. My career hasn't been conducive to long-term relationships."

"Just short-term ones, hmm?" She switched back to banter mode, hoping that would help ease the ache in her heart that memories of Grant always stirred up.

"I think I'm going to employ those verbal judo techniques you mentioned. How about we settle on a time for that cold drink?"

"Evading my question, huh?"

With a chuckle, he lifted his arm to check his watch. "No comment."

As he angled away from her to shade the face of his timepiece from the sun, a persistent yellow jacket buzzed her. Sidestepping it, she flapped her hand to shoo it away.

"The bees are bad this summer—"

The distinctive crack of a rifle shot shattered the early morning stillness, cutting her off in midsentence.

The next thing she knew, Mark lunged at her, taking her to the ground with a powerful thrust.

As her body slammed against the unforgiving pavement, the bizarre reality slammed into her with equal force.

Someone was shooting at them.

His adrenaline surging, Mark shielded Emily with his body as he scanned the area. They needed cover.

Fast.

A stone bench stood a few yards away. In the other direction, a grouping of boulders behind a flower garden offered more protection. Neither option was optimal. But they were the only barriers available to put between them and the shooter.

Without loosening his grip on Emily, Mark half rolled, half dragged them behind the bench as another shot rang out. He felt the vapor bulge of the bullet—a lethal whisper against his cheek that was far too close for comfort—before it chipped the concrete corner of the seat, shattering it into rough shards.

Hoping the backless bench wasn't anchored to the ground, he wrapped his fingers around the top edge and pushed.

Nothing.

Exerting as much force as possible, he tried again, his muscles straining. To his relief, the bench tipped. He kept a tight grip as it fell to ensure it didn't turn upside down and leave them exposed. A metallic reflection in the wooded area at the perimeter of the park caught his attention an instant before the bench blocked his view.

"Curl up and stay down, Emily."

He barked out the order as he edged her in tight behind the concrete barricade and tucked himself beside her.

He took another look at the boulders, which would offer more substantial cover, calculating his chances of getting them both there alive.

Not good, he concluded.

The shooter's aim was too accurate.

Unarmed, he had no defense except to lay low and hope help arrived before the sniper found a position that would give him a cleaner line of sight.

On the positive side, he had his phone. And the stand of trees on the far side of the adjacent baseball field, where he pegged the shooter to be hiding, gave way to more open ground on each side—backyards of homes in the residential neighborhood bordering that side of the park. The man's mobility was limited if he wanted to remain hidden.

It wasn't much of an advantage, but he'd take it.

Pulling out his BlackBerry, he jabbed in 911. As soon as the dispatcher answered, he gave her a rapid-fire download.

"This is Special Agent Mark Sanders with the FBI. I'm in Hardin Park in Oakdale, and I have an active shooter on the east perimeter in the woods. I'm not armed. I've taken cover behind an overturned bench, but I need backup as fast as you can get it here."

"Is the shooter still firing?"

"Nothing since the first two shots."

"Any casualties?"

In his automatic response to the gunshot, Mark had taken Emily down hard. On some instinctive level he'd tried to absorb the brunt of the fall, but he didn't think he'd succeeded. Pressed close against her, he could feel her shuddering, and her breath was coming in shallow gasps. "My friend may need some assistance. Hang on."

Taking one more sweeping survey of his surroundings, he shifted and spoke in her ear.

"Emily, are you okay?"

No response.

"Emily?"

Silence.

Scanning the deserted park and woods once more, Mark eased back as much as he dared. If the shooter was still out there, he would be waiting for an opportunity to take another shot. But in light of the approaching police sirens, Mark's gut told him the man had already disappeared.

And he was certain it was a man. Most shooters of this type were.

Emily was curled into a ball on the asphalt, facing him. Her hair had come out of its elastic band to spill across her face, and with gentle fingers he brushed it aside. Her dazed eyes were open, and there was an abrasion on her cheek—a souvenir of her slide across the rough asphalt. But it was her pallor that alarmed him.

She blinked once, twice, and reached out a shaky hand toward his shirt.

"Blood." The word came out in a weak whisper.

He looked down. She was right. The large, red stain on his gray T-shirt was blood.

But it wasn't his.

His alarm escalating, Mark eased back another couple of inches and gave her a swift, comprehensive scan. She had a skinned knee, but that wouldn't account for the blood on his shirt.

Setting the BlackBerry on the ground, he rolled

her toward him to check behind her—and found the source of the blood.

As his breath hissed out between his teeth, he grabbed the phone.

"We do have a casualty. The woman I'm with has been hit."

2

Nothing in Mark's years of training and field experience prepared him for the panic that kicked in as he watched Emily bleed. He'd been in plenty of situations where people got hurt. He'd learned to steel himself against blood and terror. But he wasn't used to feeling helpless. And he wasn't used to having someone he cared about—or had once cared about—in the line of fire.

Punching the speaker button, he laid his BlackBerry beside him again and eased Emily onto her back, keeping his head low.

"How bad is it?" The dispatcher's clipped voice came over the line.

He assessed the wound. It was on her left arm, halfway between her shoulder and elbow. The flow of blood was heavy and steady. Not good, but better than spurting from an artery.

"The bullet went all the way through her arm. I think it nicked a major vein." He needed to stem the flow of blood. She was losing too much too fast, and they weren't going anywhere for the next few minutes.

"I'll alert the EMTs. You should be seeing some activity at the perimeter momentarily. There was a patrol car three minutes away."

He took a quick look around as he stripped off his T-shirt, noting the flashing lights on the road bordering the park in the distance.

"I see the car. I also need you to contact Steve Preston at the St. Louis field office ASAP." He recited Steve's phone number.

"I copy that."

Working in the restricted area behind the bench, Mark folded his T-shirt into a long strip and wrapped it around Emily's arm, exerting as much steady pressure on the wound as his prone position allowed. It wasn't his first choice for a dressing, but it was all he had.

When Emily drew a ragged breath, he touched her cheek. The gesture was meant to comfort her, but instead it elevated his alarm. Her skin was cool and clammy. Her eyes, though open, were starting to glaze. And her breathing was becoming shallower. Classic signs of shock. She needed more help than he could provide.

"Hang in there, Em, okay?" He tucked her hair behind her ear, maintaining the pressure he was exerting on the wound with his other hand.

"W-what happened?"

"Someone decided to use us for target practice."

"Are you hurt?"

She's bleeding to death and she wants to know if I'm hurt.

He had to swallow past the lump in his throat before he could speak. "No."

"Good. I wouldn't want to miss that cold drink with you."

Her voice was fading.

"I have Officer Fisher from Oakdale on the line, Agent Sanders. He was first on the scene. I'm going to patch him in." There were a few clicks as the dispatcher connected the call. "Go ahead, Officer Fisher."

"Agent Sanders, I'm on the south side of the park, and I have you in sight. We're securing the perimeter, focusing on the wooded area on the east end where you pinpointed the shooter. Have there been any additional shots?"

"No. I suspect he's long gone. And I need medical assistance. Now!"

"Understood. We're preparing to send in two paramedics. In the meantime, we're sweeping the perimeter of the woods, and a chopper is on the way to do a thermal scan."

As the man spoke, Mark heard the thlump-thlump-thlump of rotors in the distance. The rapid response meant the helicopter must have been close by on a training mission or doing aerial photography. One lucky break, at least.

But they could use a few more. Emily's blood

had soaked through his shirt, and the flow wasn't showing any signs of abating. Mark's gut clenched, and he drew a shaky breath. For a brief instant he considered praying. He was that desperate. But in his twelve years with the FBI, he'd seen too much. Somewhere in the blood and gore and man's inhumanity to man, he'd lost touch with the loving, compassionate God of his youth. Yet he'd never needed divine intervention more than at this moment.

As the seconds crept by with agonizing slowness, Mark was tempted to ignore the lay-low advice he would give to anyone else in his situation, pick up Emily, and run toward the flashing lights in the distance. But he'd been too well trained to take that chance. If the shooter was still in the woods, a rash action like that could be a death sentence for both of them. He had to follow protocol, no matter what his heart was telling him to do.

"Mark?"

Emily's voice was growing weaker as she began to drift in and out of consciousness. When he touched her cheek, her eyelids flickered open, and she turned her head toward him. He was close enough to see the gold flecks in her green eyes. Close enough to feel her breath on his lips. Close enough for memories of their brief summertime romance to flow back. And to make him wonder why they'd ever lost touch.

"I'm here, Em." He hated being powerless. He was trained to take charge of situations like this, to be in control, to solve problems. The role of victim didn't suit him. A slow anger began to build inside him. He would find whoever did this and—

"Remember Wren Lake?"

Emily's unexpected comment jolted him. During her six-week visit to her grandmother's house two decades ago in his Tennessee hometown, Wren Lake had been "their" place. A quiet spot for swimming, picnicking—and kissing. They'd done quite a bit of the latter during the summer of his seventeenth year. Enough to give them both a first, tentative taste of physical intimacy. Mark hadn't thought about Wren Lake in years, but the memory was sweet now that she'd reminded him.

"Of course."

"Everyone should have a Wren Lake," she whispered.

She was drifting now. Her eyelids fluttered closed, and she let out a long breath. Fear gripped him, and he pressed his fingers against the carotid artery in her neck. A steady pulse tapped out a rhythm against his skin, but it wasn't as strong as he'd like.

"Agent Sanders, we're coming in."

A quick look confirmed that help was on the way, and a surge of relief shuddered through him. A police car was moving across the grass toward them, protective vests jury-rigged over the far windows. It stopped a few feet away, providing additional cover between the bench and the woods. Two EMTs exited, crouched low, and ran toward Mark and Emily. Two officers with automatic rifles took up positions behind each end of the car, their weapons trained on the woods.

The EMTs dropped down to flank Mark as he rose to a kneeling position. While one of them wrapped a blood pressure cuff around Emily's good arm, the other snapped on a pair of latex gloves and reached toward the bloody T-shirt.

"I can take over now."

Mark eased his hand off the makeshift dressing as the EMT slid his in.

"I think the bullet hit a vein. She's been bleeding steadily for seven or eight minutes," Mark told him.

"Pressure's low. She's shocky." As the other technician spoke, he prepared to start an IV line, sparing Emily's injured arm a quick look as he addressed his partner. "You'll need a pressure bandage on that."

For several minutes Mark watched them work—until he felt a hand on his shoulder.

"The thermal scan indicated the woods are clear."

Turning, Mark wasn't surprised to find that Steve had already arrived. The lean, mid-fortyish agent might have a few flecks of silver in his dark hair, but he showed no signs of slowing down. As supervisor of the reactive squad, he was known for his rapid-response mentality—and he expected no less from the agents who reported to him.

"You got here fast." Mark gave Emily one more look and stood.

"I was at a meeting in Clayton." He inclined his head toward Emily. "I understand she's a friend?"

"Yeah." Mark took a deep breath. "I haven't seen her in twenty years. Not exactly the way I would have planned a reunion."

More EMTs arrived, with a gurney in tow. Steve and Mark stepped aside to give them room to work.

"You need to get that taken care of." Steve nodded to Mark's forearm.

Frowning, Mark examined the expanse of skin that had been scraped raw from his slide on the asphalt. "Later."

"Now." Steve caught the attention of one of the EMTs standing by the gurney. "We'll talk while he works on you."

It wasn't worth arguing about, Mark decided. He turned his attention to his St. Louis boss as the EMT began treating his arm. "I take it the shooter got away?"

"For now. The chopper's going to hang around and do some aerial shots, though. The ERT and the county CSI unit are on the way. We'll sort things out when they get here."

It didn't surprise Mark that Steve had called in

the FBI's Evidence Response Team. The St. Louis County Crime Scene Investigation unit was good, but when one of their own was involved, Steve would want to use FBI resources. Once everything was "sorted out," Mark suspected the ERT would take over the crime scene.

"Is the perimeter secure?"

"The tape and barricades were being put up as I arrived."

Mark winced as the EMT cleaned a particularly sensitive area.

"Sorry. You've got a lot of dirt in there," the man apologized.

"It's okay." He'd endured far worse. And he'd learned how to distance himself from physical pain.

"I called the Bureau and talked to your boss in Quantico. He wants to set up a conference call as soon as possible. And we need you to debrief the team. We're going to have to decide how to coordinate this with local law enforcement."

In general, a shooting like this would be handled by the local cops. When a federal officer was involved, however, the FBI would play an integral role in the investigation. Mark assumed they'd consider it a joint investigation with the Oakdale PD, at least until they got a better handle on the target and motive. In the meantime, his high-profile position and recent media exposure would mean serious involvement from the higher-ups back East.

As the EMT working on Mark's arm taped a final strip of gauze in place, Mark's roommate joined them. He tossed a T-shirt at Mark and shook his head. "And you thought St. Louis would be quieter than Quantico."

Mark pulled the shirt over his head and scowled at Special Agent Nick Bradley. With his startling blue eyes, sandy hair, and lean, athletic build, he was the epitome of the all-American boy—and he'd taken plenty of ribbing for that at the academy, where he and Mark had been in the same new agent training class. When Nick had offered him a spare bedroom in his house for the duration of his St. Louis assignment, Mark had accepted without hesitation.

"They're setting up a command center over there." Steve indicated a cordoned-off area surrounded by emergency vehicles, shielded as much as possible from the media trucks already converging on the scene. "Let's head over and get Quantico on the phone."

"Give me a minute."

Without waiting for a response, Mark turned toward Emily. The EMTs had put her on the gurney and were preparing to transport.

"How is she?" He addressed his question to the closest technician.

"The bleeding's under control and she's stable. But she lost a lot of blood." The man took a look at Mark's hands, withdrew a pack of sterile wipes from his kit, and held it out. "Some of it's on you."

For the first time, Mark noticed the burgundy stains on his skin. He took the pack and ripped it open, cleaning up as best he could. But it would take a thorough washing to remove the traces of Emily's blood from his hands. And he had no idea how to wash away the taste of fear that lingered in his mouth.

"Is she conscious?"

"Barely."

"Can I have thirty seconds?"

"No more."

Moving beside her, Mark took her hand. She remained pale as death, and her tank top, pristine white half an hour ago, was soaked with blood on one side. Leaning close, he brushed the hair back from her forehead and spoke softly.

"Em?"

Her lashes fluttered, and she struggled to focus. "Mark?"

"Yeah. The EMTs are going to take you to the hospital now. I'll come by and see you later."

"Give me a . . . rain check on that frappuccino, okay?" She tried to smile.

"You got it."

The EMTs moved into place, and after an encouraging squeeze, Mark released her hand.

"You ready to try and find this guy?" Nick moved beside him as they watched Emily being wheeled away.

"Oh yeah." Mark's mouth settled into a grim line. "More than ready."

The command center was teeming with activity when Mark and Nick ducked under the yellow police tape. Steve was already putting through the call to Quantico, and he placed his hand over the mouthpiece. "Go ahead and pick up the other line, Mark. We're both patched in."

Mark took the phone from the communications specialist. A few seconds later, Les Coplin's familiar, gruff voice came over the line. A one-time green beret and former HRT operator, he'd headed the Hostage Rescue Team for the past three years. His stocky build, close-cropped gray hair, and square jaw—plus his tenacious determination—had earned him the nickname Bulldog.

"You there, Mark?"

"Yes."

"Okay. Steve's filled me in on the basics. What's your take on this?"

The man's clipped, cut-to-the-chase attitude reminded Mark that while he might be a victim in this incident, he was also expected to provide a professional assessment.

Shifting gears, he considered Les's question. His initial theory had been that the shooting was random, perpetrated by some nut who'd decided he'd had enough and wasn't going to take it any-more. Someone who wanted to send a message to the world.

But that didn't fit, Mark realized. Shooters who wanted to attract attention tended to seek crowded, very visible places to make their statement. Places where they could inflict the most amount of damage in the least amount of time. And in general they expected to be caught—or to take their own life rather than surrender.

Today's shooter had chosen an isolated park on a quiet Saturday morning. Only two people had been in range when he'd opened fire. His aim had been sound. And he'd made a fast getaway.

That led to a very disturbing conclusion.

"I don't think this was a random shooting," Mark said slowly.

"Explain."

When Mark provided his rationale, there was a moment of silence on the line before Les spoke. "Steve, what's your take?"

"I don't want to jump to any conclusions without some preliminary findings from the crime scene investigation. But I think Mark's reasoning is sound."

"So do I. We could be dealing with a sniper who has a very specific target. I'm going to brief the CIRG team as soon as I hang up."

Again, Mark wasn't surprised. The HRT was part of the FBI's larger Critical Incident Response Group, which was charged with crisis management in large-scale, volatile situations. Some of the group's resources would be tapped to assist with this investigation because of Mark's involvement.

The sound of shuffling papers came over the line. Mark pictured Les squinting, as he often did in tense situations, his ever present unlit cigar clenched between his teeth.

"Until we get a better handle on this, I want security on Mark 24/7. I'll send Coop out there to assist."

Cringing, Mark imagined his teammate's reaction to bodyguard duty. They'd worked a few dignitary protection details together through the years, and those had been among Coop's least-favorite assignments. "I think we can handle this with existing manpower."

"The decision's not open to debate. You and Coop have worked together for four years. He knows you—and your habits—better than anyone. He'll be there this afternoon."

Coop did know him well, Mark reflected. They'd been on the same assault team since Mark joined the HRT, and when a mission called for partners, they were usually paired. It was unofficial, but that's how Mark always thought of Coop—as a partner. And friend.

"I'm also going to have Christy take another look at the hate mail and phone calls we got after your shooting incident and review her risk assessment," Les continued. "See if she missed something."

Unlikely. Christy Reynolds was a top-notch profiler in the Behavioral Science Unit. She was good at what she did, and she didn't miss much. But this time Mark kept his mouth shut.

"I know everyone will be on this 24/7. Keep in touch over the weekend, and let's regroup first thing Monday via conference call," Les concluded. "By then we should have some data from the crime scene to add to the mix. Get any evidence to Quantico ASAP. In the meantime, Mark, pull up recent prison releases for cases from your days as a field agent. Anything else we need to discuss?"

After a quick look at Steve, Mark responded. "No. We don't have enough information yet."

"You okay?"

"Yes."

"How's the woman doing?"

"She was stable when the EMTs took her out."

"Good. Keep me in the loop if anything comes up before the conference call."

The line went dead.

As Steve replaced the receiver, he quirked an eyebrow. "He doesn't waste words, does he?"

"No. But he knows his stuff."

Steve turned to Nick, who'd moved off a discreet distance during the call, and waved him over. "Do you have room for one more in that pile-of-bricks rehab you call home?"

"Sure. I can move some drywall and lumber aside." Nick rejoined them. "What's up?"

"The Bureau is sending out one of Mark's teammates. Until we get a handle on this, I want one of you on him whenever he steps outside your door. It will be easier if you're living under the same roof."

"You think this was a hit on Mark?"

"It's a possibility. The MO of this incident doesn't fit a random shooter."

"Steve . . . sorry to interrupt, but the press is clamoring for info."

The three men turned to Ellen Levine, who handled media relations for the St. Louis office.

"I want to get with Oakdale before we say anything, but I'd prefer to stick to the basics—a shooter in the park, one victim with injuries, no other details available yet. You okay with that?" Ellen asked.

"Fine with me," Steve replied.

"Can we keep Emily's name out of this?" Mark directed his query to Ellen. After pulling her into this mess, the least he could do was protect her privacy.

"We can try. The press was all over the ambulance as they took her out. I don't think they got a look at her, but they'll figure out where she is."

"We have an agent with her," Steve told Mark. "He won't let anyone except medical personnel get close. Until we sort this out, I want security on both of you. Okay, let's do a quick debrief with the team here."

Steve rounded up Clair Ellis, the ERT lead inves-

35

tigator, along with detective Captain Carl Owens from Oakdale and the agents from the St. Louis FBI office who had arrived on the scene. Once the group had gathered, Mark walked them through the events leading up to the shooting. Carl and Steve agreed that both FBI and Oakdale resources would be used in the investigation, and that the FBI's ERT would handle evidence collection and analysis. Tasks were assigned, and Oakdale officers were paired with FBI agents to begin an immediate canvas of the residential area around the wooded area where Mark had pinpointed the shooter.

As they wrapped up, Clair turned to Mark. "I could use some input in the park."

"Sure." Mark followed her, with Nick and Steve close behind.

A casual onlooker would be surprised by the apparent lack of activity inside the yellow police tape, Mark speculated. But he'd been impressed with the St. Louis ERT during his brief tenure. Already one crime scene investigator was sweeping a fifty-yard radius around the shooting site with a metal detector, searching for the two bullets. In the woods, he knew the hunt would be on for spent shell casings. Once the shooter's position was identified, a technician would check for fingerprints, footprints, trace evidence. Another technician was beginning to videotape the area and would follow up with digital photos. No detail would be overlooked. If there was evidence to find, the ERT would discover it.

Clair led them toward the overturned bench and took out a sketchpad. Mark tried to ignore the bloodstains on the concrete.

"I need an exact placement for you and your companion." She directed her comment to Mark. "Can you walk me through your positions?"

"While you do that, I'm going to see what's happening in the woods. Stay tight." Steve looked at Nick.

The agent acknowledged the order with a nod.

Mark sent his friend a disgruntled look. "This is overkill. The place is crawling with police. The shooter is long gone." Already he was feeling smothered.

"He's the boss." Nick lifted one shoulder and stood his ground, folding his arms across his chest.

Turning his back on Nick, Mark recounted the minutes leading up to the shooting and showed Clair where he and Emily had been standing as the first shot was fired. Another technician took measurements, and Clair incorporated those into her diagram. They ran through the same drill near the bench.

As they finished, Steve rejoined them.

"Did they find anything?" Mark asked.

"Not yet."

"I've got something."

At the announcement, all heads turned toward

the technician with the metal detector. Clair set aside her sketchpad to join him, followed by the technician with the camera and video equipment. As she placed a number on the grass beside the bullet that was lodged partway in the ground, her actions were recorded on video. With the camera running, she extracted the piece of lead with long pincers. Slipping it into an envelope, she sealed the flap. After signing the envelope, she recorded the same number on the outside and jotted that ID in the evidence log.

"One down, one to go." Steve planted his hands on his hips and surveyed the park. "We'll need statements from you and your friend, as soon as she's up to it."

"I can take care of mine now." Mark checked his watch. "But I want to talk to the hospital first."

"I'll do that while you get started on the statement." Steve inclined his head toward a waiting detective. "He's chomping at the bit." Turning toward Nick, he opened his mouth to speak. But the agent beat him to it.

"I know. Stay tight. Got it."

His response earned Nick a cool perusal through narrowed eyes. "I like guys who listen."

As Steve walked away, Nick grinned at Mark. "Looks like you're stuck with me."

"Don't rub it in. It's bad enough that I have to live in your construction site."

"Hey, it's a great house."

"Maybe someday."

Without giving Nick a chance to respond, he headed to the command center.

By the time Mark finished his statement, Steve had returned.

"She's doing okay. They're moving her to a private room as we speak. Her blood pressure's low, and she lost a lot of blood, so they want to keep her overnight. I understand she's not happy about that."

"I'll talk to her when I stop by. Is there any reason for me to hang around here?"

"No. The ERT has center stage today."

"Okay. I'm going to swing by the house to shower, then stop by the office and check my prison releases. But I don't think I've had any in the past few months."

"Good. That will be one class of suspect we can rule out. I'll call you if anything breaks." With a wave, Steve headed toward the woods.

Mark glanced back toward the bloodstained bench. In a flash, the horror came rushing back. Along with anger. And fear. Emily could have died in his arms this morning.

"My car's over by the command center." Nick stepped into his line of sight, blocking his view. "Let's get out of here."

His jaw clenching, Mark turned away. "Yeah. Let's."

3

It was almost five o'clock when Mark wrapped up at the office. As he'd anticipated, his computer search for recent prison releases from his field days had been a wash. Though he'd been less diligent about monitoring them after joining the HRT, he did check on a periodic basis. It paid to watch your back.

Standing, he clipped his BlackBerry onto his belt and snagged his jacket off the chair beside his desk.

"Ready to go?"

At the familiar voice, he turned. Coop stood at the entrance to his cube, one shoulder propped against the partition, arms folded over his chest. Tall, dark, and imposing, Evan Cooper still looked every bit the Division I quarterback he'd been in his college days. But it was his keen judgment and team orientation as much as his athletic prowess that had earned him a coveted spot on the HRT. Mark always felt lucky to draw him as a partner on missions.

"When did you get here?"

"I walked in about ten minutes ago. Looks like my timing was perfect."

"Sorry about the bodyguard gig. I tried to talk Les out of it."

"Not a problem. I don't mind a little easy duty on

occasion. And Monica sends her thanks. She's glad there won't be any deployments of unspecified duration to unknown destinations in my immediate future."

"How's she doing?"

"Beginning to get uncomfortable. If it was up to her, she'd have gone straight from four months to birth."

Grinning, Mark slid his arms into the sleeves of his jacket. "Have you talked to Les about taking some time off after the baby's born?"

"We've had a few discussions." Coop pushed away from the partition. "Where are we off to?"

"I want to stop by the hospital."

"Steve said you know the woman who was shot."

"Yeah. We go way back. But I haven't seen her in twenty years. And after a reunion like this, I wouldn't blame her if she never wanted to see me again." A muscle clenched in his jaw.

"If you hadn't been there and reacted as quickly as you did, she might be dead."

"If I hadn't been there, the shooting might not have happened."

"I've been thinking about that." Coop shoved his hands into his pockets and regarded Mark. "You're guessing this is related to the convenience store incident. That you were targeted."

"It seems like a logical conclusion. A random shooter doesn't pick a deserted park and fire just two shots."

41

"Do you jog there every day?"

"No." He'd been indoctrinated to avoid patterned behavior. "But I do go there a couple of times a week. If someone was after me, they could show up a few days in a row and wait."

"That would raise the risk of detection exponentially."

"We may not be dealing with a rational person."

"I'm not sure I buy that. From what I've gathered, the shooting sounds like a very deliberate, well-thought-out attempt to take somebody out. And according to the latest update from the crime scene, the shooter managed to disappear without leaving much evidence. That suggests he didn't want to becaught and knew how to avoid detection. Sounds rational to me."

"Then how do you explain the risk he took, hanging around maybe several days in a row, waiting for me to show?"

"I can't. It doesn't make sense. But neither does the random theory." A beat of silence ticked by. "Tell me about your friend."

Mark paused in the process of sliding his Glock into the holster on his belt, momentarily thrown by the change of subject. "Emily?"

"Yeah."

"She's a clinical psychologist."

"Any enemies that you know of?"

The question jolted him. "She's not the kind of person to have enemies."

"How do you know? You haven't seen her in twenty years."

"I talked to her this morning. Trust me. She's still not the kind of person to have enemies."

"Steve's running a background check on her."

"That's a waste of time."

"I'd do the same in his place. You would too, under normal circumstances." Coop gave him a speculative look. "Maybe you're too close to this one, Mark."

Taking a deep breath, Mark secured his gun in his holster. "Okay. You're right. Every possibility does need to be looked at—dead end or not. You ready to head out?"

"Lead the way. I took a cab from the airport. I didn't think I'd need a car, since Les's orders were clear that I was to be your shadow until this thing gets sorted out."

"You realize that may not happen overnight." Mark wove his way to the rear of the building.

"Yes. That's why I reminded Monica as I left that absence makes the heart grow fonder."

"I bet she loved that." Mark reached for the door, only to feel Coop's restraining hand on his shoulder.

"Hand over the keys and let me go first."

Frustration tightened Mark's features as he turned toward his partner. "This is going to get old really fast."

"Understood. But humor me, okay? If anything happens to you, my neck's on the line."

With a disgruntled look, Mark fished the keys out of his pocket and stepped aside. Coop disappeared through the door, returning two minutes later to motion him outside. "We're clear."

"Thanks."

"You're welcome." Coop's sarcasm matched Mark's.

The drive to the hospital was quiet. Mark knew Coop was checking for tails—just as he was. If this kept up, he was going to be more paranoid than he already was.

They stopped once, at a florist shop, and Coop insisted on the same security drill. But at least he didn't comment on the oversized bouquet of roses Mark purchased. Unless a raised eyebrow could be construed as a comment.

In any case, Mark ignored it.

At the hospital, Coop parked near the service entrance in the back to avoid the press vans staking out the main entrance. Again, Mark waited until Coop did a sweep of the area before he got out of the car. Deciding humor rather than anger or frustration might be the easiest way to deal with the awkward situation, he grinned as he stepped out of the car and leaned back in to retrieve the flowers.

"I could get used to this. It makes me feel important."

Coop gave him a dry look. "Don't let it go to your head."

With a chuckle, Mark headed inside.

They found a fellow agent sitting outside Emily's door, and Mark did the introductions as Coop flashed his credentials.

"I'll take over for a while if you want to stretch your legs," Coop offered.

"Thanks. I'd appreciate it." The man turned to Mark. "Steve said to let him know if you think she's up to an interview. Oakdale would like to get a statement today."

"Okay, thanks."

As the agent disappeared down the hall, Mark turned to Coop. "I won't be long."

"Don't rush on my account." Coop settled into the chair. "In light of the fact that I'll be sleeping in a construction zone, I'm in no hurry to leave."

"I take it you talked to Nick?"

"Yeah. I ran into him in the office when I arrived. He hasn't changed much since you and I were in Richmond with Monica a year and a half ago. Anyway, he warned me about the house."

"It's not that bad."

"It is if you're allergic to drywall dust."

"Seriously?" After four years working in often too-close quarters with his partner, he thought he knew all of Coop's idiosyncrasies.

"Don't worry. I came with some heavy-duty medication. I'll live."

"If you're trying to make me feel even guiltier, it's working."

"Good. You'll owe me." Coop grinned and eyed the flowers. "Now go see the lady."

Shaking his head, Mark turned and tapped lightly on the door, cracking it a few inches. "Em? It's Mark. May I come in?"

There was a rustle of sheets before she responded. "Of course."

He stepped inside, shutting the door behind him. The top of the bed was hidden from his view, but he confirmed with a quick glance that the agent protecting Emily had drawn and closed the vertical blinds. It was a standard security and privacy measure. Reporters would do almost anything to get video for the evening news, and a plate glass window wouldn't stop a sniper if he could get a clear line of sight.

The latter scenario didn't sit well with him, and he pushed it aside. Forcing his lips into a smile, he moved into the room.

To his relief, Emily's pallor had been replaced with near-normal color, and her eyes were alert. Strain had tightened her features, but considering the sizeable bandage on one arm, the IV in the other, plus her multiple abrasions and bruises, that didn't surprise him.

"We have to stop meeting like this, you know." She managed a weary smile as she greeted him.

"I don't know. I kind of like those pajamas." Grinning, he moved beside the bed and gave the pink satin top an appreciative inspection.

Warmth tinted her cheeks. "You've gotten pretty bold since the old days."

"More flush too. As I recall, a bouquet of daisies was about all I could afford back then." He leaned over to set the vase of pink roses on the nightstand, moving a worn Bible aside to clear a space for them.

"Could you let me smell them first?"

"Sure." He switched direction. She attempted to sit up, but when she stiffened and drew in a sharp breath, he put a hand on her shoulder and pressed her gently back.

"I have a better idea."

Setting the vase on the nightstand, he withdrew a single long-stemmed pink blossom and handed it to her. She lifted it to her nose and inhaled, closing her eyes as a contented smile softened her lips. "I love the smell of roses. Thank you."

"You're welcome." He drew the side chair close to her bed and sat. "Tell me how you're doing."

"I tried to convince them to let me go home."

"I heard."

"They said my blood pressure was too low."

"I heard that too. You lost a lot of blood."

"Is there anything you haven't heard?"

He grinned. "Being with the FBI has its advantages."

"I'm beginning to realize that. And I hope that means you can fill me in on what happened. No one's told me a thing."

"There isn't much to tell yet. The incident is being investigated as we speak. We think it was a single shooter. He was gone before the police arrived."

"Who would do a thing like this?"

"We aren't sure."

"Was it someone trying to make some sort of statement, like you hear about on the news once in a while?"

"It's possible. But not likely. Those kinds of shooters tend to pick crowded places and try to inflict as much damage as possible. He only fired two shots, and there was no one around except you and me."

Some of the color left her cheeks. "You think he was shooting at us specifically?"

"That's one of the theories we're considering."

"Why?"

He debated how to answer, choosing his words with care. "In my line of work, you make enemies."

"Do you have a suspect?"

"No. But we have some ideas about where to start looking for one." He hadn't planned to bring up the convenience store debacle, but he saw no reason to keep it from her. Once his connection to today's shooting was discovered by the press, she'd hear about it anyway. "I was involved in an incident several months ago that generated national press—and a lot of hate mail to me and the Bureau."

Her brow furrowed. "I don't remember seeing anything in the media. I would have recognized your name. When did this happen?"

"Early May."

"That explains it. I was in Europe for a conference. I must have missed the coverage."

"Just as well. The media frenzy died down in a few days, but the public reaction continued for quite a while."

She fingered a velvety petal. "Is that why you're in St. Louis instead of Quantico?"

"Yes. The powers that be wanted to let the dust settle. And I needed a few weeks to recover."

"Is that new-looking scar on your leg a souvenir of the incident?"

"You were looking at my legs?" He tried for a teasing tone, hoping a touch of levity would ease the tautness in her features.

"It seemed fair enough. You were looking at mine." A smile whispered at her lips.

He chuckled. "Guilty as charged. And not the least bit repentant."

"You *have* changed. Whatever happened to that shy boy I knew once upon a summer?"

"He grew up."

"I noticed." A dimple flashed in her cheek, but before he could respond, she shifted the conversation back. "You haven't answered my question about that scar."

"Yes. It's a souvenir. I was shot."

"Do you want to tell me about it?"

In truth, he'd rather forget the whole thing. And her gentle question suggested she wouldn't press the issue if he declined to talk about it. But he'd learned that refusing to discuss it wouldn't make it go away. And that forgetting wasn't an option.

"My partner Coop and I were on our way to work very early one Monday morning. We stopped at a quick shop for some coffee. I went in, and while I was filling the cups, a guy pulled a gun on the teenage clerk and demanded the money in the cash drawer." He swallowed. Cleared his throat.

"I was one of three customers. The others were an older man and a pregnant woman. The gunman had the clerk in a choke-hold, and he told us he'd kill him—and us—unless we did exactly what he said. From the way he was sweating and the wild look in his eyes, it was obvious he was an addict in desperate need of a fix. The situation was volatile, and I knew it wouldn't take much for him to use that gun."

Mark rested his forearms on his thighs, clasped his hands between his knees, and kept his gaze fixed on the floor as the tragedy replayed in agonizing detail in his mind. "The clerk—his name was Jason Wheeler—tried to open the cash drawer, but it stuck. That infuriated the gunman, and he put the gun to the kid's temple and said he had five seconds to open the drawer or he'd pull the trigger. To demonstrate he had no qualms about using the

50

weapon, he took a shot in our direction. It didn't hit any of us, but I knew we couldn't expect to be as lucky if he fired again."

Mark took a deep breath. This was where it got really difficult to maintain an impassive tone.

"While all this was happening, Coop decided to grab a bagel to go with his coffee. When he opened the door and the bell jangled, the guy turned, giving me a clear shot. I drew my gun. Unfortunately, Jason chose that instant to make his own move. He jerked away from the gunman as I pulled the trigger. My bullet hit him instead of the target." Mark closed his eyes. Waited a few seconds. Opened them. "Coop took the guy down, but not before he managed to put a bullet in my leg."

"What happened to the boy?"

At Emily's soft question, Mark stared at his hands. "He didn't make it."

The silence in the room was heavy, mirroring the burden that weighed down his soul. When he felt a touch on his shoulder, he forced himself to look up.

"I'm so sorry, Mark."

"Yeah." The word rasped out, and he cleared his throat. "I am too."

"I can tell the physical wound is healing. What about the emotional one?" The question was soft. Caring.

He tried to smile, but his lips wouldn't cooperate. "You're being a psychologist."

"No. A friend."

Nodding, he accepted that. With gratitude. "That's taking a little longer."

"Have you talked to anyone?"

"A psychological assessment is required after an incident like this. The counselor didn't think I was ready to rejoin the team. I didn't argue."

"What team are you referring to?"

"I work in a division of the Critical Incident Response Group. We deal with large-scale, high-profile crises."

She searched his face. "You're on the Hostage Rescue Team, aren't you?"

"You know about that?" His eyebrows rose in surprise. Most civilians had never heard of it.

"I read a book a few years ago by a former HRT sniper. It was . . . eye-opening."

"I'm not a sniper. I'm on an assault team."

"That's just as dangerous. Maybe more so."

"We're well trained, Emily."

"Grant was too." Her eyes grew distant, and a flash of pain echoed in their depths. "Training doesn't eliminate danger. Or risk."

In silence he reached for her hand and laced her cold fingers with his, unable to refute her statement.

With an obvious effort, she refocused her attention on him. "Sorry. We were talking about you. Tell me about the letters and calls."

Shrugging, he tried to downplay them. "Some

people have long memories, and Waco and Ruby Ridge didn't engender a lot of positive public sentiment for the Bureau. We do everything possible to avoid the use of excessive force, but even in a situation like the convenience store—where a tactical resolution is justified—we get beat up."

"It sounds like you took the appropriate action, given the circumstances."

"That's what the review board concluded."

"But it doesn't bring back Jason Wheeler."

"No." He should have figured Emily would zero in on the guilt that had been gnawing at his gut for close to three months. Even before she'd become a psychologist, she'd had good insights. "He was seventeen. An honor student. He had a great future ahead of him."

She thought about that for a few moments. "Would you do anything differently if faced with that situation today?"

It was a question he'd asked himself many times. And he gave her the answer he'd memorized. "No. I did what I had to do, despite the tragic outcome."

He knew in his head that was true. But his heart was still struggling to accept it.

"How did his family react?"

"I don't know. They were fully briefed on what happened by senior people in the Bureau while I was in the hospital. And I sent them a letter, carefully vetted by Bureau lawyers, who were convinced we'd be sued." A mirthless smile twisted

53

his lips, and he shook his head. "But we never heard a word from them."

"Not everyone is litigation-happy. Perhaps they recognized that you did your best."

"It's possible, I guess." He knew his disheartened tone suggested he didn't hold out much hope of that, and he gave her an apologetic smile. "Sorry. I didn't intend to get into all of this today."

"I'm glad you told me."

He was too. But it was time now to talk about the present. "Do you feel up to giving a statement to the police?"

"Yes. Although I doubt I can tell them much."

"That's okay." He pulled out his BlackBerry as he spoke. "They won't expect a lot. I couldn't help them much, either. Except to suggest that the shooting might be connected to the convenience store incident." He punched in Steve's number. It was answered on the first ring. "It's Mark. I'm with Emily. She's ready to talk to the police."

"Good." Steve sounded relieved. "Oakdale is pushing. I'll let them know they can send someone over."

As Mark said good-bye and slid the BlackBerry back into its holder, a nurse entered to offer another round of pain medication.

"Is it going to knock me out again?" Emily asked.

"That's a possibility."

"Can I wait a bit?"

"Sure. Press the buzzer whenever you're ready."

Watching the woman exit, Emily wrinkled her nose. "I hate medicine. Besides, your visit is far more effective than a pill in distracting me, anyway."

"I'm flattered. And the feeling is mutual, by the way."

She smiled. "You always were a charmer."

As he looked at her across the bed—and across the years—Mark suddenly couldn't remember why they'd lost touch. "How come we didn't stay in contact after that summer?"

"We did for a while. But a serious relationship wasn't on our agenda in those days. We had other priorities."

"The foolishness of youth," he murmured.

Giving him a quizzical look, Emily asked a question of her own. "How is your family? Do they still live in Tennessee?"

"Yes. Dad died a few years ago, but Mom's doing well. My sister has three kids now and lives close to her. I get down as often as I can."

"Tell me about them."

She plied him with questions, and he was able to conjure up a few stories about his nieces and nephew that elicited some much-needed laughter. When he ran out of those, he turned the tables on her.

"How about you, Em? How's your dad?"

She'd had little family, he recalled. The summer

she'd come to visit her grandmother, a few months after her mother died, it had been just her and her dad, a military officer. She'd spent her youth moving every few years as her father's assignments took him all over the world. Six months after her visit to Tennessee, her grandmother had suffered a fatal stroke. The last time he'd seen her was at that funeral.

"He died ten years ago," she told him.

Meaning she was alone. Emily had told him once that with all the moving, she'd never had a chance to build long-term friendships. He wondered if she had fared better on that score after settling in St. Louis. Good friends would have helped sustain her through the loneliness and the losses.

He took a back-door approach to that question. "We're going to try to keep your name out of the media, but we may not be successful. Is there anyone you need to notify about this before they hear it on the news?"

A slow shake of her head answered his question before she spoke. "No. I've already called my secretary and my pastor, who has my medical power of attorney. There's no family. And Evelyn knows."

"Evelyn?"

"My neighbor. A wonderful widow lady in her seventies who's like an adopted grandmother. She took me under her wing when I moved into my condo after . . . when I lost Grant. She's the one who brought over my pajamas."

No mention of close friends her own age, he noted. Why not?

A knock on the door interrupted them. And as Mark rose to admit the detective who had come to question Emily, he realized he had a lot more questions of his own.

4

"Dr. Lawson? Sergeant Montgomery, Oakdale PD. Sorry to bother you with this, ma'am. I'll try to keep it brief."

"No problem, Sergeant." As the detective took the chair Mark had vacated, Emily looked at the man who'd made this day bearable—and who was now heading out the door. A wave of panic swept over her. "Aren't you staying?"

Mark paused. "It's not protocol to have two victims or witnesses in the room together when one is being interviewed."

"But you've already given your statement. Please . . . I'd feel better if you'd stay." The trauma of the past twelve hours had shaken her secure little world, and she needed the moral support his presence would provide.

His gaze dropped to her hands, which clenched the sheet into a tight wad, and he exchanged a look with Sergeant Montgomery. "It's up to you. But she might be more relaxed if I stay. I can leave at any point if either of you wants me to."

The man considered Emily's tense posture. "Okay. Let's try it this way."

With a nod, Mark propped one shoulder against the wall and shoved his hands into his pockets.

The detective recorded the basic information first, for which Emily was grateful. It gave her a chance to calm down a little before he began asking about the morning's events. But her pulse ratcheted up again as his questions got more specific.

"Do you walk in that park every morning, ma'am?"

"Yes. With rare exception."

"Did you notice anything out of the ordinary prior to the shots being fired?"

"No."

"Is there anyone in your acquaintance who has a grudge against you, or has threatened you?"

That query threw her, and she shot Mark a startled look.

"It's a routine question in a case like this, Emily," he told her.

She looked back at the detective. "No. I have no enemies."

"Is there anyone in your acquaintance who you consider to be capable of violence?"

"You mean, someone who might shoot me?" Incredulity rippled through her voice.

"Anyone you think capable of violence of any kind. Friends, family, co-workers, clients, the guy who cuts your grass . . . any person you've had any contact with."

Jack Hanley.

The name flashed across her mind like a neon light, jolting her.

Jack Hanley wasn't happy with her, but taking out his frustration with a gun? She couldn't imagine it.

At her hesitation, Mark frowned and pushed off from the wall.

"What is it, Em?"

"Nothing. I just . . . I do have one client who's rather peeved. A referral from a corporate employee assistance program. But shooting at me . . . the whole notion is surreal."

Mark exchanged a look with the detective and took a step closer. "Tell us about this guy."

"He's a senior-level manager who didn't appreciate being sent to me by his company's EAP three weeks ago. Nor did he appreciate my suggestion that he enroll in an anger management course. When he elected not to take my advice, I recommended he be put on paid leave until he worked through his issues."

"Why?" Mark asked.

"With workplace violence at an all-time high, it's best to diffuse potentially risky situations."

"In other words, you thought this guy was capable of violence."

"Not necessarily. But I didn't think it was wise to take any chances. My recommendation was more precautionary than anything else. The leave was intended to send him a strong message about his need to get help. In any case, I can't see him as a shooter."

"When did all this take place?" Sergeant Montgomery asked.

"He was notified of the leave yesterday."

The two men exchanged another look.

"Has he ever threatened you?" Mark asked.

"He called to rant a little yesterday after HR informed him of the company's decision. But he's never threatened me."

"We need to check him out."

Emily shook her head. "I can't reveal a client's name. That would compromise the confidentiality my work is based on."

"Confidentiality can be breached if criminal activity is involved," Mark said.

"We don't know that there is." Emily understood the legalities of her profession. And the ethics. Her instincts, as well as her professional training, told her Jack Hanley hadn't been the shooter. Yes, his explosive outbursts and callous treatment of his direct reports was what had brought him to the attention of his management. But she didn't believe he would pick up a gun to express his anger. Identifying him would not only be wrong, it would add unneeded stress to a life that was already crumbling.

"Where there's a reasonable suspicion that a

person may present a danger of violence to others, you're under no obligation to protect his identity," Mark reiterated.

"I don't think there is a reasonable suspicion," Emily countered, holding her ground.

Mark regarded her for a moment. Then he turned to the sergeant. "What else do you need?"

"I'm done."

"I'll walk you out."

The detective stood. "Thanks for your help, Dr. Lawson. We'll be in touch if we have any additional questions."

As the two men disappeared out the door, Emily closed her eyes and drew a shaky breath. The interview had taken a turn she hadn't expected. Or liked. Until a few minutes ago, she'd assumed the shooter had been either a fanatic or someone after Mark. It had never occurred to her that she might be his target.

Even now, the whole notion was ludicrous. Aside from Jack Hanley, there was no one in her life capable of *thinking* about shooting her, let alone doing it. And she was certain the troubled executive wouldn't take such extreme measures, either.

However, given the look on Mark's face, she suspected that convincing him of that was going to be a formidable challenge.

"We need this guy's name." Sergeant Montgomery turned to Mark as the door shut behind them.

"I know."

Coop rose as the two men stepped into the hall. Mark filled him in as they clustered outside Emily's room.

"We can always resort to legal means to get his name, if necessary," the detective pointed out.

"I'd rather not go down that road if we can avoid it. Let me work on it."

"Besides checking this guy out, I don't see any obvious reason why Dr. Lawson would be a target."

"Me neither. I'll be in touch, Sergeant. Thanks."

With a wave, the man headed toward the elevators.

"The background check on her may be finished by now," Coop offered. "We could ask Steve to have someone fax it to Nick's house."

"I doubt it will be much help, but let's take a look. I'm heading back in to give this one more try."

"I'll call Steve. Good luck."

The determined set of Emily's jaw as Mark reentered her room wasn't a good sign. But he was more concerned about the drawn, pinched look around her mouth and her lack of color. She needed the pain medication. Now.

Moving beside the bed, Mark perched on the edge instead of taking the chair. The Bible that had been on the nightstand rested in her hands.

"Still a believer, I see."

"You aren't?"

He shrugged. "I've seen a lot in my job, Emily. Too much. It's hard to reconcile most of it with a loving God."

"I'm sorry, Mark." Regret pooled in her eyes. "I can't imagine walking through life without God by my side."

He refrained from asking her where God had been a few hours ago when a bullet had ripped through her arm and she'd almost bled to death. Or where he'd been when her husband had perished in a fire. Faith wasn't a topic he wanted to discuss tonight.

Instead, he reached over and tucked her hair back behind her ear, the whisper of a smile touching his lips.

"It's been quite a day, hasn't it?"

He sensed the subtle relaxing of her muscles. She'd been prepared to do battle to protect her client, and he'd disarmed her by stepping back from the fight.

"Before all this happened, I was looking forward to a very quiet Saturday."

"I'm sorry it didn't turn out the way you planned."

"So am I. But I'm not sorry our paths crossed again. It's been good catching up."

"We're just getting started. I'm not about to let you disappear again when it's obvious fate brought us together. I hear you'll be released tomorrow. How about I give you a ride home? We could stop on the way and have that cold drink we never got around to this morning."

A smile curved her lips. "My neighbor volunteered to pick me up, but I think I like your offer better."

"Good." He needed to tackle the hard stuff again, but he wished he didn't. He would have much preferred a simple, uncomplicated reunion. "There's something else I need to discuss with you."

"Okay." She gave him a cautious look.

"Until we get this thing figured out, the Bureau would like you to have some security."

"Explain that."

"We want to assign an agent to you."

"A bodyguard?"

"That's one way to describe it."

She searched his eyes. "Is that really necessary? I've been by myself all day today."

"There's been an agent with you ever since you left the scene. He's outside your door now."

Shock rippled across her face. "You think this guy might try again?"

"We can't rule out that possibility."

"What about you? It seems to me you're the more likely target."

"I'll have someone with me too."

She stared at him. "They're putting protection on

an HRT member who's trained to handle worst-case scenarios?"

For a second, he hesitated. He didn't want to freak her out—but he also needed to drive home the danger. "Yes."

"Wow." She let out a low breath. "Okay. I guess I'll take it too."

He hadn't expected her to acquiesce so easily, but he was grateful she'd realized the gravity of the threat. "Good."

There were other security measures he needed to talk over with her, but they could wait until tomorrow. If the deepening lines of strain around her mouth were any indication, she'd had about all she could take today. "Why don't you get that pain medication from the nurse." He handed her the call button.

She gave him a wary look. "Aren't you going to push me about the client I mentioned?"

"Would it do any good?"

"No."

"That's what I thought. But consider this, Emily. We're very adept at making discreet inquiries. He'll never know we ran a background check."

"But he'll know if you ask him for an alibi."

"True. But we're dealing with an attempted murder." He waited a few seconds to let the full impact of his words register. "In that kind of investigation, no stone is left unturned. The man knows he has an anger problem. He knows he's mouthed off to you. It's not unreasonable the police would want to check him out. In any case, we're not obligated to identify the nature of the investigation or the parties involved when we question someone."

After considering his comment, she shook her head. "I'm sorry, Mark. It doesn't feel right. He could put two and two together. And trust is essential in a counseling relationship."

"Did he choose to come to you?"

"No."

"Would you say there's much trust now?"

She conceded his point with a shrug. "Not a lot. But there'll be less if I identify him as a client."

He'd forgotten about her stubborn streak. And the way she could dig in her heels when it came to her principles, no matter the cost to herself.

"I understand your concern. But there are extenuating circumstances." He laid a gentle hand on her bandaged arm. "This was too close for comfort, Emily. If you are a target, he may not miss the next time."

She frowned and reached up to massage her temples. "Can I sleep on it?"

After a brief hesitation, Mark nodded. "Okay. I'll be by in the morning." He scrutinized her and pushed the call button himself. "You waited too long to ask for the pain pills."

"They put me to sleep."

"Sleep is good. You'll feel better when you wake up."

"What can I do for you, Dr. Lawson?" The nurse's voice came over the intercom.

"I think I can use that pain medication now."

"I'll be right in."

As Mark moved the call button aside, he gave Emily a sympathetic look. "Nights are always the worst for pain."

She dredged up a smile. "The voice of recent experience."

"Unfortunately."

"Have you been shot before this last incident?"

"I have my share of battle scars."

"You're dodging the question."

He was saved from having to reply by the appearance of the nurse, who moved beside the bed.

"We can do pills or I can administer the medication through the IV, which is faster-acting. Any preference?"

"The IV."

Emily's immediate response confirmed Mark's assessment that she'd waited far too long to ask for help with the pain.

The nurse injected the medication and smiled at Emily. "You'll feel better in a few minutes."

As she exited, Emily turned to Mark. "You probably have places to go. It's Saturday night. You might be able to salvage a few hours."

"If I leave now, Nick will have me wielding a paintbrush within the hour."

"Who's Nick?"

"My roommate. A classmate from the FBI Academy who works in the St. Louis office. He's rehabbing an old house, and in exchange for a place to stay, he puts me to work every chance he gets. He'll have Coop climbing ladders too, before he's through."

"Your partner's here?"

"Yes. My boss in Quantico sent him in to help with the case, and he's staying with Nick too. Except I found out today he's allergic to drywall dust." He gave her a rueful smile and shook his head. "He's never going to let me live this down."

She gave a soft laugh. Already she was drifting. "I'll have to meet him."

"Tomorrow."

There was silence for a couple of minutes. Her eyes flickered closed, and Mark was relieved to see her features relaxing as the pain medication began to take effect.

"Mark?"

"I'm still here, Em."

"You're the only one who ever called me that, you know." Her lips lifted into a wistful smile, but her eyes remained closed as she reached out to him. "Would you mind holding my hand?"

He cocooned her slender fingers in his. "I've had harder duty."

"Mmm. That feels good. Thanks."

"It's my pleasure, Em."

And in truth, it was.

• • •

Darkness hadn't diminished the oppressive heat, but at least he'd gotten rid of the long sleeves. Unfortunately, his T-shirt exposed more flesh to the thick swarms of hungry mosquitoes that called the mud flats along the river home.

As he stepped into the boat and pushed off from the small dock, he slapped at a few of the bloodthirsty insects that were unfazed by the liberal coating of DEET on his skin. Under normal circumstances, he wouldn't venture out onto the river at night. However, today had been anything but normal. And the heavy blackness of the overcast, starless sky provided the perfect cover for his task. But the darkness wasn't a problem. He'd fished this river hundreds of times through the years and could navigate it blindfolded.

The muffled putt-putt of the outboard motor, throttled low, echoed in the stillness as he headed downstream. Given the late hour and the dark windows in the few weekend cabins he passed, he doubted the precaution of traveling to an isolated area was necessary. But he'd thought through every step of his plan and saw no reason to change it. He couldn't afford to get caught.

Especially since the job wasn't finished.

According to the evening news, one person had been wounded this morning. That hadn't surprised him. He was a good shot. But an unexpected move by his quarry just as he pulled the trigger had sabotaged his aim. His second shot had been a gamble, and it didn't appear to have paid off. The reporter on TV had mentioned only a single gunshot wound, and indicated the victim was hospitalized but stable.

He nosed the bow of the boat toward the center of the river, turned upstream, and set the throttle high enough to keep him stationary in the rapid current. Woods ran down to the shore on both sides here, and a quick scan of the secluded bank revealed no sign of life.

As he pulled the pieces of metal from the sack under his seat, he fingered the remains of his dismantled hunting rifle. The stock had been splintered and fed into his barbecue pit this afternoon as he'd cooked a steak. The barrel had been cut into three sections in his workshop, the smaller parts hammered beyond recognition.

Now, one by one, he dropped each piece overboard, watching as they were swallowed by the dark, swirling water.

The necessity for this clandestine trip was galling, and a surge of anger welled up inside him. In a just world, he wouldn't have to cover his tracks. He would be applauded for following the Good Book, for settling this score. But the cops didn't see it that way. If he was caught, he'd be thrown into jail. And he couldn't let that happen. He wanted to right a wrong, not give his quarry a chance to commit more sins.

His failure today left a bitter taste in his mouth. But he consoled himself with the belief that it had to be part of God's design. The Lord must want revenge exacted in a different way. And it was up to him to figure it out. He'd pray about it, and when he understood what was expected, he'd formulate another plan. A better plan.

Because the next time he set his sights on his target, he didn't intend to miss.

5

"Morning."

At Coop's greeting, Mark stopped in the kitchen doorway. His partner sat at the small oak table, a sheaf of papers spread out in front of him. Judging by the half-empty pot of coffee on the counter, it looked as if he'd been there a while.

"When did you get up?" Mark moved to the counter and poured himself a cup of the dark brew.

"An hour or two ago. I already worked out. Nick has quite a home gym." He gestured to the papers. "Your friend is one busy lady."

"The background material showed up?"

"Nick found it on the fax this morning."

"Where is he?"

"Gone. He said something about having to chase down a new lead on a bank robbery."

"He's been hot on that trail since I got here. I've been working the case with him." Mark sat at the

71

table and took a sip from his mug. It had been a long, restless night, and he was feeling the effects. He needed a few jolts of caffeine to jump-start his brain. "Find anything interesting?"

"Depends on how you define interesting. Personally, I think she's a very interesting lady."

Mark gave him a wry look. "Okay. I'll rephrase that. Did you find anything that would mark her as a target?"

"Hard to say."

That wasn't the answer he'd expected. "You want to explain that?"

"In addition to her private practice, she takes corporate referrals for troubled employees from a number of EAP programs. According to the file, she's quite an authority on workplace violence. That was the subject of her PhD dissertation, and she's done a lot of additional research in that area. The results of that work have appeared in a number of prestigious scholarly journals. In her *spare* time, she hosts a radio call-in program every Thursday night for teens. She's also active at her church and volunteers as a counselor one afternoon a week at a shelter for abused women. A place called Hope House."

Tightening his grip on the mug, Mark looked at Coop. "She could have enemies as a result of some of those activities."

"That's my take." Coop took a sip of coffee. "You knew she was married, right?"

"She told me yesterday. To a fireman. He died five years ago."

Flipping through the papers, Coop pulled out a sheet that included a photo. "Grant Stephens. She never took his name. Professional reasons, maybe, since she already had an established practice when they married. It doesn't appear she has any living family."

"She doesn't."

"Nor close friends. Or a steady boyfriend."

The background check had been thorough. Given Steve's propensity for detail, that didn't surprise him. "When would she have time?"

"Good point. I'm not even sure how she works sleep into her schedule."

Mark scanned the sheet on Emily's husband. Nice-looking guy, with dark hair and a firm jaw. He'd been honored with several citations for bravery, and had died after the floor collapsed while he was trying to rescue a sleeping baby from a second-floor bedroom. True hero material.

Setting the sheet down, Mark toyed with his mug. "Emily's workplace violence expertise and her involvement at the shelter worry me. We already know about one guy who's not happy with her because of a job issue. And if she's talked any of the shelter's clients into leaving a partner, there could be a disgruntled boyfriend or husband out there."

"I agree."

"What's your assessment of imminent risk?"

"Low. No matter who the target is. Whoever did this appears to have had a plan that took into account behavior patterns and provided a high probability of a clean escape. Given the level of planning, I suspect he was confident he'd succeed. He could have a fully formed plan B, but my gut tells me he doesn't. He'll either throw in the towel or go back to the drawing board."

"To come up with a plan that won't fail the next time."

"Yes." Coop cradled his mug in his hands and leaned back, stretching his legs out under the table. "You need to get Dr. Lawson to tell you who her unhappy EAP client is."

"That's my top priority today. And I want to talk with her about the women she's counseled recently at the shelter." Mark checked his watch. "You ready to head over to the hospital?"

"If you're willing to stop for a sausage biscuit on the way. That chicken Caesar salad Nick put together last night for dinner was good, but it didn't stick with me."

"Tell me about it. He's beginning to go overboard on this health-food kick he's on." Mark drained his cup. "Let's go."

No media vans were staked out in front of the hospital as they pulled in, but Coop chose to park near the service entrance again in case a reporter or two lurked in the lobby.

Following the pattern they'd begun yesterday, Coop got out first, signaling Mark to follow a couple of minutes later.

Another agent was on duty outside of Emily's room today. He stood as they approached, shaking Coop's hand as Mark introduced them.

"Everything quiet here?"

"Quiet is a relative term," the man responded. "No problems from a security standpoint. But the lady had a rough night."

Alarm tightened Mark's gut. "Did she start bleeding again?"

"No. Nightmares."

The tension in Mark's shoulders eased. Nightmares weren't good, but neither were they unexpected. He'd awakened twice last night in a cold sweat himself. And for once, he hadn't been able to blame it on the convenience store shooting. This time, it hadn't been a teenage boy bleeding in his arms, but Emily.

"I'll cover for you if you want to grab some coffee," Coop told the agent.

"Thanks. I wouldn't mind stretching my legs a little."

As Coop settled into the chair, he nodded toward the closed door. "Go to work. We need names."

With a nod, Mark cracked the door. The lights were off, and instead of knocking he moved quietly into the dim room. Emily was sleeping, her head turned to one side, her face in shadows.

While he'd admired her trim, toned figure yesterday, today she looked fragile and vulnerable beneath the white sheet outlining her slight body.

Unwilling to wake her after her rough night, Mark rejoined Coop.

"She's sleeping."

"No problem. My time is your time."

"You know, you're going to be bored out of your mind in forty-eight hours. You didn't join the HRT to be a bodyguard."

"You might be surprised. I'm mellowing with age."

While Coop's comment was delivered with a grin, there was more than a hint of truth to it, Mark realized. Since meeting and marrying Monica—and somehow rediscovering his faith along the way—Coop had been more laid-back. More content. It hadn't dulled his on-the-job skills, but Mark sensed he no longer craved the adrenaline rush of tactical operations that had once been an outlet for his restless energy.

"I think I'll give Steve a call and—"

A sudden, sharp cry from inside the room brought Coop instantly to his feet. On instinct, both men drew their guns as Mark pushed through the door.

Light from the hallway spilled into the room as the heavy metal door slammed against the wall, but it took no more than one quick glance to determine the cause of Emily's alarm. Blinking against the sudden light, she was sitting up, her eyes wide with terror, her chest heaving.

They were holstering their guns as the third agent joined them from behind after sprinting down the hall.

"I went through this drill twice last night," he told them quietly.

As Mark moved beside Emily, the other two agents exited in silence. He sat on the edge of the bed and smoothed the hair away from her damp face, his gaze assessing. Her pallor was unsettling, and the dark smudges beneath her eyes were mute testimony to her difficult night.

She groped for his hand and squeezed his fingers, her grip strengthened by residual terror. "I . . . I'm sorry. I had a bad dream."

"No need to apologize. I'd be more surprised if you didn't have a nightmare or two." *Or three. Or thirty.*

He wished he could tell her there was a way to stop the dreams. But if there was, he hadn't found it yet. The only remedy the counselor had offered was the distance from the event that the passage of time would bring.

It took several minutes for her respiration to moderate, and once it did, he helped her ease back down against the pillow.

She managed a shaky smile. "I'll be okay once I'm in familiar surroundings and life gets back to normal."

The normal part wouldn't be happening in the next few days. But Mark saw no reason to tell her that yet. She'd find out soon enough.

"When are you getting sprung?" He stroked his thumb over her knuckles.

As if on cue, the surgeon entered. Mark rose and introduced himself.

"You have a patient who's very anxious to go home," he told the man.

"Can't say I blame her." He addressed his next comment to Emily. "Hospitals are for sick people. You don't qualify. Your blood pressure is back to normal, and you aren't running a fever."

"How bad was the damage?" Emily asked.

"You were lucky. The bullet went through cleanly. It did clip a large vein, which accounted for the heavy bleeding, but managed to miss major nerves and muscles. Other than a small scar at the entry site and a larger one at the exit site, you shouldn't have any lasting effects." He moved closer to the bed. "If everything looks okay, we'll change the dressing and you're out of here."

"I'll wait outside," Mark said. With a wink at Emily, he exited as a nurse entered.

Coop rose as Mark stepped through the door. "What's the verdict?"

"We should be good to go soon."

"And our agenda is . . . ?"

"I promised Emily we'd stop for a cold drink on the way to her place. A rain check for the date we were arranging yesterday when we were rudely interrupted."

"I'm good with that. As long as it's someplace very public, since our shooter appears to prefer isolated locations. And don't pick a spot either of you frequent."

"Gee, thanks for the tip." Mark smirked at him.

"You know, this bodyguard gig would be easier if you weren't such a smart aleck."

"But much more boring."

A soft chuckle rumbled in Coop's chest. "I can't remember too many times when our partnership has been boring."

Despite Coop's grin, Mark sensed a subtle, odd undercurrent that was too vague to classify. But it was troubling in some way. "Is everything okay?"

Whatever had been there a moment before was gone. "Nothing a quick wrap-up here won't cure. I miss Monica already." He winked. "You should try this marriage thing sometime. It has distinct advantages."

At times Mark still found it hard to believe his partner had followed through with his announcement thirteen months ago that he was getting married. Sure, he'd known Coop was interested in Monica when they'd been assigned to her security detail. But she'd been one in a long line of women Coop had dated through the years.

Besides, neither he nor Mark had been in any hurry to tie the knot. They had about all the excitement they could handle in their jobs, and given the 24/7 nature of their work, its unpredictability and danger, plus the extended missions away from Quantico, they'd agreed that marriage would only complicate things—and add pressures, guilt, and distraction to a life that required absolute focus. Besides, they'd seen the marriages of too many of their colleagues crumble under the stress.

Then Monica had come along. And the rest, as conventional wisdom said, was history.

"Why don't you call her? You can keep an eye on me from down the hall."

"I think I'll do that." With a grin, Coop moved off a few yards, withdrawing his BlackBerry as he walked.

Mark took his seat, his expression thoughtful. Much as he and Coop had shared during the past four years, his partner had never been one to talk about emotion. He had a wicked sense of humor, strong opinions on most subjects, and an ability to rapidly dissect any problem with astounding thoroughness. He played hard—and worked harder. When the chips were down, he was an absolute professional. Mark had never worried about putting his life in Coop's hands, and had done so on several occasions. The reverse was also true.

Though he'd never verbalized his feelings, Mark missed him. Before Coop's marriage, they'd often hung out together after hours. While Mark was a frequent dinner guest at his friend's house, and he and Coop managed to grab a few hours together here and there, things were different since he'd married. Not to mention the fact that Coop's new contentment had served to magnify the essential loneliness of Mark's life.

The elevator door slid open, and Nick stepped out. Spotting Mark, he strode toward him.

"What are you doing here?" Mark queried.

"The bank robbery lead went nowhere. I've got protection detail for your friend for the rest of the day." He spotted the agent who had spent the night outside Emily's door and lifted a hand in greeting. "I'll be back in a minute," he told Mark.

Several minutes passed before anyone reappeared, and Mark welcomed the momentary solitary interlude. But as the nurse exited Emily's room after changing her dressing and helping her gather up her things, Coop and Nick rejoined him.

"She says she doesn't want a wheelchair," the woman informed them.

That didn't surprise Mark. He thought back to the spunky teen who had insisted on walking out of the woods herself rather than wait for help after spraining her ankle on one of their hikes. One corner of his mouth hitched up.

"I think we have enough able-bodied men here to get her safely to the car."

"Lucky her." The nurse gave the three of them an approving look and grinned. "She's all set."

"It's about time we get to meet this mystery woman," Coop said.

"This *pretty* mystery woman," Nick chimed in, adjusting his jacket.

Mark narrowed his eyes, and the other man shrugged.

"Hey, the background stuff came in on my fax machine. Her picture was right on top. You had your chance twenty years ago."

"You're here to protect her. Nothing more," Mark reminded him.

Nick gave a mock salute, grinned, and patted his gun. "Reporting for duty, sir. I'll be happy to take the night shift."

"I knew I liked this guy." Coop chuckled. "Even if he is a health-food nut."

Nick turned to him. "Don't bite the hand that feeds you."

"I wouldn't think of it."

"If you two are finished, why don't we talk about a plan?" Mark knew Nick was kidding around. He was a pro on the job. But he was all man off the job, according to his colleagues, with a playboy image to match.

Yet now that Mark had lived in his house for six weeks, he was beginning to suspect that image was more illusion than reality. As far as he could see, Nick spent every spare hour lavishing his love on the pile of old bricks he was restoring rather than on a bevy of women. Nevertheless, Nick's obvious appreciation of Emily's considerable physical charms disconcerted him.

"While we stop for that cold drink you promised the lady yesterday, Nick could pick up any prescriptions she needs filled, go on to her condo, and do a sweep. That will expedite things once we get there," Coop suggested.

"Good idea. You okay with that?" Mark turned to Nick.

"Sure."

"Okay. Let's do it." Leading the way, he gave a discreet tap on the door and stepped inside.

Emily was sitting on the edge of the bed, dressed in a khaki skirt short enough to reveal an appealing length of leg and a crisp, white sleeveless blouse. She had a gauze patch on her knee, a smaller one on her cheek, and a bulky bandage on her left arm. Plus assorted bruises in varying shades of purple and green.

"Ready to leave?" Mark smiled at her.

"More than ready."

He stepped aside and introduced Nick and Coop.

"It's nice to meet you." Emily took their hands in turn. "Mark's already told me about both of you."

He ignored the suspicious looks they sent his way.

"Nick's going to go on to your place while we stop for that drink. If you're up for that."

"Just try to talk me out of it. I'm not letting you off the hook because of a little gunshot wound."

She dug around in her purse and handed over her keys. "You'll need my security alarm code too. Let me find a piece of paper and write it down." She began to rummage through her purse again, but Mark touched her arm.

"Just tell us. We'll remember."

"Okay." She recited it.

"Got it." Mark passed her keys to Nick. "We convinced the nurse to forgo the wheelchair."

"Thanks."

She scooted to the edge of the bed, and Mark moved beside her. "On the condition that you lean on us."

"That's no hardship." She angled a look at Mark but turned to include Nick and Coop as well. "I can't recall ever having had this many handsome men at my beck and call."

"Flattery will get you everywhere." Coop grinned and moved beside her as she and Mark reached the end of the bed. Nick picked up her overnight case in one hand and juggled the vase of flowers in the other.

They escorted her down the hall, but when she paused at the bank of elevators, Mark urged her forward. "We're taking that one." He indicated the service elevator ahead.

"Why?" She looked up in time to catch the glance Mark exchanged with Coop over her head, and her puzzled frown eased. "Never mind. It must be a security thing."

"That, plus we're trying to avoid any press that might be hanging around. So far we've managed to keep your name out of the paper."

"I appreciate that."

At the basement service entrance, Mark handed Nick his keys. The agent exited first, depositing Emily's case in the trunk of his car and propping the flowers on the passenger seat. He did a quick sweep of the parking garage before motioning them out. They didn't linger getting into Mark's car.

As Coop put the car in gear, Mark spoke from his place beside Emily in the backseat. "To the coffee shop, driver."

Coop glanced at Mark in the rearview mirror. "Watch it, buddy."

"What? You don't like being a chauffeur?"

"I prefer to think of myself as a chaperone. So behave back there, or I'll have to ground you both."

"Restricted to quarters with Emily. I'm not sure that would be such a bad thing." Reaching for her hand, Mark entwined his fingers with hers.

She laughed and shook her head. "Are you two always like this?"

"Like what?"

"Funny. Irreverent. Sparring. I didn't expect that, considering the serious nature of your work."

In truth, that lighthearted banter was what got them through their toughest, most serious jobs,

Mark reflected. It was a good technique for diffusing tension in stressful situations. And Emily was stressed to the max. If they could help her relax for an hour or two, she might be able to regroup and regain her equilibrium. To feel a bit more normal.

Even if her life wasn't. And wouldn't be for a while.

Soon, Mark would have to remind her of that. And he hoped this brief interlude of laughter and teasing would help make the hard stuff to come more palatable.

6

As she took the final sip of her double chocolate chip frappuccino, Emily smiled at Mark. "Thank you for following through. And for giving me a pleasant interlude in the midst of all this craziness. It's been fun to reminisce."

He leaned back in his chair and returned the smile, flicking a quick glance at Coop, who sat a few tables away. His partner had chosen a seat close enough to allow him to respond instantly if the need arose, and far enough away to be discreet, with a clear line of sight to the front door and a good view of the coffee shop overall. Mark had placed himself against the wall, where he, too, had a comprehensive view. Emily sat across from him, her back to the comings and goings in the shop.

"I never break a promise."

"Oh, I don't know about that."

He redirected his attention to her but remained alert to the activity in the shop. "What do you mean?"

"I remember a young man telling me once at Wren Lake that I was the only girl he'd ever love. And that no matter what happened, we'd never lose touch."

Although Mark didn't recall making that exact promise, there were quite a few gaps in his memory when it came to the hours they'd spent at Wren Lake. His most vivid recollection was Emily's silky hair tangled in his fingers, her supple lips stirring beneath his, her soft skin tantalizing his fingers. Twenty years later, it was enough to stir the embers of that long-ago attraction.

"Did I say that?"

"More than once." Her gentle smile told him she didn't hold his lapse in memory against him.

"I can only offer two excuses in my defense. Youth and hormones."

A soft laugh whispered at her lips. "It's hard to argue with that rebuttal. Those are powerful forces."

"Can I say I'm glad our paths crossed again? And mean it this time?"

"You can."

He leaned forward to rest his elbows on the small table. Linking his fingers, he studied her, liking what the passage of years had done to her eyes. The sweet innocence of youth had given way to compassion, diffused energy to focus, searching to contentment. Her clear gaze had always radiated principle. Now he saw character, and a depth forged of experience—and loss. But he also sensed a fundamental loneliness . . . and wondered if he was attuned to that because it mirrored his own.

"Why isn't there someone new in your life?"

His quiet question startled her for a second before she smiled. "How do you know there isn't?" When he didn't respond at once, her smile faded. "Never mind. I think I can guess."

"The office ran a background check," Mark conceded. "But I would have figured that part out on my own."

"How?"

"I don't know." He didn't disclose his theory about shared loneliness. "Call it male intuition. Is it because of loyalty to your husband?"

"No." Her answer came quick and sure. "Grant loved life and believed in living every day to the fullest. He wouldn't want me to mourn forever. If he could talk to me today, he'd tell me to move on."

"Yet you haven't."

"No."

He waited for an explanation, but when she didn't offer one he respected the line she'd drawn.

Instead, he changed the subject. "Can we talk about the game plan for the next few days?"

Renewed tension tightened her features. "I'm beginning to recognize your FBI face."

"I'd rather not have to bring up the heavy stuff, Em. But it's there, and ignoring it would be both foolish and dangerous."

She drew in a slow breath, let it out. "Okay. I'm listening."

"You lead a very busy life."

"Doesn't everyone these days? And I would have been glad to tell you about it myself if you'd asked."

"You weren't in any shape to debrief us in a timely manner."

She accepted his explanation with a nod and a quick lift of her shoulders. "Okay. So you know everything about me. Now what?"

"Any chance you could get out of town for a week or two?"

"Not without inconveniencing a lot of people."

That was the answer he'd expected. "Then let's talk about your routine. It's too predictable."

She considered that for a moment. "I'm not sure I like that assessment. Predictable sounds boring. I prefer to think of it as organized and structured."

"You need to unstructure it a little."

She shifted in her chair, and he could tell she was uncomfortable with his request.

"Is that a problem?"

"I wouldn't call it a problem exactly. More like a challenge. After all my years of military living, of constant packing up and starting over, I like stability and consistency. It's very unsettling to me when my routine gets disrupted."

Given her background, Mark could understand that. But her physical safety had to come first for now.

"Is there anything you can put on hold for a week or two?"

"I have regular office hours. I can't let my patients down. They count on me. And I'm sure you know about my other commitments."

"A weekly radio program. And counseling at a domestic violence shelter."

"I also go to church every Sunday. I'm surprised you missed that one."

"It was probably in the file. I only had a chance to give it a quick look this morning." His lips quirked into a smile.

"In any case, I'd prefer not to give up any of my commitments."

"Okay." He'd expected that response too. "But we need to come up with some ways to let you honor them without putting yourself in the line of fire."

"I have a treadmill in the spare bedroom I use in bad weather. I could switch to that for my daily walk."

"That's a start. How about church? Are you flexible about which service you attend?"

"Yes."

"Can you vary your schedule at the women's shelter?"

"I could alternate afternoons."

"Would the radio station consider broadcasting your show from a remote location?"

"It's a small, local operation. That would be difficult for them."

"Okay. We can live with that as long as someone accompanies you there. Do you always see patients in your office?"

"Yes. With rare exception."

"But you could vary your hours a bit, right?"

"To some degree."

"That would help. And we'll check out the office for security issues. Let's talk about living arrangements. Is there anyone you could stay with for a few days, or someone who could stay with you?"

"No one I'd want to impose on." She gave him a distressed look. "How long could it take to find this guy?"

"It's hard to predict. I'll have a better idea after the briefing tomorrow with our people and the Oakdale police." There was no reason to tell her that unless the shooter had made some mistakes, left them some leads to track down, they might never find him. Unless—or until—he struck again. "For the next twenty-four hours we'd like to keep tight security on you. We'll revisit our plan after the meeting tomorrow." He moved his empty cup aside. "Have you thought any more about giving us the name of that EAP referral?"

She sighed. "I knew that topic would come up again."

"We can get it if we need to, Emily." There was apology in his voice, but he let the steel come through too. "There are legal routes we can take if you don't feel you can cooperate."

"I know." She stared into her cup. "Divulging his name just goes against everything I believe about doctor/patient relationships. Being questioned as part of a police investigation will add to his stress, even if he doesn't connect it to me."

"I'd rather add to his stress than take a chance with your life."

Silence greeted his blunt rebuttal. He waited, hoping she'd recognize the necessity of his request and honor it without forcing him to take official action.

With a resigned sigh, she looked up. "Jack Hanley." She named his company.

Relieved by her capitulation, Mark filed the name away in his memory. "We can get everything else we need on our own."

"He's not going to be happy about this."

"We can deal with that."

"I'm not sure he can."

Reaching out, Mark enfolded her hand in his. "I wish you'd worry about yourself as much as you worry about your patients."

"The person I'm most worried about at the moment is you. Between the two of us, you're the more likely target."

"I've got Coop watching my back. I'm not concerned."

She looked over her shoulder to check out his partner. Mark didn't have to. He knew what she was seeing. Coop would appear relaxed as he lingered over his drink, ankle crossed over knee, one arm stretched along the top of the chair next to him. No one in the shop would suspect he was assessing every person who came through the door, that he was ready to spring into action at the slightest hint of danger. Or that the flap of his suit coat hid a lethal weapon.

"He strikes me as very competent."

"The best."

She turned back. "Have you been partners long?"

"Four years." He examined her face, noting the deep lines of weariness around her eyes, the strain at the edges of her mouth. "Much as I'd love to prolong this, I think you need to go home and rest."

A winsome smile tipped up the corners of her lips. "I'd forgotten how easy it is to be with you, Mark. I feel like our summer together was weeks, not years, ago."

"Hold that thought until all this is over." He gave her hand a squeeze, then stood and reached down to help her up. "Don't make any fast moves. You could be a little lightheaded for a few days, and the last thing we need is for you to nosedive into the floor."

She accepted his help—and his advice. "You know, even as a teenager, you were a sensitive guy. And I think you've improved with age."

Her words warmed him, but he hid their effect with a grin. "Thanks. But don't tell Coop, okay? I'd never live it down."

"Not a macho thing, huh?" she teased.

Over her head, Mark nodded to Coop, who moved to the door to scan the parking lot. "Not in the HRT. Okay, let's get you home."

As Mark lifted his finger toward the bell, Nick opened the door to Emily's townhouse condo.

"Everything okay?" Mark ushered Emily inside while Coop took one more look behind them before shutting the door.

"No problems."

Emily paused in the small foyer and gave a contented sigh. "It's good to be home." She angled toward the shadowy living room on her left, where all the shades and drapes had been drawn. "Why is it so dark in here?"

Mark followed her as she moved into the room, giving the space an appreciative scan. Soft white walls formed a neutral backdrop for her impressionist prints and cobalt blue couch. Inviting side chairs upholstered in cream, blue, and rose stripes were styled in clean, simple lines. A piece of contemporary blown-glass art in vivid jewel tones was centered on the glass-topped coffee table.

Classy, he concluded. Just like the lady who called this home.

As she headed toward the window and reached for the pull on the shade, he moved behind her and put a restraining hand on her shoulder. "It's safer this way."

Mark watched her contented expression morph to apprehension as her illusion of home-turf safety evaporated. He wished he could restore it. Wished he could guarantee her this was a safe haven. But the only way to ensure her security was to catch the guy who'd lined them up in the sights of his rifle.

"I put your bag in the bedroom, Emily." Nick broke the tense silence. "We're going to need a few minutes to sort things out here, if you want to unpack."

"Okay. Thanks." Her words came out shaky. "There are sodas in the fridge if anyone gets thirsty. Did you get those prescriptions, Nick?"

"Also in the bedroom."

"Thanks."

The three men watched her slow progress toward the steps, her fingers skimming the wall to steady herself. When they heard her door on the second floor click closed, Nick spoke.

"She's pretty banged up."

"Inside and out." Coop frowned. "This whole situation reminds me of Monica."

"But that turned out okay," Mark reminded him. And himself.

"Yeah." Coop shoved one hand in the pocket of his slacks and turned. "Okay, Nick, what have you got?"

"The security here isn't bad." He settled on the edge of the couch, and the other two men sat as well. "She has a good alarm system and deadbolts on the outside doors. The windows are double-paned. She's also got a very attentive neighbor in the attached unit, who cornered me as I was opening the door. An older woman. She was quite protective until I showed her my creds."

"That would have to be Evelyn."

"Evelyn Martelli. How did you know?"

"Emily told me about her. The grandmotherly type, from what I gather."

"Yes. But she's not afraid of confrontation. And it was obvious she keeps an eye out for your friend. I checked the parking situation too. Not so good. An isolated garage in back covers this whole unit. The spots are numbered, meaning it would be easy to target a car."

"The visitor parking in the front would be safer. Plus, there's a lot more activity out there," Coop noted.

"I agree. In terms of surveillance, much as I'd like to suggest we put an agent inside—and I'd be happy to volunteer for that duty," Nick offered with a grin, "it makes more sense to monitor the building from the parking lot. From the front we can scan the whole area and watch for anyone who might be stalking her. Plus, we could be at her door in seconds."

"Sounds like a plan," Coop concurred.

"I also got an update from Steve. The guy left a clear route through the woods, thanks to broken branches and trampled underbrush, but not much else. The lab's working on what they have, but no results yet. They promised to have more by the briefing tomorrow."

A door opened upstairs, and Emily came down the steps a few moments later. She'd changed into shorts and a T-shirt, and her feet were bare. If anything, she looked more vulnerable than ever. Mark's throat tightened, and he had to restrain the urge to close the distance between them and wrap her in a comforting hug.

She hesitated in the doorway of the living room, grasping the door frame with one hand. "Am I interrupting?"

Mark rose. "Not at all. We need to talk with you, anyway."

She joined them, and with Mark's assistance gingerly lowered herself into one of the striped chairs. She flashed him a smile as he took his seat. "Why do I think you gentlemen have been planning my life for me?"

"Nick volunteered to sleep on your couch," Coop told her.

"We voted him down," Mark added. "He'll be in the parking lot."

"You can't blame a guy for trying." Nick grinned, eliciting a smile from Emily.

"We'll regroup after the briefing tomorrow, but in the meantime we'll have an agent in the visitor lot out front. What are your plans for tomorrow?"

"I have appointments, but I'm going to reschedule them for later in the week and stay close to home. I think I'll sleep most of the day."

"Good plan," Mark approved. "By end of day, we may have some additional information. We do need one more thing from you. Names of the women you've counseled at the shelter in the past four weeks."

Emily sent him a puzzled look. "Why?"

"Abusers are not nice people. And when thwarted, they can be dangerous. If any of the women you spoke with told her spouse or boyfriend that your counsel convinced her to leave him permanently, he could be very upset. How many women would you estimate you've coun- seled in the past month?"

"Eight, maybe. Some weeks I only talk to one, other weeks two or three."

"Can you get us their names? We'll check them

out, see if they've mentioned your name to their significant other."

"You'll be discreet?"

"Always."

"My notes are at my office. I can have Maria, my secretary, check my file tomorrow. She could also call the shelter to get additional contact information. Is that okay?"

After a brief hesitation, Mark agreed. "Today would be better. But we can wait until first thing in the morning. Have her fax the information." Mark withdrew a small notebook from his pocket and jotted down a number, glancing at the other two men as he handed it to Emily. "Anything else we need to cover today?" When the other two agents shook their heads, he gave Emily his full attention. "Then we're going to let you get some rest."

"I'll be across the parking lot, in the black SUV," Nick told her, rising.

"I'll wait for you outside." Coop followed Nick to the door.

"Thanks, guys." Emily started to stand, but Mark restrained her.

"They can find their way out."

Waiting until the door clicked shut, he moved to the ottoman across from her and took her hands. "We're going to do our best to find this guy, Em."

"I know." She squeezed his fingers. "Some reunion, huh?"

"Yeah." A humorless smile twisted his lips. "But we're going to make up for this after the dust settles. And that's a promise I won't forget."

For an instant, Mark was tempted to lean close and seal his pledge with a kiss. Emily had been right earlier. The years had melted away, and Wren Lake seemed like yesterday. He, too, felt as if they'd picked up where they'd left off.

But twenty years had passed, and you couldn't step back into a relationship that easily, he reminded himself. They were different people now, with histories that had shaped and changed them in the two decades that had elapsed since they'd shared their first kiss. She'd loved again, and mourned that loss. He'd shied away from commitments, unwilling to take on the inevitable stress of trying to juggle a relationship with his demanding career. Reconnecting wasn't that simple. Especially when he was slated to return to Quantico in four short weeks, and her life was here.

Restraining his amorous impulse, Mark gave her fingers one more squeeze and rose. "Lock the deadbolt behind me."

He helped her up, and she followed him to the door.

"Be careful, Mark."

"I will. And keep the shades and curtains closed."

"Okay."

He lifted his hand and touched her cheek. Hesitated. And then he stepped through the door and pulled it closed, waiting until he heard the soft click of the lock before joining Coop.

Emily took a long, slow breath and rested her forehead against the door as quiet descended in her condo.

If the last thirty-six hours had left her reeling, the last thirty-six seconds had sucked the air from her lungs.

Unless the pain medication was totally addling her brain, she'd swear that Mark had wanted to kiss her just now.

Unsettling as that was, she was more unnerved by her reaction.

She'd wanted him to.

Pushing away from the door, she forced her lethargic legs to carry her back up the stairs to her bedroom. Sinking onto the mattress, she stretched out with a sigh. She'd tried to disguise her discomfort as much as possible around the three agents, but she was hurting. Badly. Every muscle in her body ached, and her arm was throbbing. The pain medication she'd downed as soon as she'd arrived home hadn't yet kicked in.

Yesterday, she'd used the word surreal to describe her present situation. And it fit. Despite the bulky bandage, she found it difficult to believe she'd been shot. Things like this didn't happen to people like her, who lived quiet lives, pursued safe careers, abided by the law. Crime and violence weren't supposed to be part of her world anymore, now that Grant was gone.

She turned her head on the pillow, toward the photo on her nightstand. It had been taken at Grant's birthday party a week before the fire that had claimed his life and destroyed their future. She'd known when she'd married him that his job carried some risk. But he'd assured her accidents were rare, that the safety net of his training would protect him 99 percent of the time.

Neither of them had counted on Grant running into the 1 percent sort of situation where it wouldn't.

Lifting the photo from the nightstand, she gazed at Grant's face, recalling their first meeting. She'd shared an elevator with him when he'd come to do a safety inspection at her office building. His energy and intensity had reminded her of Mark—a surprise, considering she hadn't thought much about her summer beau in the years before meeting Grant.

It wasn't that she and Mark had had a falling out. They'd stayed in touch for a few months after that idyllic summer, and she'd seen him again at her grandmother's funeral, but they'd both had plans, and the letters had gradually dwindled, then ceased. Nevertheless, she'd tucked the memory of her first, sweet taste of romance in her heart, expecting someday to find the man who would take it to the next level.

But for years, she hadn't. Always goal oriented, she'd devoted herself to her schooling with a singular focus that allowed no room for other pursuits. She'd received her PhD at twenty-six and gone on to work with a seasoned pro, opening her own practice after he retired two years later. There'd never been any time for romance.

Until Grant had convinced her to *take* time.

And in truth, it had been an easy sell, she reflected. With his teasing smile, he'd always been able to coax her away for a day of fun, convince her to leave the office before seven and share a pizza, or cajole her into taking a walk through the autumn leaves. He'd helped teach her the value of balance in her life, the importance of carving out time for relationships.

It was a lesson that had been long overdue for an army brat who'd never been in one place long enough to form lasting friendships. As much as she counseled her clients to take time for themselves and the people who were important in their lives, she hadn't followed her own advice until Grant came along.

Since his death, she'd fallen back into old habits, using work to fill the empty place in her life—and to keep risk at arm's length. If you didn't let anyone trespass on your heart, you couldn't get hurt. She'd been down the road of loving and losing once; she didn't want to travel it again. Instead, she'd counted on work to sustain her.

What she hadn't counted on was Mark reappearing in her life.

He would have liked Grant, she speculated, tracing the image of her husband with a loving touch. They shared common traits. A ready smile. Integrity. Honesty. A teasing manner that hid a serious side revealed only to people in whom they had absolute trust.

Under different circumstances, Emily might have considered exploring the possibility of picking up her relationship with Mark. He'd been up-front in his interest, said he didn't want to let her slip away again. And their shared history gave them a solid base on which to build.

But there was no way she could ever again get involved with someone in a high-risk profession.

And from everything she'd read, high-risk defined the HRT.

As the medication began to take effect and her eyes drifted closed, she hugged the photo of Grant to her chest. In their brief months together, he'd given her enough memories of love to last a lifetime. She didn't need to create any more. Yes, it had been good to run into Mark. She'd enjoyed their reunion, would look forward to seeing more of him in the next few days. But they had no future together.

Even if Mark thought otherwise.

7

"Okay, if everyone's ready, let's get started."

As Carl Owens called the Monday morning briefing to order, Mark surveyed the table in the conference room. Reps from the ERT were present, as were the detectives and agents working the case. Although it was a joint investigation, Carl and Steve had agreed that today's briefing would take place at Oakdale police headquarters.

"Les, are you with us?" Steve verified.

"We're hooked in." Les Coplin's voice had the typical disembodied sound of a conference-call connection.

"We met a couple of times over the weekend. No breakthroughs. But the evidence team has a preliminary report." Steve turned to Clair. "You're on."

The ERT lead investigator rose and moved to the front of the room, flipping on the overhead projector.

"The shooter didn't leave much. No casings, but we did find the projectiles. They're 30-06, suggesting they were fired from a common deer rifle. Both are distorted." She put the photos of the bullets on the screen. "Ballistics ran their rifling parameters through the general rifling characteristics database and thinks the rifle may be a Winchester."

She replaced the bullet shots with one of a footprint. "It was fairly easy for the detectives on the scene to identify the shooter's route through the woods and his firing position, based on broken branches and compressed ground cover. There were no fibers at the scene, but we did get a partial footprint in an area of damp ground. Size eleven, common work boot. Not enough there to verify wear pattern. We did take a soil sample from the footprint, and there appears to be some material in the dirt that is inconsistent with the soil in that area. Quantico is working to identify it as we speak."

The footprint transparency was replaced by one of a tire track. "We found this impression in some mud at the edge of the woods, where the shooter exited. We can't verify it's from his car, but it was at the far end of the church parking lot, in an area that wouldn't be used by members of the congregation unless there was an overflow crowd. Also, since it rained the day before the shooting, we know it was a recent track. There's not much here, but enough to tell us the shooter drove a midsized car."

Clair tucked her short blonde hair behind her ear and adjusted her glasses. "This diagram is interesting." She centered it on the projector. Picking up a laser pointer, she aimed it at an X at the edge of the woods. "This marks the shooter's location. Note where the two victims were standing at the time of the shooting." She indicated Mark's and Emily's positions southwest of the shooter. "They came together from opposite directions; Agent Sanders from the north, Dr. Lawson from the south." She traced their routes with the pointer.

The room went silent, and Mark's stomach clenched as he exchanged a look with Coop. He'd passed directly in front of the shooter as he walked toward Emily, and the man hadn't taken a shot.

"This would suggest Dr. Lawson was the target." Steve voiced the obvious conclusion. "But if she was, why wait until she and Mark were together to fire?"

"If he was focused on Dr. Lawson, it's conceivable he didn't see Mark until it was too late to get a clear shot," Carl weighed in.

"What were you doing immediately before the first shot was fired?" Coop directed his question to Mark.

It took Mark a second to re-create the moment in his mind. "We'd just talked about getting together for a cold drink, and I was checking the time. I had to angle away from the sun to cut the glare on the face of my watch."

"In other words, you shifted enough to the right to potentially open up a line of sight for the shooter to Dr. Lawson."

"Yes."

"Let's not be too hasty here," Steve interjected. "What about that row of bushes along the path,

Clair? Wouldn't they have prevented the shooter from getting a clear shot at Mark?"

She indicated the bushes with her pointer. "These are about six feet high and spaced four feet apart. They run along the path for thirty yards. They wouldn't have blocked the shooter's view, but they could have been an impediment to shooting if Agent Sanders was moving at a fast pace. And when he emerged from behind them, he would have been directly across from the shooter, presenting a less-than-optimal side view as a target."

"The guy might have been waiting until Mark got past the bushes and moved away from him, planning to aim for his back." Carl studied the diagram and shook his head. "I don't think this gives us a clear answer about the target."

"Or if there was one," Steve pointed out. "We can't discount the possibility that we're dealing with a random act of violence. What we've learned suggests otherwise, but it's too early to rule anything out."

"Agreed. Anything else, Clair?" When she shook her head, Carl picked up a notepad. "Let's move on to the interviews. We finished canvassing the neighbors in the vicinity of the church, and with the exception of several families who were on vacation, we talked to someone in every household. No one saw anything out of the ordinary that morning, or noticed any activity at the church. The investigators also asked residents and the pastor of the church about surveillance cameras but came up blank there too." He set the notepad down. "What about suspects . . . enemies, people who are holding grudges, recently released criminals?" He turned to Mark.

"I've checked my recent releases. There haven't been any in the past few months. I've also spoken with Dr. Lawson." He filled them in on the contacts from the shelter she would provide that morning. "Did anyone track down Jack Hanley yet?"

"No." One of the detectives on the other side of the table spoke. "No one's been home since you passed his name on to us. I'm heading there again after the briefing."

"That brings us back to Mark." Steve looked toward the speakerphone. "Les, do you want to chime in here?"

"I've got Christy Reynolds with me. She's the profiler in our Behavioral Science Unit who evaluated the hate mail we got after the convenience store incident. I asked her to take another look at that material in light of the shooting. Christy."

Folding his arms across his chest, Mark leaned back in his chair as she began to speak.

"All the overtly threatening feedback we received was anonymous. Assuming the shooter was one of those people, logic tells us there was nothing to prevent him from taking action sooner if he lived in the East. The fact that the shooting occurred in St. Louis suggests that if Mark is the target as a result of some of that feedback, and if the shooter was following his movements, proximity might now give him an incentive to act. As a result, I focused on letters and emails from the Midwest. I'll fax you the names of St. Louis area people who signed their letters, but we're not able to identify the authors of the more hostile feedback."

"What's your risk assessment, based on the content of the communication?" Steve asked.

"Marginal. Most people who spout off like this are the same people who write nasty letters to the newspaper or get into shouting matches at board of aldermen meetings. They blow off steam that way versus taking any direct action. That doesn't mean there aren't exceptions to that rule, but I saw nothing in any of the material I reviewed to suggest we're dealing with the kind of deep-seated hate or mental imbalance that would pose an imminent danger to Mark. Nor was there more than one communication from any single individual, which might have suggested a fixation or vendetta."

Steve rested his elbows on the table and knitted his fingers together. "What about the family of the boy who was killed at the convenience store?"

"We've already done a cursory check on them," Les responded. "The parents are model citizens, churchgoers, gainfully employed, civic volunteers.

The remaining two children are ten and fourteen, good students, no apparent problems. Last weekend they were all on vacation, visiting family in Michigan."

"Did any leads surface based on the media coverage?" Coop threw in that question.

"No." Carl ran his fingers through his bristly salt-and-pepper hair, shook his head, and let out an audible breath. "I'm not seeing anything substantive. Steve?"

"I agree."

"I suggest we finish the remaining interviews as soon as possible," Carl continued. "Steve, it sounds like Christy's list will cover multiple jurisdictions. Do you want to have your people tackle those?"

"Okay. And Mark and Coop are going to handle the interviews of Dr. Lawson's domestic abuse shelter clients."

"We canvassed the park this morning, talking to everyone who came through," Carl noted. "We'll be there again tomorrow, and next Saturday. There's a chance one of the regulars saw something out of the ordinary on Saturday."

"You'll get us the lab report on the material you found in the shoe print ASAP?" Steve turned to Clair.

"Yes. I hope to have it later today or tomorrow."

"What's your security protocol?" Carl directed the question to Steve.

"We're covering Mark. Most of you met Evan Cooper before the meeting." He nodded to the dark-haired agent, who lifted a hand in response. "He works with Mark on the HRT. I've also assigned one of our people to him as Coop's backup."

"What about Dr. Lawson?"

"We've got someone on her now, but if things remain quiet, we'll reduce our coverage in a day or two."

That news didn't surprise Mark. He didn't like it, but he knew Steve was already doing more than was required. The FBI didn't provide protection for targets. Federal marshals often worked security details, but they focused their efforts on high-profile witnesses and judges. And the local cops didn't have the personnel to provide round-the-clock protection. Once the case began to cool—and in light of the sparse evidence and lack of leads, that was happening with alarming speed—Emily would be on her own. Unless he could convince Steve to let him and Coop step in.

"Assuming nothing breaks sooner, let's regroup this afternoon about four," Carl said. "Thank you all for coming."

As the meeting concluded, Steve signaled to Mark and headed out the door. Mark followed him to an empty interview room, and Steve waved him to a seat as he shut the door. "What are your thoughts?"

"I don't like pulling security off of Emily."

"I didn't think you would." Steve took a chair at right angles to Mark.

"There's too much we don't know yet. I know we can't cover her 24/7, but for the immediate future I'd like to give her some company when she ventures out."

"I can cut you loose from some of your day-to-day work to focus on this case—and to provide some security for Dr. Lawson. Coop can back you up. I can also give you Nick now and then to fill in. That's the best I can do."

Some of the tension in Mark's shoulders dissipated. It was more than he'd hoped for. "I understand. And I appreciate your willingness to let me work this."

"You'll be gone in four weeks anyway. No sense getting you involved in anything new here." Leaning back in his chair, Steve gave him a steady look. "Unless we could convince you to stay."

The out-of-the-blue remark surprised Mark, and he wondered if Steve might be kidding. But the man's tone and demeanor suggested he was very serious.

"I was a case agent before I joined the HRT." He chose his words with care, watching the other man. "I don't think I'd want to step back into that role."

"I hoped you might consider it if the role was . . . enhanced." Steve paused to give his vibrating BlackBerry a cursory look, then slipped it back on his belt. "This is confidential, but Dave Sheldon is retiring to take a job as police chief in California at the end of September. I need to fill his slot. I like what I've seen of your work on the reactive squad here, and I know you have the tactical and special weapons experience to do the job."

Stunned, Mark stared at Steve. The man was offering him the chance to head the St. Louis FBI SWAT team.

"I wasn't planning to leave the HRT."

"Understood. But things have a way of changing. Think about it." He rose, signaling the end of the discussion.

"Okay. And . . . thank you."

His hand on the doorknob, Steve turned. "I like to surround myself with good people. If it works for you, great. If not, I understand."

Mark gave himself sixty seconds to regroup. When he stepped into the hall, he found Coop waiting, arms crossed over his chest, one shoulder propped against the wall.

"Everything okay?" Coop raised an eyebrow.

"Yeah. Fine." He'd share Steve's offer with Coop eventually, confident his partner would respect the need for confidentiality. But first he had to process it himself.

"I talked to Les. He called me after the meeting to let me know he doesn't want to ease up on your security."

"Meaning we're stuck with each other."

"Like glue. Until we get this thing figured out."

"I have a feeling that may not happen anytime soon." Mark headed down the hall.

Coop fell into step beside him. "The guy didn't leave much to work with, that's for sure. But it only takes a lucky break or two to turn the tide. Let's check and see if the list of Emily's clients from the shelter has come in yet."

"Sí, cambié las citas. Pero tienes que quedarte en casa más de un día. ¡Te dispararon!"

As the rush of Spanish tumbled through the phone line in response to her question, a smile tugged at Emily's lips. "English, Maria. Despite your diligent efforts to teach me, I have no ear for languages."

"I said that I have changed your appointments for today, like you asked, but you should stay home more than one day. You've been shot . . . with a gun! ¡Que Dios nos proteja!"

"Except for being a little tired, I'm doing fine. You know I'd go stir-crazy if I sat around my condo for more than one day."

"That is because you have nothing in your life but work. Work is good. But there is more. You have been too long by yourself."

For seven years, since the day she'd opened her practice, Maria Fernandez had shared her office as secretary, receptionist, sage, friend—and matchmaker, Emily reflected. Married at twenty-two, she was the proud mother of three. She loved her work . . . but she loved her family more and couldn't understand why anyone would want to remain single.

She'd fretted about the lack of romance in her boss's life, and it had been her prodding that had pushed Emily to accept that first date with Grant. No one had been happier than Maria when Emily had married. Or more devastated when she'd been widowed. Maria had consoled, comforted, fed, supported, and—after a respectable number of months had passed—begun nudging her to establish some sort of social life again.

However, despite Maria's good intentions, Emily had no interest in taking another chance on romance. In time, she hoped Maria would come to accept her decision and quit pushing.

But that hadn't happened yet.

"I'm fine by myself, Maria. I like my own company."

"Hmph."

The muttered comment that followed was in Spanish, but Emily could guess what *mula* meant.

"I need you to check my file for Hope House and pull the names of the women I've seen during the past four weeks." Turning the discussion to business was a surefire way to deflect further personal comments. "The shelter will give you their contact information. I've already alerted Margaret that you're going to call. Once you have all that, go ahead and fax it." Emily recited the number Mark had given her.

"I will handle. You rest. Do you want me to bring you some fajitas tonight? We had them for dinner yesterday, and there is plenty left."

"No, thank you. My fridge is full. I'll see you tomorrow."

"Sí. I am sure you will." Maria didn't try to hide her resigned sigh.

"If anything comes up before then, call me and—"

The ring of the doorbell startled Emily, and she fumbled the phone.

"What was that?" Maria demanded.

Struggling to quiet the sudden pounding of her heart, Emily took a slow breath and tightened her hold on the phone. "The doorbell."

"Do not answer it!"

"I have an FBI agent watching my front door, Maria. It's probably him."

"You check. I will wait."

"Fine. I'm walking to the door now." When she reached it, she peered through the peephole. Evelyn stood on the other side, balancing a plate covered with aluminum foil. "It's Evelyn, Maria. Bearing food."

"Ah. Good. You will call later?"

"Yes. I promise."

Severing the connection, Emily flipped the lock and pulled the door open.

"Good morning, Emily. I hoped you'd stay home today. I made pot roast last night and, as usual, I cooked far too much. I was hoping you'd take some off my hands." The older woman held out the plate.

With a smile, Emily took the foil-covered offering and motioned her inside. "You're a treasure, Evelyn."

A flush rose on the woman's cheeks, deepening their natural pink color. With her white hair coiffed into a soft French twist and her twinkling blue eyes, she looked like an ad for a greeting card commercial about grandmothers.

"Thank you, my dear. But I won't come in today. I expect the last thing you need is company. Though I must say, you've had your share of handsome young men trooping through here in the past twenty-four hours."

"They were FBI agents."

"I know. I met one of them. And there's another one across the parking lot now in a black SUB."

Emily struggled to stifle the smile that tugged at her lips. Evelyn never got abbreviations right. SUVs were SUBs. DVDs were DVTs. ATMs were AMTs. But aside from being acronymically challenged, she didn't miss a trick. If any suspicious characters were lurking in the area, Emily was convinced Evelyn would spot them before the FBI did.

"They'll be around for a few days, I think."

"I should hope so, after what that crazy man did to you. How are you feeling today, dear?"

"Better." That wasn't a lie. She hadn't needed any pain medication yet, and her sleep hadn't been interrupted by nightmares, as she'd feared.

"Good. You enjoy that pot roast and call me if you need anything."

"I will. Thank you, Evelyn."

She waved a hand in a dismissive gesture. "Just following the Good Book. Do unto others and all that. Why are we here if we can't help each other? See you later."

As Evelyn trotted off, Emily closed the door, secured the lock, and tucked the phone under her arm. It rang again en route to the kitchen, and she shook her head. Good thing she hadn't tried to sleep in, she reflected as she greeted the caller.

"Emily, it's Mark. Did I wake you?"

The sound of his voice, warm and a bit husky, set off a flutter in the pit of her stomach. "No. How did the briefing go?"

"Nothing much to report." Frustration nipped at his words. "But we're still checking out leads, and the lab results aren't back yet. How are you doing?"

"Better than yesterday. I spoke with my secretary, and she'll be faxing the contact information for my Hope House clients in the next half hour."

"Good. Coop and I will check them out this afternoon. Feel like some company for dinner tonight?"

Emily looked at the plate in her hand and decided it would keep until tomorrow. "Sure. Business or pleasure?"

"A little of both."

At least he was honest.

"I'd like that."

"Great. What should I bring? Pizza, Chinese, Mexican, Italian . . . you name it."

"You pick. But if it's pizza, could you ask them to leave off—"

"The mushrooms. And add extra green peppers."

His response caught her off guard. "How in the world did you remember that?"

"It must have been stuck somewhere in my subconscious."

"That's a scary thought. What else is stuck there?"

She could hear the smile in his voice when he responded. "I have no idea. I guess we'll find out."

His flirty inflection sent a tingle zipping along her nerve endings—and prompted her to wander over to the thermostat and turn up her air-conditioning. She tried for a light, teasing tone when she replied. "That's what I'm afraid of."

"As I recall, you don't harbor any deep, dark secrets or questionable vices that you need to worry about."

"If I did, I have a feeling you guys would know about them by now. I must admit, having your life scrutinized is kind of weird. And a little scary."

"It shouldn't be, unless you have something to hide."

"Nothing the feds would be interested in."

"Hmm. That's an intriguing comeback. Maybe I'll have to brush up on my interviewing skills before tonight. What happened to that uncomplicated girl I used to know?"

"Life."

"I hear you. I suppose most people our age have their share of baggage. We'll have to continue this discussion in person."

"Or not." It would be safer to keep the conversation light and simple, Emily decided.

He chuckled. "How does seven sound?"

"Fine. I'll see you then."

As the connection went dead, Emily returned the phone to its stand and slid Evelyn's offering into the fridge. It would be way too easy to let Mark Sanders ease back into her life, she realized. During that long-ago summer, they'd clicked on some elemental level. And despite the passage of years, despite the baggage he'd referenced, despite their different lifestyles, they'd clicked again.

But she was older now. And wiser. Love wasn't about whispered promises and stolen kisses or the magic of Wren Lake. It was about risk and courage and loss. It offered incredible highs—and crushing lows. And every moment of togetherness and sharing and intimacy served only to throw the devastating loneliness of loss into stark relief, like the deepening shadows cast by a setting winter sun.

Emily had no regrets about her time with Grant, except that it had been too short. But neither did she have any desire to repeat it. She'd survived loss once. She didn't think she could do it again. It was safer to build a world she could control, one that didn't require her to expose her heart to risk.

As she moved back toward the bedroom, already in need of a nap, she paused to peek through the blinds in her office. Her gaze fell on the black SUV across the parking lot, its tinted windows hiding the occupant from passersby.

And all at once, a startling insight jolted her.

The safe, predictable world she'd created for herself, the one she guarded so fiercely, the one in which she controlled the variables, hadn't simply vanished in a heartbeat, leaving her exposed and vulnerable.

It had always been an illusion.

8

That evening, at seven o'clock on the dot, Mark pressed Emily's doorbell. He'd traded his suit and tie for khakis and a cotton shirt, but the heat was still oppressive.

Or maybe he was hot for other reasons, he reflected as Emily opened the door and his pulse took a leap. Despite the raw patch of skin on her cheek where a scab was now forming, and despite the purple bruise on her temple that refused to be disguised by cover-up, she looked fabulous. White capri slacks hugged her slim hips, and her pink and white striped knit top hinted at her supple curves. When he found himself focusing a second too long on the appealing softness of her lips, he forced himself to speak.

"Hi."

"Hi yourself." A becoming blush tinted her cheeks—which did nothing to cool him off.

He lifted a large shopping bag bearing the logo of a local gourmet takeout shop. "I come bearing dinner. Will that earn me an invitation into the air-conditioning?"

"Sorry." She stepped aside to usher him through the door. "What happened to the pizza?"

"I thought we deserved better after the past couple of days." He waited until she locked the door before heading toward the kitchen. "This will only take a few minutes to throw together—or so the clerk assured me."

Setting the bag on the table, he unpacked Caesar salad, beef tenderloin, au gratin potatoes, asparagus, rolls, and two pieces of chocolate torte.

"Wow!" Emily surveyed the feast. "You don't do things halfway, do you?"

"I considered going for sentiment and grabbing some poor boy sandwiches, like we used to take to Wren Lake. But I had a feeling you'd prefer slightly more upscale fare after being forced to ingest hospital food for twenty-four hours."

"You have my undying gratitude. What can I do to help?"

"Plates, utensils, water glasses, napkins . . . unless you want to use the paper and plastic they provided."

She wrinkled her nose. "A meal like this deserves my good china and silver. And we'll eat in the dining room."

"Light some candles too," he called after her as she headed toward the door.

She turned on the threshold. "Pretty soon you'll be wanting music."

With a grin, he withdrew a CD of easy-listening jazz from the bag and handed it to her.

Folding her arms across her chest, she tilted her head and considered him. "You are one smooth operator, Mark Sanders. How many hearts have you broken?" She plucked the CD from his fingers.

"I take the fifth."

"That's what I figured."

Five minutes later, as they sat down to enjoy their salads amid candlelight and soft music, Emily shook her head. "This is almost as surreal as the shooting. You and me together after twenty years."

"But surreal in a good way."

"Absolutely." She unfolded her napkin and placed it on her lap, then bowed her head in silent prayer.

She'd done that even as a teen, Mark recalled. While a good number of their friends had tossed out their faith as too old-fashioned and too restrictive, Emily had held on to her beliefs. He found it somehow comforting that she still did.

He waited quietly until she finished. "That's a nice habit. And it's good to know some things never change."

"Including God. He's the one constant in a world where very little can be counted on. And it's more than a habit. It's a way of life."

Unsure how to respond without offending her, Mark picked up his fork and changed the subject. "I like your hair tonight."

"Thanks. Getting ready for dinner was a challenge. Since I can't get this bandage wet"—she moved her arm, where the thick white dressing peeked below the sleeve of her top—"I had to resort to a bath instead of a shower. And trying to wash my hair one handed in the kitchen sink was no picnic, let me tell you."

He reached over and fingered the silky strands. "I would have been glad to help you."

She groped for her glass and took a long swallow of ice water. "I'll let that pass."

"Why?"

"Because it makes me uncomfortable. Just like my mention of faith makes you uncomfortable."

Dropping his hand, he focused on his salad. She'd always been too good at reading him. "It doesn't make me uncomfortable, Em. I just don't relate to it much anymore."

"Have you really seen that much bad stuff?"

Her question was quiet and gentle. But the memories it stirred up were brutal. Terrorist raids, prison riots, hyperviolent street gangs that thrived on carjacking, drug dealing, and murder. And Jason Wheeler, who had died because of a crack addict's desperate need for a fix.

"Yeah. I have."

The sudden warmth of her fingers seeped through the sleeve of his shirt, her touch a surprise—and a comfort. "I'm sorry, Mark."

He tried to smile. "Hey, I signed on for this gig. I like my job. Remember that line from *Camelot*? 'Might for right.' It fits. I don't like using force, but sometimes it's the only way to bring justice. And I believe in justice, Em."

"You always did. And it's a noble principle. God would approve."

His smile faded. "I'd like to believe that. But to be honest, I'm not convinced he pays that much attention. I can't reconcile a loving, caring God with all the brutality and callousness and disregard for humanity I've seen."

"He cares. But he also gave us free will. Meaning people can make mistakes or bad choices."

"And innocent people suffer as a result." He touched her injured arm. "Like you."

"What would you have had God do? Send down a bolt of lightning to strike the shooter? Turn me invisible? Take away that man's free will?"

Her calm response ruffled him. "How can you be philosophical about almost getting killed?"

"It's not about philosophy. It's about trust. If I think too much about what could have happened Saturday, I wouldn't be able to function. There was nothing I could do to control that situation— and there's very little I can do to control a similar situation in the future. As much as I like to think I'm in charge of my life, Saturday reminded me I can't manage every variable. All I can do is take appropriate precautions and then put it in God's hands. And the hands of the FBI, of course."

The last was tacked on in a teasing tone, an obvious attempt to lighten the somber mood that had descended. She might be trying to sound philosophical, but the discussion had shaken her, Mark realized, noting the sudden tremble in her hand, the hollow look in her eyes. He'd hoped to give her a pleasant dinner, as far removed from the terror of Saturday as possible. Instead, he'd brought it all back.

He took her hand, entwining her cold fingers in his. "Well, between God and the FBI, you're in very good hands. Now tell me about Evelyn Martelli. I met her on the way in, and considering the charming but determined way she grilled me,

I'm wondering if she might be one of our under-cover people."

His change of subject and humorous observation eased some of the tension in her features.

"That's an interesting mental image. Evelyn with a gun." Emily smiled. "She'd probably be more lethal with her knitting needles."

"So what's the scoop on her?" Mark reached for their salad plates and stood to put the main course in the microwave.

Trailing along behind him, Emily leaned against the doorway. "You mean you guys haven't run a background check on her?"

Mark flashed her a grin as he worked. "She isn't high on our suspect list."

"Good. You'd be wasting your time. Evelyn is like the perfect grandmother. Supportive, caring, available—but never overbearing. When I moved here a year after Grant died, I thought I was han-dling things okay. After all, I'm a psychologist. I, of all people, should have known how to deal with grief. I'd counseled plenty of people in situations similar to mine.

"But to be honest, I was a mess. And Evelyn picked up on that in a flash. She found ways to convince me to go places with her by saying she was tired of being alone. When she discovered my dinner often consisted of canned tuna and crackers, she began dropping off 'leftovers.' I'd find jokes she'd printed off the Internet under my door. And I never spent a holiday alone. Somehow she always finagled me into driving her to her son's in Chicago for Christmas, saying she didn't want to travel by herself, or got me to help her serve meals at a homeless shelter on Thanksgiving. She was a godsend."

The microwave pinged, and Mark withdrew their entrees. Once they carried their plates back to the table, he resumed the conversation.

"You seem to have your act together now."

"In general, I'd say that's true. And I have a very full life."

"You do keep yourself very busy."

"It's good work, though." Her tone grew slightly defensive. "The women I've counseled at Hope House are in desperate need of sympathy and encouragement. And the radio program is important too. Did your background check give you much detail on that?"

"No. Tell me about it."

"It's a weekly call-in program called Teen Talk. My pastor's on the board of a local Christian radio station, and he convinced me to take on the project two years ago. The audience has been growing, and we've gotten some great accolades." She leaned forward, her expression earnest. "But the opportunity to provide kids with a forum in which to air their concerns is the real payoff for me. The show is a safe, anonymous way for them to get a third-party take on their perceptions, which can be distorted by hormones and peer pressure. I like to think I've made a difference in the lives of kids who otherwise might not have had a resource to turn to."

"And who do you turn to, Emily? Besides Evelyn?"

At his soft question, she shrugged and tucked her hair behind her ear. "Maria, my secretary, is a great sounding board."

He waited, but when she offered nothing else, he gave her a quizzical look. "That's it?"

"I can always talk to my pastor if I need some guidance. And prayer has been a mainstay." She took a sip of her water and turned the tables on him. "Let's talk about you for a while. You know almost everything about me, but you've managed to tell me very little about yourself. All I know is you're on the Hostage Rescue Team."

"I can't offer much more than that. My missions are often classified."

"What about when you aren't on missions?"

"I train. Work out. Hang around with the guys on the team. Eat dinner with Coop and his wife, Monica."

She chewed the last bite of the savory tenderloin. "How come I didn't hear any mention of dating?"

"I'm trying to be discreet."

"Don't worry. I didn't think a man like you would lack for female companionship."

Grinning, he removed her plate. "I'll get the dessert and coffee."

"I'm not letting you off the hook this easily, you know," she called after him as he headed for the kitchen.

"I didn't think you would. I'm just buying myself a minute to come up with some good answers."

He heard her laugh as he deposited the plates on the counter. In truth, though he'd had his pick of women who'd been impressed by the glamour of his profession—which was more perceived than real—there had never been anyone special in his life. He enjoyed casual dating, but he'd never been tempted to move any relationship to a more serious level. And he was always honest about that. Most women accepted whatever he was willing to offer. The ones who couldn't broke things off.

After putting their cake and coffee on a tray he found in her cupboard, he returned to the table. Emily watched him, her chin propped in one hand.

"Where's Coop?"

"He dropped me off and headed back to Nick's. He'll pick me up later."

"You could have invited him to join us."

"No, I couldn't. I'm not sharing you with anyone else tonight."

"I thought he was your friend."

"He is. And friends know when to disappear. Besides, he's returning a favor." Taking a sip of his coffee, he dug into his cake, surprised she hadn't returned to the subject of his social life.

"How so? And this is delicious, by the way. You can ply me with chocolate pastry anytime."

He chuckled. "Still a chocoholic, I see." Spearing a bite of cake, he answered her question. "Coop and I were assigned security duty for Monica. That's how they met. Once sparks began to fly, I tried to stay in the background."

Her speculative expression told him she'd caught his implication that sparks were flying in their situation as well. But she ignored it. "Why did she need protection?"

Hesitating, Mark told her as much as he could. "She was the daughter of a diplomat and was targeted by an extremist group. They ended up kidnapping her."

"Oh." She looked down and toyed with her cake, her expression troubled.

"And to answer your earlier question . . ." He surprised himself by bringing up his dating life again, but he wanted to erase the lines of worry that etched her features. "I date on a regular basis when I'm home. More now that Coop is married. But I've never had a serious relationship."

The ploy worked. Emily lifted her chin and studied him. "Why not?"

"That's a pretty personal question." His teasing tone took the edge off the comment.

"Turnabout is fair play."

"Touché." Leaning back, he cradled his cup in his hands. A grin tugged at the corner of his mouth as he gave her an appraising look. "I could say I've been carrying a torch for you all these years and no one else ever compared."

She laughed, doing her best not to choke on her coffee.

"I'm deeply wounded by your cynicism." He feigned a hurt expression.

"Where do you get these lines? I think I'm beginning to understand why you've never married."

Smiling, he took a sip of coffee. "Okay, the truth. It's like I told you in the park. My career doesn't lend itself to wedded bliss."

"It didn't stop Coop."

"I guess he's better at juggling commitments than I am. Plus, he found a woman who could live with the long absences. And the risk."

She regarded him for a moment, her expression pensive and touched with regret. Then she pushed her empty plate aside and checked her watch. "You said when you called earlier that tonight was both business and pleasure. I've enjoyed the pleasure part very much, but I'd hate to be responsible for keeping Coop up past his bedtime. I guess we better talk about the business."

She hadn't liked his answer, Mark concluded. Her retreat, though subtle, had been deliberate. For Emily, as for most women, the absences and risk inherent in his job weren't acceptable long-term. And logic told him they would be bigger stumbling blocks for her than for most women. She'd already loved—and lost—one man in a high-risk profession.

In a way, he should be grateful for her withdrawal. He wasn't in the market for commitments. Much as he'd once cared for Emily, there was no guarantee the old chemistry resurrected by their unexpected meeting could be sustained after the initial novelty wore off. Not that it wasn't pleasant while it lasted. He'd like nothing better than to tuck her close beside him on the couch tonight and share some laughs as they watched a vintage movie, like the ones they'd enjoyed during a classic comedy film festival in that Tennessee summer of their youth.

Beyond that, who knew? In less than four weeks, he'd return to Quantico and she'd go back to her normal life. One that didn't include him. It would be best to enjoy any stolen moments they had together in the midst of this craziness and expect nothing more.

Leaning forward, he folded his hands on the table and switched gears. "It's not the policy of the FBI or the local police to provide round-the-clock security for citizens who face violent threats. However, I've talked to my boss, and he's agreed to let me and Coop, plus Nick on occasion, be available to accompany you to and from your various commitments. For the near-term, anyway."

"Meaning the agent in the SUB—as Evelyn calls the surveillance vehicle in the parking lot—is going to disappear?"

He heard the trepidation beneath her attempt at humor. "He left when I arrived."

When she lifted her cup of coffee, he couldn't miss the tremor in her hand—and knew she was going to have a long, tense night.

"Why don't you tell me what the plan is?" She took a sip and pushed the cup aside.

"Coop and I, or Nick, will accompany you to your various commitments. All you need to do is give us a schedule and we'll be there as you move from place to place. We'd prefer you not venture out alone."

"For how long?"

"Until we solve this, or until we can conclude with reasonable certainty that the shooter has decided not to try again. Why don't you run me through your agenda for tomorrow? And it would be helpful if you could give us your schedule for the rest of the week ASAP."

"On Tuesdays I arrive at the office by eight to review my cases for the day. I see my first patient at nine. Since I often catch up on paperwork at noon, it's no hardship to stay in. I'll take a sandwich for lunch. I see my last patient at four, and Maria leaves at five. I usually stay until about six."

"Long day."

She lifted one shoulder. "It's interesting work. I don't mind the hours. Anyway, tomorrow I need to leave early to get the dressing on my arm changed."

"One of us will take you there too. Now let's run over some security protocols. Nick checked out your office this afternoon."

"Why am I not surprised?"

"Forewarned is forearmed. He said Maria was very helpful."

"She would be. She worries about me way too much."

"Someone needs to." He went on without giving her a chance to respond. "The building isn't very secure, Emily."

In truth, based on Nick's description, that was an understatement, Mark reflected. Located in the heart of Kirkwood, the small, single-story brick building that had been Emily's professional home for the past three years housed four office suites. Parking was in the rear, and the suites opened off a single center corridor. Other than an alarm system that could be set each night by the last occupant to exit, it was wide open.

"We've never needed to worry about that. It's generally a safe part of town."

He let her comment pass. For him, safety was always relative. "Nick said there are two doors into your private office."

"That's to preserve confidentiality. My current

patient can exit directly into the hall without having to go back through the waiting room and run into the next patient. The hall door is unmarked and always locked from the inside."

"That's what Maria told Nick. He also talked to the landlord, who agreed to install a peephole tomorrow in both hall doors. We need you to keep the reception room door locked too. We've instructed Maria to check all visitors before opening it, and not to let anyone in she doesn't recognize. And we want you to check the hall as patients exit your office before you open that door."

He leaned forward, his gaze intent. "This is all predicated on the assumption that you have absolutely no reservations about any patient other than Jack Hanley. If you do, Emily, this is the time to tell me."

"No." Her response was immediate. "I have no qualms about any of them. And very few about Jack."

After scrutinizing her for a few more seconds, Mark sat back. "Okay. How about if we come by for you about 7:30?"

"If you can manage 7:15, I'll treat you both to Starbucks. There's a shop near my office. And I love their vanilla lattes in the morning."

"Sold."

A sudden yawn caught her unawares, and she stifled it with an embarrassed laugh. "Sorry about that."

"I can take a hint." Grinning, he stood and began to clear the table.

"Leave everything." She rose and picked up a water glass. "The least I can do after that gourmet meal is—"

A soft tap sounded on the front door and she jerked, sloshing water on the tablecloth.

"It's Coop." Mark rested a reassuring hand on her shoulder. "I told him to come at ten."

Moving to the door, Mark checked the peephole and pulled it open. "Give me five minutes."

Coop stepped back into the shadows. "No problem."

When he returned to the dining room, Emily was standing where he'd left her, the water glass still clutched in her hand. It didn't take a genius—or a psychologist—to figure out she was scared.

He wanted to take her in his arms, assure her she would be safe. Except he could offer no such guarantees. Instead, he shoved his hands in his pockets and stayed where he was.

"If anything—and I mean anything—spooks you tonight, call 911. Don't hesitate. Promise me that."

"I will. Thank you for the fabulous dinner."

He heard the slight catch in her too-perky voice and hesitated. "I could sleep on the couch, Emily."

She managed a smile. "Then Coop would have to stay too, since he's assigned to protect *you*."

"He wouldn't mind a reprieve from the drywall dust."

"I only have one couch. And it's not big enough for either of you. Go home, Mark. I'll be fine. I have good locks and a good security system. Nick said so himself."

"Right."

"And don't forget, secret agent Evelyn is a knock on the wall away."

His lips tipped up. He admired Emily's spunk. He always had. "Tell her to keep those knitting needles handy."

"I'll do that." Setting the glass on the table, she rubbed her palms on her slacks and led the way toward the hall. "Let me show you out."

When she reached the door, Mark's hand closed over hers on the knob. As she turned to him in the dim foyer, looking vulnerable and in desperate need of comforting, he knew at once that touching her had been a mistake. And he wasn't sure what he should do next.

What he *wanted* to do was crystal clear.

And dangerous.

Earlier in the evening, when Emily had changed the subject after he'd mentioned the risk inherent in his job, her message had resonated. She didn't want to get involved with someone like him. And he understood that. While he might consider a brief romance, similar to the one they'd enjoyed during their Wren Lake days, Emily's world had been turned upside down once by loss. She wouldn't walk away unscathed if things escalated between them.

And in all honesty, he didn't think he would, either.

It was better to back off now. Before it was too late.

Removing his hand took every ounce of his willpower, but he managed it. "Keep the shades drawn and all the doors locked, okay?"

"I will." She didn't sound any steadier than he felt after that brief contact.

"I'll see you in the morning."

And before the temptation to pull her into his arms and taste her lips became too strong, he eased the door open and slipped outside, clicking it shut behind him.

"Everything okay out here?" He turned to Coop.

"Fine. Everything okay in there?" He nodded toward Emily's condo as he stepped out of the shadows.

"Yeah. Why?"

"I've been on a lot of missions with you, and you don't shake easily. But you look shook tonight."

Warmth crept up his neck, and Mark turned toward the car. "I'll be fine."

Coop fell into step beside him. "That's what I said too."

"What are you talking about?"

"Monica had the same effect on me."

For a moment, Mark considered refuting his partner's conclusion. But in the end, he decided against it. There was no point.

Coop knew him too well.

9

"Let's focus on lab results first. Clair, did you identify the material on the shooter's boot?" Steve turned to the ERT technician, who sat halfway down one side of the table in the Oakdale PD conference room for the Tuesday morning briefing.

"Yes. The lab actually found two different things. Concrete and manure."

"Is the manure from a deer?" Carl asked. "They're taking over out here."

"No. Based on preliminary results, it's looking like bovine. The sample was fresh, so there wasn't a lot of degradation in the DNA. The lab should have a positive ID today or tomorrow."

"Interesting. Sounds like our shooter lives in or frequents a rural area. And he's also been around wet concrete recently. It's not much, but it's more than we had yesterday." Steve consulted his notebook. "We managed to track down several of the people on Christy's list. They all check out so far. We have three more to question." He looked at Coop and Mark. "How are you doing with the women's shelter interviews?"

"There were nine women on our list." Coop

leaned forward. "We talked to five of them yesterday. Four haven't had any contact with their spouses or boyfriends since they spoke to Dr. Lawson, and one has gone back to her husband. We'll talk to the other four today, assuming they're in town."

"What about Hanley?"

"His alibi checked out," the detective who'd been assigned to question Emily's troubled client responded. "He was out of town with his son all weekend at a soccer camp. On Saturday morning, he was helping coach one of the teams. His story checks with all the witnesses he identified."

"So much for that lead. Anything else we need to discuss?" Carl directed the question to the group.

As Mark glanced around the table, there was a bit more discussion about next steps, but the options were limited. Three days into the investigation, most of the leads had been dead ends, and no new evidence had surfaced. The case was chilling as fast as his skin had years ago after a springtime plunge into icy Wren Lake.

"We'll schedule another briefing if anything substantive breaks. In the meantime, stay in touch by phone." Carl rose and gathered up his notes.

As the meeting broke up, Steve joined Mark and Coop in one corner of the conference room. "How's Dr. Lawson doing?"

"Okay. She went back to work today. Coop and I escorted her and laid out some ground rules for the next few days." Mark raked his fingers through his hair and shook his head in frustration. "We're nowhere with this."

"The shooter didn't leave us much to work with," Steve concurred.

"He wears a size eleven shoe, drives a midsize car, and has a passing acquaintance with cows and cement." Coop stuck one hand in his pocket and propped a shoulder against the wall. "We also know he's careful. He doesn't want us to find him."

"And we may not, unless he made a mistake we haven't found yet. Or tries again," Steve noted.

Sitting around waiting for the latter possibility held no appeal for Mark. "What do you think about releasing some additional information to the press? I know we didn't get any leads from the initial coverage, but maybe someone will see it who missed the original story."

"It might be worth a shot. Let me run it by Carl and see what he thinks. I'll be in touch."

As Steve headed across the room to talk with the detective captain, Coop turned to Mark. "Let's go check out the rest of the Hope House contacts."

At the knock on her door, Emily looked up from the patient file on her desk. "Come in."

A moment later, Maria's head appeared around the office door. "You are alone, yes?"

"Yes. Mr. Barlow left a few minutes ago." She

checked her watch. "Why are you still here? I thought you had to pick up Carlos early from school today."

"Sí, I know. But I do not like to leave you here alone."

"I have locks on all the doors. And peepholes now, too, thanks to Nick. Mark and Coop will be here soon. I promise not to open my door to strangers before then."

"You are sure?"

"Yes. Go. I'll see you tomorrow afternoon."

"I am glad you have no morning office hours on Wednesday. This way, you can sleep in."

"Trust me, I'm looking forward to it. Now go get Carlos."

"Okay. After I finish one letter."

A few minutes later, when Emily heard the muted sound of a male voice through her thick door, she assumed Mark and Coop had arrived to escort her to the doctor. Locking the patient file in her desk drawer, she rose, glad to call it a day. In the past hour her arm had begun to throb, and exhaustion had sapped her energy. After she got her dressing changed, her agenda for the remainder of the day was simple: take a warm bath, eat a light dinner, go to bed. And the sooner the better.

Gathering up her purse and briefcase, she threw her jacket around her shoulders. But as she flipped off the light in her office and pulled open the door, she froze.

A red-faced Jack Hanley stood on the threshold of the hall door, his path blocked by all five-foot-three inches of Maria, who had a white-knuckled grip on the door on one side and the door frame on the other. It was clear she had no intention of moving as she glared at the man who towered over her by a good ten inches.

When Jack caught sight of Emily, however, he shouldered his way past Maria, throwing her off balance.

"He was on the other side of the door when I opened it to leave," Maria told Emily, anger flashing in her eyes as she steadied herself on the doorframe. "I told him you were not seeing anyone else today, but he would not go away."

"It's all right, Maria." Emily did her best to keep her face and tone placid, though her stomach was churning. "Mr. Hanley, why don't you call tomorrow, and Maria will set up an appoint—"

"Did you send those cops to interrogate me?" He planted his fists on his hips and glared down at her as he bit out the words, his face inches from hers.

Although Mark had said the officers and agents wouldn't reveal details of the investigation, Emily wasn't surprised Jack had connected it to her. She'd been his nemesis of late, and he knew she had detailed information about his problems. Logic would suggest to him that she was somehow involved with, or had knowledge of, his encounter with the police.

"I'm aware they were planning to talk with you."

Her answer fueled his anger. "That's what I thought. Look, lady, I have enough trouble already. I don't need the cops hanging around. I haven't done anything illegal."

"Then you have nothing to be concerned about."

"Since the day I met you, I've had nothing but trouble."

"The trouble was already there when we met, Mr. Hanley. I'm trying to help you work through it."

"And sending the cops to my house is a way to do that? What kind of therapist are you, anyway?"

She eased away from him. "I think you should leave. We can schedule an appointment for tomorrow when you're calmer."

"I want to talk now." He raised his voice. "I'm tired of being jerked around. Tired of people telling me what to do and how to live my life. And don't try to brush me off." He reached out and snagged her jacket as she turned away, as if to restrain her, but succeeded only in pulling it from her shoulders.

The next few seconds were a blur. Emily heard pounding footsteps in the hall. Maria started hitting Jack with her purse. Mark and Coop appeared, guns drawn. As Coop whipped Jack around and barked out an order, Mark stepped in front of Emily, keeping his Glock trained on Jack.

"What the . . ." Jack's complexion reddened as Coop flashed his credentials and proceeded to do a thorough pat down.

After he finished, Coop backed off and lowered his gun, but he didn't put it away. Nor did the grim line of his mouth ease. "He's clean."

Turning, Mark holstered his gun and eased Emily into the chair beside Maria's desk. Maria hovered close, muttering in Spanish, and handed her a glass of water.

As she lifted it to her lips, Emily realized she was shaking. When the water sloshed dangerously close to the rim, Mark closed his hand around her cold fingers. She was grateful for his warm, steady touch as she took a sip.

"You're okay now." Leaning down, he stroked her hair, her cheek, his gaze probing hers.

"What's going on here?" Jack glared at Coop.

"He has a solid alibi for Saturday. But you have every right to press harassment charges for this little incident." Mark ignored Jack's question and kept his voice low as he spoke to Emily.

"No. That would only complicate his life further. I shouldn't have given you his name. I knew it would backfire."

"Now that I've seen him in action, I'm not sorry we checked him out. Are you sure about the charges?"

"Yes." She gave a jerky nod.

He hesitated a second, then straightened and

turned to Jack. "You're a very lucky man, Mr. Hanley." His tone was icy. "Dr. Lawson has elected not to press harassment charges. And for your information, she was extremely reluctant to reveal your name to us, even though she was wounded by a sniper on Saturday."

"She was shot?" Shock rippled across Jack's features, and some of the color drained from his face. Angling his head, he looked past Mark. For the first time, he seemed to notice the thick white dressing on Emily's upper arm that extended below the sleeve of her blouse.

"Yes. Now I suggest you leave before she changes her mind about the charges . . . or before we change it for her."

"Look, I'm really sorry about . . . I had no idea." He moved toward the door, turning when he reached it to address Emily, his tone subdued. "I guess maybe I do need that anger management class. Thank you for not . . . for not taking any legal action today."

At least something good had come of this episode, Emily reflected. Jack had acknowledged his anger problem. And recognized that he'd narrowly averted serious trouble as a result of it.

"Just get some help, Mr. Hanley," she told him.

With a brief nod, the man slipped through the door. Coop moved to the threshold, watching until he exited the building.

Dropping down to balance on the balls of his feet

beside her, Mark took her hand. "Let's get you to the doctor, then home, okay?"

She managed a smile. "How is it you always manage to make such dramatic entrances in my life?"

"Frankly, I could do with a little less drama." He turned to Coop, who had stepped back inside the office.

"He's gone," Coop confirmed.

Maria moved closer, concern etching her features. "Can I do anything else for you, Emily?"

"No. Thank you for coming to my defense. That purse can be a lethal weapon. I know how much it weighs." She managed a shaky smile.

"You take good care of her," Maria addressed the two men.

"That's the plan." Mark rose.

"I am sure you will try. But it is not always easy to do. She can be terca . . . stubborn." Maria turned to Emily. "You do what they say, and I see you tomorrow. And from now on, I will look even if I think no one is there. I will not make this mistake ever again. Buenas noches."

As Maria disappeared out the door, Emily stood. Her legs felt like rubber, and she was grateful for Mark's hand under her elbow. She reached for her purse and briefcase, but Mark beat her to them.

"How about you concentrate on hanging on to me instead?"

That was no hardship. She could feel his muscles

bunch beneath her fingertips as she slipped her hand through his arm, and his rock solid steadiness gave her a sense of strength and security. Two things she was in desperate need of tonight.

Especially after he told her on the way home that none of the interviews or leads had produced any suspects. And that they were no closer to finding the shooter now than they had been three days before.

He almost missed the follow-up story. If someone hadn't left Wednesday's newspaper on the table in the lunch room, he would have.

As he nuked one of the last homemade chicken potpies Ruthie had frozen, he scanned the head-line: "Police Continuing to Check Leads in Park Shooting." Information on the incident had been sparse until now. An initial story short on detail, plus some TV coverage the first day that consisted of nothing more substantive than video footage of the park. That had been it.

The reason for the lack of coverage was obvious. The police didn't have a clue who was responsible. And this latest headline was a crock. There weren't any leads to check. If there had been, he'd be in jail by now. The care he'd taken to cover his tracks had paid off.

The microwave pinged, and he withdrew the potpie, settling at the table with the newspaper in the empty lunch room. He'd started eating later than the other guys in the past few weeks. Their chitchat had begun to get on his nerves.

"Smells good in here."

He looked up as Red entered. Pushing sixty, the foreman had a shock of thick white hair that always needed combing, and the ruddy complexion that had earned him his nickname was redder than ever after the summer construction season.

"It's one of Ruth's potpies."

It didn't surprise him when that response discombobulated his boss.

"She was a good cook." Red busied himself at the coffeemaker and changed the subject. "You gonna bowl with us again this fall? League'll be starting soon."

"Not this year."

Turning, Red looked over at him. "Listen, I know you've had some really tough months. You okay?"

"I'm fine."

For a moment, he thought Red was going to say more. Instead, the man added some cream to his coffee and headed for the door. "Don't forget to read that note from George on the bulletin board. Take care, pal."

Pal.

Red wasn't his pal. Not like Ruthie had been. Or his son. Nor were any of the guys at work. They weren't there when he went home at night. They didn't cook him great meals and listen to his problems or shoot baskets with him or help with the chores. They went home to their own families.

And he didn't blame them. That's what he used to do too.

When he had a family.

A savory piece of chicken from the potpie stuck in his throat, and he pushed the food away, struggling to blink the moisture from his eyes. He couldn't break down. Not yet. He had a job to do first. The Lord had spoken to him about it. And until he finished that assignment, he needed to keep a clear head. Grief could come later.

Lifting the newspaper, he scanned the story. Until now, neither of the victims had been identified. But today's article listed one by name and the other by profession—FBI Special Agent Mark Sanders and a prominent local psychologist. According to the piece, the investigators were focusing on Sanders as the target because of a high-profile shooting in which he'd been involved.

Looking up from the newspaper, his gaze fell on the employee bulletin board next to the refrigerator. He'd already read the note from George Aiken, general manager, about a new Missouri Department of Transportation project the company had been awarded. And he'd read the letter next to it from big-time builder Mike Evans, commending the team at Aiken for its work on his latest housing development. The man had even personalized it with some handwritten kudos at the bottom.

He'd worked on that project. Done a good job too.

As he considered Evans's note, he suddenly realized that the tools to further deflect attention from his real target were staring at him.

It was like a message from above.

And once everyone was focused on protecting the FBI agent, it would be much easier to finish his job.

The next time, Emily Lawson would die.

10

Signaling to the waitress, Mark pulled out his wallet to pay for the late lunch he and Coop had wolfed down after spending a long Thursday morning following up on some leads for Nick's bank robbery case. As it turned out, those had been far more productive than the ones they'd pursued for the shooting. And now, after five days, the latter had dried up. The news story in yesterday's paper identifying Mark as one of the targets had produced two calls, but both had been dead ends.

"Let me get this." Coop reached for the bill as the waitress set it down.

"Nope. My treat. It's the least I can do for keeping you and Monica apart."

"True." Coop retracted his hand with a grin.

"However, you must be getting used to these separations by now."

His grin faded. "As a matter of fact, I'm not. And imminent fatherhood isn't making them any easier."

Surprised by Coop's candidness and serious demeanor, Mark looked at him. In all the years they'd worked together, his partner had rarely talked about personal issues. And he reserved serious discussion for job-related topics. Everything else got the glib, irreverent treatment.

"How does Monica feel?" Mark decided to test the waters, open the door if Coop wanted to talk.

"The same."

Coop played with his coffee mug, and Mark sensed a sudden tension in the air. Instinctively, he braced.

Grasping the mug with both hands, Coop looked over at him. "I'm leaving the HRT, Mark."

For an instant, Mark stopped breathing. For four years, he and Coop had spent most of their waking hours together. They'd trusted each other with their lives on numerous occasions, suffered together through long, uncomfortable missions, pushed each other to do their best during countless training simulations. They'd covered each other's backs and put their lives on the line for one another more times than Mark cared to count. They shared a bond born of mutual dependence—and respect— that few ever experienced.

And now their partnership was coming to an end. Because of Monica. And a baby.

Resentment clawed at Mark's gut. "I guess this is why I never got married."

"I had a feeling you'd look at it that way. And marriage was one factor in my decision. But not the only one." Coop pushed his mug aside and leveled a direct gaze at his partner. "I'm thirty-nine, Mark. I've been on the HRT for five years. There are only two operators from my class left on the team. You know as well as I do that four or five years is the average tenure. And we both know this is a job for younger men. It's time for me to go. With or without Monica and the baby."

Struggling to control his roiling emotions, Mark considered Coop's words. Everything he'd said was true. Most HRT operators lasted four years, max. And the job was designed for younger bodies. The intense training and often-difficult working conditions took a physical toll. Mark didn't bounce back as quickly from injuries as he had in the past, and some had caused permanent damage. Coop had suffered a broken leg three years ago during a mission, and Mark knew he continued to fight the lingering pain and effects— and that the grueling training often aggravated the old injury.

Logic told Mark that Coop's decision was a good one. But it didn't make him feel any better about it. He was losing a partner. He was losing a part of himself. And life would never be the same again.

"When are you leaving?" Mark managed to ask the question with reasonable calm.

"The end of September."

"What will you do?"

"I've lined up a teaching job at the academy."

At least he was staying with the FBI. Meaning their paths would continue to cross. It wasn't much of a consolation, but it helped.

"It sounds like you've given this a lot of thought."

"I have. It wasn't an easy decision, Mark. But it's the right one."

Taking a sip of his tepid coffee, Mark tried to smile. "I guess that means I'll have to break in a new partner. Maybe I'll luck out and get one who doesn't snore."

"I probably should have warned Monica about that, huh?" Coop grinned.

"I could always tell her my secret for making you stop."

"A jab in the ribs with a blunt instrument? Forget it. Besides, she has a different technique. And it's far less painful." A slow, lazy smile lifted his lips.

"I don't suppose you're going to expound on that." Mark quirked an eyebrow.

"Not a chance."

"That's what I figured." Mark withdrew a credit card from his wallet and waved it at the waitress, who took it as she passed. "Seriously, Coop, I wish you well. I understand your reasons for leaving, but it won't be the same without you. It's been a . . . we've had a good run."

"Yeah. We have." Coop drained his cup and cleared his throat. "But you're not rid of me yet. We still have a shooter to find."

"I'm not too hopeful on that score."

"If he tries again, we may have another chance."

"Much as I hate loose ends, I'd prefer that to risking a life just to catch this guy."

"Agreed. However, given the planning that went into the first attempt, the guy strikes me as determined."

"True. The most frustrating part is not knowing why he's determined or who he's after. The one good thing is that it's looking less and less like he's after Emily now that Jack Hanley is out of the running as a suspect and none of our shelter interviews turned up anything suspicious."

"Depends on how you define good. If he's not after her, that puts you in his crosshairs."

"Better me than her. I've got you watching my back."

"No pressure there." Coop gave him a dry look.

The waitress returned with Mark's card, and after he signed the check and pocketed the receipt, he stood and faced his partner.

"I'm not worried. You're the best. And I trust you with my life."

Emotion had no place on the HRT. Nor did sentiment. And he and Coop had avoided both, on the job—and off. The closest they'd ever come to acknowledging their feelings for each other had been when Coop asked Mark to be the best man at his wedding, choosing his partner over his brother.

Until now.

Though Mark's comment reflected his professional opinion of Coop, both men knew it resonated with deeper meaning.

Rising, Coop held out his hand. "You can count on me, Mark. Always."

As they left the restaurant, Mark felt a little less depressed. He'd miss Coop. No one could ever take his place as an HRT partner. But he was confident that on another level, their partnership would continue long after Coop moved on to other things.

"This is the best Chinese food I've ever eaten." Mark helped himself to another scoop of chicken broccoli.

"I discovered this place when I was in college, and I still stop and get takeout on a regular basis." Emily leaned over to grab a few paper napkins from the center of her kitchen table. "I hope you guys don't mind eating in. I thought it would be faster, since I have to be at the studio by 7:15. And it has to be easier from a security standpoint for us to eat here than in a restaurant."

"Much." Coop took the last crab rangoon.

"What's the plan for tonight?" Mark polished off a spear of broccoli.

"Once I arrive, we'll do a few sound checks. The program goes live at 7:30. We're on for an hour."

"Let's get there by seven. I want to take a look around first," Coop said.

Glancing at her watch, Emily rose. "In that case, let me run a comb through my hair and touch up my makeup."

"I thought it was a radio program," Mark said.

"I still like to look nice."

"You always look nice. With or without makeup." He grinned.

She rolled her eyes, matching his light tone. "Help him work on his lines, would you, Coop?"

Chuckling, Coop wiped his hands on some paper napkins. "I've tried, Emily. He's a lost cause."

"I'll have you know that most ladies like my lines." Mark gave them both an indignant look, enjoying the repartee.

"Not too discriminating, are we?" Emily countered.

Coop tried to hide his laugh behind a cough.

"I'll be back in a few minutes, gentlemen."

As Emily exited, Coop turned to Mark with a grin. "I like her."

"So do I." The whisper of a smile twitched at Mark's lips.

"I know."

At his partner's amused expression, Mark narrowed his eyes and lowered his voice. "This isn't going anywhere, Coop."

"Uh-huh."

"It's not. My work is in Quantico. Emily's practice is here. Besides, she's not interested in a relationship with a man in a high-risk profession. She's been down that road once, and I got the distinct impression she doesn't want to travel it again."

"Love changes things."

Taken aback, Mark eyed Coop. "What's that supposed to mean?"

"I thought I was speaking English."

"I haven't seen Emily in twenty years. And she's only been back in my life for five days. Love doesn't happen that quickly."

"Maybe it was there all along."

Mark shot him a skeptical look. "We were sixteen and seventeen. She came to visit her grandmother one summer for six weeks. We clicked. We had a great time. She left. End of story."

"Sorry. Don't buy it. You guys obviously had chemistry twenty years ago. And trust me, you still do."

"Since when did you become an expert on love?"

"Ask Monica." He gave Mark a smug smile.

"Oh, give me a break."

"All I'm saying is that as someone who found himself in that state in the not-too-distant past, I recognize it in other people. Or the potential for it, anyway."

"I'm not in the market for a serious relation-ship."

"Tough. They show up when you least expect them."

Mark gave up. It was clear he wasn't going to change his partner's mind. "Okay, fine, believe whatever you want. But do me a favor, okay? Don't share your theories with Emily. She's already nervous enough when the two of us are alone together."

"I rest my case."

An hour later, as Coop did another walk-through in the small studio, Mark leaned back in the sound booth and watched as the headphone-wearing technician fielded incoming calls and patched them through to Emily, who was visible through a glass window in front of the control panel.

"Hi, Lauren. What can I do for you tonight?"

Speakers in the sound booth allowed Mark to listen in on the chat session, and he'd been impressed with Emily's deft handling of the teen callers. Her advice had been sound, her empathy real, her candor sincere. She had an amazing ability to connect with the teenagers, and quite a few were repeat callers, taking her up on her invitation to let her know how they'd fared in their attempts to resolve whatever sticky situa-tion they'd talked with her about on a previous program.

Lauren's problem involved pressure from her boyfriend to "prove" how much she cared for him. He was pushing her toward higher and higher levels of intimacy. Curious how Emily would respond, Mark gave the conversation his full attention, analyzing her comments as she spoke.

"Adam sounds like a nice guy, Lauren." *She didn't dis the boyfriend and risk raising Lauren's defensiveness. Smart.* "And it's normal to want to express your feelings in a physical way if you care about someone." *She acknowledged the validity of the girl's emotions.* "What you have to decide is whether you're ready for that kind of commitment. And it's good you're asking yourself that question." *She let Lauren know her concerns were legitimate, and that she had choices.* "The thing is, sometimes even people who care about us want us to do things that will make them happy, but maybe won't make us happy in the long run." *She was subtly instilling a doubt about the boyfriend's motives.* "It can help to ask ourselves how we'll feel about this down the road. Let's say you and Adam break up in three months. How will you feel then if you go along with what he wants you to do?" *She was asking Lauren to evaluate long-term consequences.*

As Emily went on to discuss options and strategies with Lauren, Mark's respect for her abilities mushroomed. She was masterful. When at last Lauren hung up, with a promise to call back next week and give Emily an update, it was clear the teen was having serious second thoughts about giving in to the pressure from her boyfriend.

The door to the small sound booth opened, and Coop slipped in, taking a seat beside Mark in the cramped space.

"She's impressive, isn't she?"

"You were listening?"

"They broadcast the programming throughout the office."

"Hi, Kyle." Emily took the next call. "Thanks for waiting to talk with me. What's on your mind tonight?" When there was no response, she looked toward the sound booth. The technician checked some dials and gave her a thumbs-up. "Kyle? Are you there?"

"Yeah."

"Good. We thought we lost you for a minute. What's going on?"

"I don't . . . I'm not sure where to start."

"Is there a problem at school? Or at home?"

"Yeah."

"Both places?"

"Yeah. Like, everywhere. My parents split a month ago, and my grades stink, and my brother shipped out to the Middle East last week. My life sucks. It just doesn't seem worth it some days, you know?"

Frowning, Mark looked over at Coop. The kid sounded like he was teetering on the edge.

It was obvious Emily had come to the same conclusion. She checked the clock in the studio. They were down to the final five minutes of the program.

Signaling to Andy at the sound controls, she responded, "I hear you, Kyle. Life can throw us a lot of curves, that's for sure. And you've got a plateful right now. Can you do something for me? Can you stay on the line while I take one more caller? We're about to wrap up the program, and I'd like to talk with you some more as soon as I'm off the air. Will you wait on the line for me?"

"I guess."

Again, Emily signaled to Andy, who patched through the last caller of the evening.

While Emily took the final call, Andy spoke to Kyle. It was obvious he'd been through this drill before, buying time for Emily, keeping someone on the line who she felt needed extra attention and more in-depth counseling than her program allowed.

Once Emily signed off, Andy transferred the call back in to her, shut off the sound, and removed his headphones.

Through the window, Mark watched as Emily gave her full attention to Kyle, her expression intent as she scribbled notes, twin grooves furrowing her brow.

"Does she get callers like that very often?" Coop addressed the question to the technician.

"Now and then." He swung around in his swivel chair and crossed an ankle over a knee. With his longish, gray-streaked hair, threadbare jeans, and T-shirt emblazoned with the station logo, he looked like a heavy metal junkie. "But Emily's cool with them. More often than not she manages to get their names and set up some counseling for them, or she'll get them to promise to call back if they're really down. If they won't do that, she gives them her cell number and tells them to call anytime." He angled his head and gave her an admiring look. "A lot of people talk about compassion and Christian charity. Emily lives it."

While Andy shut down the studio for the night and set up the recorded programming that would fill out the evening schedule, Mark mulled over the technician's comment as he watched Emily talk to the troubled boy. Her posture was taut, her face a mask of concern, her eyes filled with empathy and caring. Andy was right, Mark thought. She lived what she believed. And if she could be this caring, this committed, this intent on doing the right thing for a youthful stranger, how much love would she lavish on someone to whom she'd given her heart?

The thought filled him with awe.

"I'm heading out." Andy swiveled toward them and rose. "All you need to do when you leave is flip the light switch and pull the door shut behind you."

"Andy." Coop's voice stopped him. "Do you track the source of these calls?"

"No. My guess is most of them come in on cells. These kids don't want their parents listening in on the home phone."

"Okay. Thanks."

With a wave, he left.

"What was that all about?" Mark gave Coop a quizzical look.

"That kid she's talking to sounds disturbed."

"And . . . ?"

"Disturbed people can do dangerous things."

It was obvious where Coop was heading, but Mark was skeptical. "That could be a stretch. These are teenagers. Our shooter was methodical. Someone who knew how to handle a gun. And how to disappear without a trace. A kid like that"—he nodded toward the studio—"would make mistakes. And I'd be more concerned about him taking his own life than someone else's."

Coop shrugged. "It was just a thought."

Forty-five minutes later, when Emily at last took off her headphones, Mark watched as she pushed her hair back from her face and rubbed her temples. The weary slump of her shoulders reflected a full caseload of patients today, an hour-long program with teens that required her to be at the top of her game every second, and a taxing, emotional session with a very troubled young man.

"We need to get her home. She looks ready to fold."

"I agree. The lady's had a tough week." Coop rose.

Emerging from the studio, Emily gave them an apologetic smile. "Sorry about this. After most shows I'm out the door in five minutes."

"No problem." Mark stood too. "That kid sounded like he needed a sympathetic ear."

"He needs more than that."

"Did you convince him of that?"

"I think so. He promised to talk to a counselor at school tomorrow and call back next week. And I gave him my cell number."

"Andy told us you get calls like that now and then. How often is now and then, Emily?"

Shrugging, she reached for her purse. "I have a kid like this every month or two. Some of them call me several times before I convince them to get face-to-face help or they trust me enough to give me their full names. Some call for a while, and then I never hear from them again. I had a kid like that a couple of months ago. Bryan. Several calls, each more desperate than the last, then nothing." She shook her head, distress etching her features. "Those are the ones I worry about most."

"Well, tonight I'm more worried about you. You've had a long day." Mark looked at Coop.

"I'll do a quick check outside. Hang tight till I get back."

When the door closed behind Coop, Mark smiled at Emily. "I was impressed. You're good."

A soft flush colored her cheeks. "For the most part, I listen. That doesn't take any special skill."

"Real listening does. And giving direction and guidance by letting people think they're reaching conclusions on their own takes tremendous talent."

She tipped her head. "Now I'm impressed. You've nailed my technique."

"It's more than technique. What you do also takes a lot of caring and empathy. But you had those qualities way back in our Wren Lake days too. I remember the time we went hiking and you found that laminated, old-fashioned photo of a woman. You insisted on turning it in at the ranger station because you were certain it meant a lot to someone. And you were right, based on the note the ranger forwarded to you later from that World War II veteran."

She stared at him and shook her head. "I haven't thought of that in years."

He hadn't, either. The memory had surfaced out of nowhere. But it reminded him yet again of how special Emily was.

A coded knock sounded on the door, followed by the sound of Coop's muffled voice. "We're clear."

Putting his hand in the small of her back, Mark guided Emily out into the night. Once inside the car, he leaned across to help her with her seat belt.

"I'll be glad when I can manage this again on my own."

Her breath whispered against his ear as he bent his head to secure her belt. "I'm not sure I will. You won't need me anymore."

Mark had meant the remark to come out teasing. Instead, there was a wistful quality to it that surprised him. He opened his mouth to follow up with a humorous comment to lighten the atmosphere, but the words died in his throat when Emily reached for his hand and twined her fingers with his.

If he didn't know better, Mark would have thought she was sending him a message. Telling him that even after she'd recovered, she'd still need him. Yet only a few nights ago she'd been clear she wasn't like Monica, a woman who could overlook the absences and risks inherent in a job like his.

Mark didn't like mixed signals. On the job, or off. They confused him.

And that was exactly how he felt now.

Confused.

About a lot of things.

11

As Emily said good-bye to Mark and Coop the next day and locked the office door behind them, she turned to find Maria watching her with a pleased expression.

"What's with the look?"

Tilting her head, Maria folded her arms across her chest. "He is a nice man."

"They're both nice men." Emily knew where Maria was heading, and she didn't want to go there. Turning, she moved toward her office.

"How is your arm?"

Surprised her assistant hadn't followed up with another comment about Mark—and there was no doubt in Emily's mind the "he" in Maria's comment referred to Emily's long-ago beau—she paused and looked back. "Feeling better, thanks." Mark and Coop had taken her to the doctor again before escorting her to the office, and she was pleased that her bulky dressing had been exchanged for one much less obtrusive.

"Good. Everything heals in time."

Her assistant was talking about more than her arm, and Emily knew it. "But scars remain. As reminders to proceed with caution."

"Caution is fine. But proceeding is important. Otherwise you get stuck in a rut."

"I'm not stuck in a rut."

"Did I say you were?"

"You think I am."

"It is not what I think that matters. It is what you think."

"I think I'm fine. My life is perfect the way it is."

"Life is always better when it's shared."

A pang of loss echoed deep inside Emily. Maria was right. But sharing was risky. And left you even lonelier when it ended. "Been there, done that. Once was enough."

"I still say he is a nice man."

They'd come full circle in their conversation. This time, Emily didn't pretend not to understand Maria's meaning. "I appreciate your concern for me, Maria. And I like Mark. I always have. He *is* a nice man. He's also going back to Virginia in three weeks. Besides, he's in a very dangerous profession."

"And yours is so much safer? You are the one who got shot, not him."

"That was a fluke. An aberration. I was in the wrong place at the wrong time. Mark had to be the target."

"That is why you have an FBI escort, I guess."

"It's a simple precaution. In a few days they'll decide it's not necessary anymore."

"Hmph." Maria turned back to her computer and began clicking the keys at a furious pace. She always took her stress—and frustration—out on the keyboard. And at the rate she was going, it wouldn't be long before she wore this one out, Emily reflected as she entered her office.

The case files for her Friday patients were waiting for her review, pulled earlier by Maria. But instead of flipping the first one open, she leaned back in her chair and glanced toward the window.

In general, she kept the mini blinds slanted, closed enough to ensure privacy for her patients, but open enough to give her a glimpse of the trees on the edge of the parking lot. Today, they were shut tight, as they had been since the shooting, restricting her view of the world. Nick had taken care of that on his scouting visit.

Nevertheless, she took some comfort in the restful décor of her office. The cream-colored walls were hung with landscapes, the cherry desk and credenza were polished and uncluttered, the small rose damask settee and side chairs striped in rose and teal in the seating area were tasteful, the dove gray plush carpet soft and nonclinical. She'd always felt comfortable here. It was a world of her own making, where she could help troubled people sort out their problems.

But had her refuge also become a place to hide? A place where she filled her time assisting others while dodging her own issues related to pain and sorrow and loss?

Maybe, she conceded. She might be good at helping other people see the value of admitting their own foibles and dealing with their issues, but she was far less adept at following her own advice.

At least when it came to matters of the heart.

She'd dragged her feet with Grant because she'd been unwilling to divert focus from her career.

She was dragging her feet again with Mark because she was unwilling to embrace the risk that caring for him would entail.

But perhaps caution in this case was good, she reassured herself. Mark had given no indication he was interested in anything serious. They'd flirted a little, enjoyed some lighthearted banter, had some fun and some laughs. Yes, there was chemistry. That hadn't faded one iota through the years. But time—and experience—did change people. Those changes might not be apparent at once. Nor were they necessarily all good. Only time would tell.

So for now, she would enjoy this interlude with Mark and expect nothing more, Emily decided.

No matter how hard Maria pushed.

"I heard an interesting rumor yesterday."

Wiping his forehead on the sleeve of his paint-splattered T-shirt, Mark looked over at Nick and rested the roller in the pan at his feet. While he was spending his Sunday painting the ceiling, his host was focused on smoothing out the drywall seams on the far wall in what Nick claimed would soon be a formal dining room. As far as Mark was concerned, the room had a long way to go.

"Want to share it?"

"According to sources I can't disclose, Dave Sheldon is retiring and heading west to take some cushy gig in a local police department."

Keeping his expression bland, Mark reached for the damp rag slung over the rungs of a nearby ladder and wiped his hands. The news of Dave's departure had leaked faster than he'd expected. He hadn't even shared Steve's offer yet with Coop. "Good for him."

Nick angled a glance his way. "I thought you might be interested."

"Why?" Mark busied himself pouring some more paint into the pan.

"The SWAT team leader job will be open. As well as a spot on the reactive squad. You've got the credentials."

"I have a job, Nick."

"I know." Nick concentrated on the seam he was disguising. "But guys don't stay on the HRT for more than a few years. And Coop told me he's leaving. I figured you might be looking around for another slot too."

"I haven't given it a lot of thought. Besides, when I do leave, I'll probably look for a job closer to Tennessee. My mom's not getting any younger, and it would be nice to see her and the rest of my family more."

"St. Louis isn't that far from Tennessee."

"I have no connections to St. Louis."

"I can think of one—wrapped up in a very pretty package."

"If you happen to be referring to Emily, she and I are old friends. Nothing more."

"Uh-huh."

Aiming a disgruntled look toward Nick, Mark set the paint can back on a tarp. "Since when have you become a matchmaker?"

"Hey, just trying to be helpful. You're not getting any younger, you know."

"Who are you to talk? I don't see you planning a walk down the aisle."

Turning, Nick grinned. "Wow. You're farther gone than I thought if you have marriage on your mind."

"I didn't start this. You did."

"I never mentioned marriage. I was thinking more along the lines of exploring an old attraction. I see it's already moved beyond that."

Annoyed, Mark shook his head and picked up the paint roller. "You're nuts."

"Uh-huh."

All at once, Mark was sorry he'd accepted Coop's offer to escort Emily to church this morning while he and Nick worked on the house. At the time, he'd considered it a blessing in disguise. He had a feeling his lack of interest in church could be a point of contention between him and Emily, and he didn't want to risk shaking the still-fresh foundation of their renewed friendship. Plus, he owed Nick for taking Emily to Hope House for her counseling session Friday afternoon while he and Coop sat in on an HRT meeting via conference call. Putting some time in on the rehab had seemed like a good way to pay back the debt.

In light of the present conversation, however, he no longer considered Coop's offer a benevolent gift from above.

Since ignoring Nick's comment seemed to be his best option, he turned away and dipped the roller in the pan of paint.

"Why is it so hard for you to admit you care about Emily?"

Stifling a groan, Mark focused on the blank wall in front of him. He'd forgotten how persistent Nick could be. And how open. Unlike Coop, who went out of his way to avoid talking about feelings, Nick dove right into the emotional stuff. Mark wasn't always comfortable with that—like now—yet Nick's comments often prompted him to think. Especially when he didn't want to.

"I haven't seen her in twenty years, Nick."

"Uh-huh."

"Will you stop with the 'uh-huhing'?"

"As soon as you stop denying the obvious."

"What's it to you, anyway?"

Shrugging, Nick set his trowel on the makeshift workbench balanced atop two sawhorses. "Friends watch each other's backs."

"Okay." Mark's tone was cautious. "But I don't see the danger here."

"That's the problem." Nick gave Mark his full attention, no trace of his customary humor in evidence. "The danger, my friend, is that unless you're very careful, you could let a great opportunity slip through your fingers. Take it from someone who's been looking for a while. Women like Emily don't come along every day."

Mark's eyes narrowed. "What did you two talk about during your little excursion to the shelter, anyway?"

"Enough to tell me my original impression about her being a special lady was right on. And to conclude her feelings for you run a lot deeper than you—or she—might think."

"When did you become Dr. Phil?" Mark gave him an annoyed look.

"I'm no expert on what makes people tick. That's Emily's specialty. But I do pay attention to feelings. And vibes. You ought to give it a try."

Turning back to the wall, Nick resumed his work. For a few moments Mark watched as his friend applied drywall compound over the taped seam in smooth, steady strokes. Nick was good at the work, patient and thorough. After the wall was painted, it would be impossible to tell where one board ended and the other began. The two would be joined by the touch of a master's hand in seamless unity.

Kind of like the way a man and woman were united in a good marriage, Mark reflected. One blessed by God.

Startled by that unexpected analogy, Mark applied the paint roller to the ceiling, determined to give the task his undivided attention.

But two thoughts kept intruding.

First, God hadn't been on his radar screen in years, and it was more than a little disconcerting to find him popping up now. He supposed he could thank Emily and her trust in the Almighty for planting that seed in his mind.

And second, it appeared Nick was right, after all.

He did have marriage on his mind.

As his BlackBerry began to vibrate, Mark slid it out of its holder and pressed it to his ear. "Sanders."

"Mark, it's Steve. We've got a new development on the shooting. Where are you?"

"Coop and I were running down some leads for Nick on the bank robbery. We're on our way back."

"Come to my office as soon as you get in."

The line went dead, and Mark returned the device to his belt.

"What's up?" Coop kept his attention on the road as he negotiated the Monday lunch-hour traffic in downtown St. Louis.

"Steve's got something on the shooting."

178

Ten minutes later, when he and Coop appeared in Steve's doorway, the senior agent motioned them in. "Take a look at this." He handed Mark two clear plastic sleeves.

The first contained an envelope addressed to him at the St. Louis FBI office, postmarked Saturday and mailed from a suburb in South St. Louis County. The address had been written on a label and affixed.

The second was a single sheet of paper, about six by eight, containing five handwritten words. "Next time I won't miss."

A muscle in his jaw clenched, and Mark sent Steve a questioning look as he handed the items to Coop.

"It came in the morning mail," Steve supplied. "As soon as Rose opened it she called Clair. No one else touched it. We'll get this to Quantico for analysis as soon as possible, along with the elimination prints for Rose. Clair copied it and the envelope, and I've couriered them to Carl in Oakdale. Here's a set for you. I put in a call to your boss, but he hasn't gotten back to me yet."

As Steve handed the copies over, he motioned Mark and Coop into seats and hit the intercom button. "Clair, you can come get the originals now. Put them on the earliest possible plane." He turned off the intercom and regarded the two agents seated across from him. "It would appear our man still has killing on his mind."

"But why would he tell us that?" Mark frowned as he examined the copy of the note, his shoulders tense. Something didn't feel right.

"By now he's concluded we don't have any good leads. If we did, we'd be breathing down his neck. It could be an in-your-face, yank-your-chain kind of thing."

"Or it could be a red herring."

At Coop's comment, both men turned to him.

"That's possible," Mark acknowledged as he played out the possibilities in his mind. "It could also be a hoax. Somebody who saw the media coverage and wants to stir things up for laughs. But if it is legit, it surprises me. The shooter was careful not to leave us much to work with after his first attempt. Why drop a piece of evidence into our laps?"

"Cockiness, maybe. Which can translate to mistakes. This could be a big one." Steve held up the plastic sleeves. "And if it is, let's cross our fingers that Quantico finds it."

Resting an arm on the wooden gate that led to the pasture, he took a sip of coffee as he watched the two grazing cows in the distance. He'd always enjoyed raising his own beef, taken pride in his well-cared-for vegetable garden and carefully pruned fruit trees, liked eating scrambled eggs laid in his own chicken coop. It was good to be self-sufficient. A sign of strength. Providing his family with everything they'd needed had always been a matter of honor for him.

But he didn't much care about any of it anymore. He'd sold the chickens a month ago. They laid too many eggs for one man to eat. Weeds were taking over the garden, and the birds and squirrels were feasting on the ripe tomatoes littering the ground under the tall stakes. He hadn't set foot among the fruit trees in weeks. Why bother to maintain the orchard and garden when Ruthie wouldn't be canning and preserving?

As for the cattle . . . he'd always sold one to the local butcher and had the other slaughtered, storing it in the deep freeze in the basement for Ruthie to turn into savory stroganoff and potpies and spaghetti sauce. But there was plenty of meat in the freezer from the spring butchering, untouched in the past two months. Enough to last a solitary man for years. He didn't need more. He should find a buyer for both cows.

Turning his back on the pasture, he let his gaze wander over the remainder of his property, ignoring the barn to his left. He hadn't been inside since . . . for eight weeks . . . except to move the livestock feed and vet supplies into the empty chicken coop and pull the mower out. It was sitting in the open now, exposed to the elements, rusting a little more with each passing day.

He focused on the small house he and Ruthie had called home for all but the first three years of their marriage. It was nothing special, just a small clap-board, one-story farmhouse painted white with a screened porch in the back where they used to sit on summer nights and count the fireflies or watch the moon rise. They'd married a bit later in life than their friends, he and Ruthie. He'd been thirty-three the day they'd said their vows. She'd celebrated her thirty-first birthday the week before. They'd both wanted to live in the country, and these ten acres had given them their dream home.

The only thing missing in their life had been children. But no sooner had they stopped praying for a family than Ruthie had found out she was pregnant. Their son had been born on their tenth anniversary, and after his birth, that day had always been a double celebration. He and Ruthie would have marked twenty-six years come November.

But there would be no celebration this year.

He took another sip of his coffee, which had grown cold and acrid. Tilting the cup, he watched as the earth absorbed the black, bitter liquid. And wished he could find a way to erase the gnawing pain inside him with the same ease.

Maybe, after he finished God's work, he would find peace. Didn't Pastor Phelps always talk about the serenity that came from following God's call? And God had called him to this task, his voice incessant. He'd first heard it in his dreams. Now it kept him awake at night. And he had begun hearing it during the day too. It was clear to him the Lord wanted the deaths avenged. And the Almighty had put the task in the hands of the man most wronged. While he didn't relish killing, he couldn't ignore God's command: an eye for an eye.

When it was over, he'd have decisions to make. Grief to deal with. All of that had been put on hold while he carried out his mission. But he couldn't lose focus now. He was too close. That's why he'd sent the note, directing attention away from his quarry. Soon God would show him the rest of the plan.

All he had to do was wait and watch for the message.

12

"Les, are you with us?"

Steve surveyed the table in the FBI's Joint Operations Center as he directed his question toward the speaker phone. Mark and Coop were there, along with Clair. Carl Owens represented the Oakdale PD at the Tuesday meeting.

"I'm here. Christy and Paul Sheehan, our handwriting expert, are with me."

"Good." Steve turned to the ERT lead investigator. "Clair, you've talked to the lab in Quantico. What do we have?"

"Unfortunately, not much." She consulted a

report in front of her. "The paper the note was written on is standard typing stock, thinner than usual, but there's nothing to distinguish it. It was pristine except for Rose's elimination prints, meaning the author wore some kind of gloves. The address was written on the same kind of thin paper and glued on the envelope. There were a few prints on the envelope, but none matched any in our database. I also checked the Missouri Highway Patrol records for new print entries that might not yet be in the national system. No matches there, either. Both the message and the address were written with a common ballpoint pen."

"Our man is still being very careful." Steve tapped his finger against the table and furrowed his brow. "What do you have from your end, Les?"

"I'll jump in here," Christy said. "Les asked me to look at this from a behavioral perspective. Assuming this note was written by our shooter, the fact that he's communicating his intent to strike again is interesting. As is the choice to handwrite the message."

"I wondered about that too," Mark said. "Why wouldn't the guy just buy a set of kids' block letters and stamp out the note?"

"Cockiness or sloppiness, perhaps," Christy responded. "If he's getting cocky, he may be starting to have fun with this and is pushing the limits because he feels invincible. Sloppiness, on the other hand, might indicate his thinking is beginning to muddle. If we're dealing with an unstable person, increasingly erratic and unpredictable behavior wouldn't be a surprise. But we have no way of knowing his motivation or mental state from the evidence we have to date. Either scenario, however, could result in mistakes."

"This could also be a harmless hoax from some nut unrelated to the shooting," Les chimed in. "But I think we have to assume worst case—that this was written by the shooter. And if it was, this guy is either a loose cannon or a meticulous killer. Either way, he's determined to finish what he started."

During this exchange, Mark watched Coop jot a few words on the notepad in front of him. His partner shoved the pad toward him when he finished.

Les is going to yank you back to Quantico.

The same thought had occurred to him. That was Les's style. The HRT chief wasn't afraid to hit hard if necessary, but he took seriously the FBI's directive to reduce risk and avoid excessive force whenever possible, always opting for a negotiated resolution versus a tactical conclusion if given a choice. In the current scenario, reducing unnecessary risk would mean removing Mark from the line of fire on the assumption he was the target.

But Mark wasn't convinced of that yet.

"Let's talk about the handwriting," Steve said.

"The letters were traced one by one from another document and linked," Paul responded. "The writer was very careful, but under magnification you can see some overlap in pen strokes at the points of connection. If we had a handwriting sample from the person who wrote the source document, we could confirm the match and use that to explore some leads. Without an original, we're left with nothing more than an apparent forgery."

"Meaning we're back to square one." Carl heaved a frustrated sigh.

There was a brief silence.

"Steve, how would you feel about cutting Mark loose early from his St. Louis assignment?" Les said at last.

"I'd prefer to see this through, Les," Mark interjected, glancing at Coop.

"The risk there is too high. Steve?"

When Steve shot him a questioning look, Mark gave a subtle shake of his head.

"He's been assisting with a major bank robbery case, Les. And we're still shorthanded here. With Coop glued to Mark and another agent filling in as backup when necessary, we've got him covered. I'd like to hang on to him unless you have an urgent need."

Silence again. Mark had no doubt Les was giving his cigar a workout, and he held his breath. The final decision rested with his Quantico boss, and everyone knew it.

"Okay. We'll revisit this in a few days. How's your friend doing, Mark?"

Les's question told Mark his boss wasn't fooled about the reason for his reluctance to return to Quantico. That the Bulldog had figured out there was a strong connection between Mark and Emily. If there wasn't, both men knew he would have hopped a plane for Virginia without protest and left the investigation in the hands of the local police and the St. Louis office.

"Better. We're keeping an eye on her too."

"Good. She's in capable hands, then. Stay in touch." The line went dead.

"How do you want to handle the next steps?" Carl refocused the group around the table.

"There's not much more we can do." Steve shook his head. "The guy's just not giving us anything to work with. I'd like to think he'd start making some mistakes—before he launches a second attack."

"Is there anything we could do to force his hand? Push him to take some action in a setting we control?" Coop proposed.

"I don't see how. Not without putting Mark directly in the line of fire."

"If that's what it takes to flush him out, it might be worth a try," Mark said.

That earned him a disapproving frown from Steve. "If your boss heard that, you'd be on the first plane back to Quantico."

"We're running out of options." Frustration nipped at Mark's words.

"I say we hold. Keep the security on Mark and wait this guy out. He sent one note. He might contact us again. Maybe next time he'll slip and tell us more than he intends to," Carl said.

"Agreed." Steve picked up the tablet he'd been doodling on during the meeting. "And in case the letter was a red herring, let's maintain Dr. Lawson's escort service for the next few days."

As the meeting broke up, Steve cut Mark off as he headed for the exit, his expression grim. "I know you want to get this guy, but no chances, okay?"

"I never take chances."

Casting a skeptical look at Coop, Steve jerked his head toward Mark. "Watch him."

Folding his arms across his chest, Coop regarded his partner as Steve strode away, a grin tugging at one corner of his mouth. "I don't think he trusts you."

"I want this guy."

"So do I."

"Getting tired of my company?"

"Missing Monica. I'm ready to go home."

"I hear you."

"How about you?"

"How about me what?"

"Ready to go home?"

There was more to Coop's question than

appeared on the surface, Mark knew. It was his way of asking him if he'd dealt with the aftereffects of the convenience store shooting—without having to directly address the emotional stuff.

In truth, Mark hadn't dwelt on that incident in the past ten days. Since Emily's reappearance in his life, his focus had been on protecting her.

As for going home . . . Mark had never thought of Quantico in those terms. It was a place he stayed between missions, nothing more. And he was in no hurry to return. Not because of the convenience store episode, though he had a ways to go before he'd feel at peace with that. His lack of enthusiasm about returning was due more to Emily, and their providential reunion. It was as if fate had given them a second chance to connect after a twenty-year separation. And he'd never been one to discount fate.

"I guess I have my answer."

Coop's comment pulled Mark back to the conversation, and he shrugged. "I still have some issues to work through. More than when I came, to be honest."

"Yeah. I know. She's a very nice lady, by the way."

Once again, Mark was reminded that his partner knew him too well.

"Pizza and a movie, as promised." Mark grinned and held up a flat box with a DVD balanced on top as Emily answered her door later that evening.

Smiling, she stepped aside and ushered him into her condo. "Where's Coop?"

"Dropped me off and disappeared."

"He could have stayed."

"Nope. Not a chance. I'm too old for chaperones on a date."

Date.

Emily tried not to give that casual reference much credence, but she couldn't quite subdue the flutter in the pit of her stomach.

"Em?"

At Mark's prompt, she closed and locked the door. "Sorry. I was feeling sorry for Coop."

"Appropriate, considering Nick plans to put him to work tonight at the construction site. Otherwise known as his house. Or, as Coop calls it, Sneeze City." Mark grinned at her over his shoulder as he headed toward her kitchen.

"Poor Coop." Emily chuckled and shook her head. "I'll have to see this place sometime. Nick told me it's a Federal-style house from the late 1800s. It sounds fabulous."

Mark's dubious expression suggested otherwise. "Let me be kind and say it has potential." He set the pizza on her counter and opened the lid. "You'll note there are no mushrooms and extra green pepper on your half."

Leaning over, she examined the savory-smelling pizza. "And olives and extra pepperoni on yours. I see your tastes haven't changed much in food."

"Or other things."

At his quiet comment, she turned to look up at him—and found herself mesmerized by his intense eyes, mere inches away. Suddenly Wren Lake felt like yesterday. As did the emotions shealways associated with it. The innocent passion of young love, restrained by deeply ingrained moral principles, straining at the leash as Mark's kisses wreaked havoc with her equilibrium and left her yearning for more.

Her gaze sought his lips, and the memory of their tender, gentle coaxing drove the breath from her lungs.

Not good. Don't look there.

She raised her head a bit, but his dark brown eyes weren't any safer. They warmed her to the core, with a heat searing and intense.

Keep going.

Unfortunately, even his hair wasn't safe. Still thick and dark, she could recall with startling clarity the rich texture of it beneath her fingers.

Fingers that itched to renew their acquaintance.

Say something lighthearted!

Reaching out in a gesture she hoped came across as playful, she brushed her fingers across the hair at his temple, unable to resist. Soft, but with great body. Just like she remembered. "If I didn't know better, I'd say you've gotten a tad grayer in the past ten days."

When his eyes darkened, Emily realized her mistake at once. Her touch had evoked passion, not play. She withdrew her hand, linked her fingers, and eased back a few inches.

She watched Mark tamp down the desire simmering in his deep brown irises. Then he summoned up a smile and rubbed his hand over his hair. "Given what's been going on, it wouldn't surprise me."

She nodded to his hands, keeping hers safely clasped in front of her. "I think I found the culprit."

Several tiny white specks clung to his fingers.

"Paint." He shook his head in disgust. "No matter how often I wash my hair, I can't get all the flecks out. Nick had me painting the ceiling."

Emily tilted her head and inspected him. "It gives you a distinguished appearance."

"Thanks a lot."

"Look on the bright side. Eventually it will wash out. Real gray isn't as easy to get rid of."

"Don't tell me you know anything about that yet." He studied her. "Your hair looks the same to me."

She gave it a self-conscious pat. "I haven't hit the bottle yet, if that's what you mean. But don't look too closely or you'll see silver threads among the gold, to quote an old song." She retrieved two sodas from the fridge and handed him one as she nodded toward the DVD. "What are we watching?"

"*Father Goose.*"

"Isn't that a Cary Grant movie?"

"Yep. An oldie but goodie."

"I'm surprised. I thought you'd go for an action/adventure flick."

There was a brief, almost imperceptible flicker in his smile. "I get enough of that in my job. Besides, this is set in World War II. I expect there will be some action."

She picked up the DVD, fingering it with a far-away look. "This reminds me of the classic movie series we went to at the Tivoli."

"That occurred to me too. I recall there was a Cary Grant movie or two in the mix."

"There was. You called them chick flicks."

"Did I?"

"But you went anyway. Earning you mucho brownie points."

"That was the plan." He gave her an unrepentant grin.

Elbowing him, she took her seat at the table. "You are so bad! What's the ulterior motive tonight?"

"Who says it's any different?"

"On that note, I think I'll pray."

Emily bowed her head, and the room fell silent. When she lifted her chin, Mark's expression took her off guard. He looked . . . envious. As if he wished he had a connection with the Lord too.

Emily was torn. She didn't talk much about her faith. It was a quiet thing, lived more than spoken. Verbal evangelizing didn't suit her temperament. Yet there were occasions when Christians were called to witness. And based on Mark's pensive expression, she felt this might be one of them.

"Does my faith intrigue you?" She kept her tone conversational as she reached for a piece of pizza, opening the door but not pushing.

He took his time answering, downing a long swallow of his soda and helping himself to a slice before he responded. "I suppose that's a good word for it. Considering all that's happened in your life, I would think your trust in the goodness of God would waver."

"It has."

"But you still believe." His questioning gaze probed hers.

"Yes. More than ever. But that doesn't mean I haven't struggled with questions. Known long periods of darkness. Doubt is part of being human, Mark. Some of the greatest saints that ever lived struggled with uncertainty. God understands that. Yet doubts can lead to deeper faith by forcing us to look more closely at what we believe. And why."

"Doubts can also cause people to turn away."

"As you did."

He shrugged an acknowledgement. "I'd like to believe. It must be a great comfort. But I've seen too much bad stuff. Too many innocent people hurt. Evil exists, Emily."

"I know that. But if you can believe in evil, why is it hard for you to believe in goodness?"

She could tell from his stunned expression that he'd never thought of it in quite those terms.

"The thing is, Mark, trying to understand the mind of God is like an ant trying to move a mountain." Emily leaned forward, intent. "His ways are so far beyond our understanding that even attempting to figure them out borders on arrogance. That's where faith comes in. At some point you have to put your life in God's hands, acknowledging you may never understand why certain things happen but trusting that he does. Accepting that you don't have to understand everything is a liberating experience. But letting go isn't always easy, even for people of strong faith."

"I hear you. In my job, control is everything. It's hard not to think in the same terms about my life."

"I struggle with that too. That's why I've had difficulty dealing with the shooting. I was convinced I'd constructed a safe, peaceful life. One that I controlled. Then one day, I go for a quiet walk in the park, and chaos erupts, changing everything in an instant. That Saturday morning was a strong reminder that we're not as much in charge of our destinies as we might like to believe."

"Strong reminder is an understatement. I could think of less traumatizing wake-up calls. By the way, I like the music."

He was changing subjects. And that was okay.

The journey to faith was rarely a road to Damascus experience, Emily knew. For most people, it was a long, slow trip fraught with detours and bumps and wrong turns. The best she could hope for was that their conversation would give Mark food for thought.

"You should. It's the jazz CD you brought to our last dinner."

Grinning, he chewed a bite of pizza. "I knew I had good taste. Now tell me how you're adjusting to the disruption in your routine."

"Not very well. As you noted early on, I'm used to a predictable life. And life has been anything but that in the past ten days. Between changing office hours, alternating days at the shelter, varying church services—even moving my car to visitor parking, not that I've been using it, anyway—I feel completely off balance." The man sitting across from her had contributed to her unsettled state too, but she kept that to herself. "When are you guys going to let me drive myself again?"

Wiping his hands on a napkin, Mark leaned back in his chair, considering her. "We need to wait a few more days."

"Why? It's been quiet. Maybe the guy decided one try was enough. I can't put my life on hold forever."

"Better on hold than at risk."

Some nuance in his voice caught her attention, and her fingers clenched around the paper napkin in her lap, wadding it into a tight ball. "You have some news, don't you?"

"Yes." He leaned forward again and rested his elbows on the table, clasping his hands together. "We've heard from the shooter."

Her heart stuttered as fear coiled in her stomach. "How?"

"A note. Addressed to me. Saying he wouldn't miss the next time."

"Oh, Mark!" Terror drove the breath from her lungs. "You need to get out of town!"

"You sound like my boss."

"Is that what he wants you to do?"

"Yes."

"Then why would you risk staying?" She grasped his hand, her grip urgent as their fingers entwined. "Please. It's not worth the chance. You have to go!"

"I can't."

"Why not?"

His gaze locked on hers. "Because I'm afraid the note might be a red herring."

It took her a few moments to process his comment, for confusion to give way to under-standing—and incredulity. "You think he might be after me?"

"We can't rule that out."

After several more seconds, she shook her head. "I don't think so, Mark. I think the note was for real. This guy's after you."

"I'm not convinced yet."

"But can't you let the local people handle it? There's no reason for you to stay and put yourself in danger."

"Yes, there is."

As he rubbed his thumb over the back of her hand, the implications of his message shook her. Mark cared enough about her to put himself in the line of fire on the off chance she was the target. He wanted to protect her. And he was willing to put his life at risk to do that.

Greater love hath no man than this, that a man lay down his life for his friends. The words from John echoed in Emily's mind. Mark might not have embraced the words of the Bible yet, but he was living the spirit of them.

In their case, however, she now knew his feelings went way beyond friendship. He'd implied as much in countless ways since their reunion, hidden under the guise of lighthearted banter. At this moment, though, there was nothing lighthearted in his demeanor. He was as serious as he'd been those many years ago at Wren Lake when he'd made his youthful promise to never love another.

Mark was all grown up now. But the look in his eyes told her he once more had love on his mind.

And, in truth, so did she. Her reaction to the danger he faced confirmed that. The depth of her terror and panic suggested her feelings for this special man went far deeper than friendship.

It was the kind of reaction a person had when a loved one was in danger.

Whatever constraints her mind had put on their relationship, whatever limits it had set, her heart had ignored them, she realized. She cared for Mark far more than she was comfortable acknowledging—and far more than was prudent after such a short reunion. They had a lot of catching up to do before things escalated, and they needed to do it under ordinary circumstances, not while one of them was being stalked by a killer and emotions were spiking way out of normal range. Logic told her that.

But logic was losing its battle against her heart, where the flame of youthful love had been fanned back to life and was growing day by day into something deep and rich and enduring.

And as she sat inches away from the man who was fast securing a lasting place in her life, more than anything she wanted to feel his strong arms close around her as they'd once done at Wren Lake.

As if reading her thoughts, he stood and held out his hand, never breaking eye contact. There was invitation . . . and encouragement . . . and yearning in their depths. But he was leaving the decision up to her. She could follow her heart and step into his arms, or listen to reason and dispel the charged atmosphere by kidding him about taking advantage of a lady in distress.

He might be disappointed if she chose the latter option, but she suspected he'd take it in stride and revert to their previous easy give and take. Yet she knew what he wanted her to do.

It was the same thing she wanted to do.

The question was, should she take that risk?

13

As he extended his hand, Mark had no idea if Emily would respond to his invitation. It had been a risk, but a calculated one, taken after careful evaluation of the situation and the signals Emily was sending. As careful as he was capable of, anyway, given that his heart was pounding as hard as it did before a dangerous mission.

Only when she rose and placed her hand in his did he realize he'd been holding his breath. As he lifted his free hand to brush a few soft strands of hair back from her face, he wasn't surprised to find that his fingers were trembling. Her nearness had always had that effect on him.

One more thing that hadn't changed through the years.

He considered speaking, but he had a feeling the words would get stuck in his throat. Instead, he tugged her gently toward him, taking care to avoid her injured arm as he enfolded her in a tender embrace.

She was trembling too, he discovered. More than

he was. Her simple step into his arms had been a quantum leap forward in their relationship. And it was scary. While the terrain was familiar, in many ways it was like visiting a favorite place from childhood after decades had passed. Often, the present reality didn't live up to the fond memories treasured—and often embellished—through the passage of years. That could happen tonight, and they both knew it.

But there was no turning back.

As the soft jazz washed over them, Mark did nothing more than hold her, giving them both a chance to adjust to the closeness, to get comfortable with the step they were taking. There was no need to rush. He'd learned to pace things through the years, to tune in to nuances and subtle messages. A skill he'd been woefully lacking during their first romantic encounter, he recalled.

After two decades, memories of how he'd botched their first kiss at Wren Lake still had the power to embarrass him. He'd been a bundle of gawky adolescent nerves driven by unruly hormones, his technique zero on a ten-point scale. Their embrace had been clumsy, at best. He hadn't known what to do with his hands, which had suddenly felt twice as big as usual. His aim for the kiss had been off, resulting in an off-center collision of lips. And somehow his watch had gotten snagged on the front of her sweater in the most embarrassing possible place. It had been a pathetic, inept romantic debut, and he'd been mortified by his fumbling of what he'd hoped would be a memorable moment.

He'd learned a few things since then. Yet all at once he felt just like that awkward adolescent of twenty years ago.

However, now, as then, Emily put them both at ease by focusing on her deficits rather than his.

"I haven't done this in a long time, Mark. I'm a bit rusty." Her unsteady voice whispered against the front of his shirt, and he recalled how she had been the one who'd apologized on that lazy summer day years ago, blaming her lack of experience for his klutzy handling of the embrace. He was as grateful to her now for taking the pressure off of him as he had been two decades before.

Relaxing a bit, he rested his cheek against her hair and inhaled her fresh, floral scent. "It's like riding a bicycle."

"That's not much of a comfort. Grant told me the same thing before we went bike riding on our honeymoon. I promptly fell off, spraining my wrist and skinning both knees. It was not a pretty picture."

A chuckle rumbled in his chest as he stroked her hair. "I promise this will be less painful." Drawing back a bit, he searched her eyes. "I've been wanting to do this ever since that first day in the park."

"I know."

"It was inevitable."

"I know."

She was shaking harder now, and he touched her cheek. "You're not sure about this, are you?"

"No. But I haven't been sure about much of anything in the past ten days. I guess I'm afraid this could be a mistake, Mark. For both of us. I don't want to jeopardize our friendship."

"It's survived a twenty-year separation. I think it should be able to survive one kiss."

Despite her nervousness, she managed a smile. "I don't remember us talking about all the ramifications the first time we kissed."

He breathed out a soft laugh. "We're older now. And wiser."

"Not to mention more wary."

"That too." He stroked a finger down the side of her jaw, his touch feather light. "But you know something? I'm done talking."

With that, he lowered his mouth to hers.

And this time, his aim was right on target.

As Mark tasted her remembered sweetness, Emily's lips stirred beneath his, responding with an eagerness and abandon that surprised—and delighted—him. He deepened the kiss, cupping her head with one hand, his fingers tangled in her soft hair. In the years since he'd left Tennessee, he'd kissed his share of women, many of them far more sophisticated and experienced than his first love. But he'd never enjoyed a kiss more. Nor felt such a strong sense of homecoming. Or connected-ness. Or rightness.

During that long-ago summer, Mark had been convinced Emily belonged in his arms for always. As the years passed, however, he'd come to look upon that conviction as nothing more than a starry-eyed reaction to a first love. Now, he had an odd feeling his seventeen-year-old heart might not have been off base after all. Emily was as appealing as she'd been two decades ago. Perhaps more so. And not merely in terms of physical beauty. Everything he'd once loved about her remained, deeper and richer and more captivating than ever—her sharp intellect, her innate kindness and unselfishness, her delightful sense of humor, and her rock-solid strength. All of these gave her dimension and character. If her adult-like maturity as a teen had intrigued him, the effect was compounded now that she'd grown into it.

Mark stretched the kiss out as long as he dared, but eventually his well-honed sense of discipline kicked in. The last thing he wanted to do was rush Emily. She was already skittish about letting their friendship escalate. And he suspected she had well-defined ground rules for relationships and intimacy—much as she had in their Wren Lake days. He respected those now, as he had years ago. Tonight he'd tested the waters. And liked her response. But he didn't intend to push his luck.

With an effort, he broke contact and drew back, keeping her within the circle of his arms.

After a few seconds, Emily opened her eyes. "Wow! You've been practicing. That was quite an upgrade from our Wren Lake days."

He chuckled. "I have a lot to make up for, as I recall. And you weren't too shabby tonight yourself."

Smiling, she toyed with the button on his shirt. "I hope we won't regret . . ."

"Hey." He lifted her chin with a gentle finger. "No second thoughts, okay? Let's just enjoy the moment. And the movie."

He guided her toward the living room, put the DVD in, and joined her on the couch. He draped his arm around her shoulders, and she scooted closer, tucking herself beside him. At first she seemed tense, but as the movie progressed he felt her relax.

He had the opposite reaction, however. Her soft curves pressed against the hard planes of his body reminded him how vulnerable she was. And how much he wanted to protect her.

Yet the reality was chilling.

No matter how many agents were assigned to this case, and no matter how many precautions they took, until the unknown gunman was identified and apprehended, safety was only an illusion.

· · ·

"Dale, George would like to see you in his office after you finish lunch."

Surprised, Dale looked over at Cindy, George Aiken's secretary. In twenty-four years on the job, he couldn't recall ever being called into the owner's office. They knew each other, of course. Aiken Concrete wasn't that large of an operation. But Red always handled official business with his crew, unless it was a very serious matter. Like when Ralph got fired a year ago for selling leftover concrete on the side to pad his wallet.

That hadn't been smart. Or honest. Much as he'd liked Ralph, Dale hadn't been able to feel sorry for the man. An honest day's work for an honest day's pay, Dale's father had taught him. And never take what isn't yours. Dale had followed that advice all his life.

"Dale?" Cindy gave him an impatient look.

"Okay. I'll go see him now."

With a nod, she exited.

There was no reason to be nervous, Dale told himself as he headed down the hall toward the office suite at the front of the main building. He was a good worker. Red knew that. Had complimented him on countless occasions, in fact. This summons couldn't be anything bad.

But when he knocked on George's door and stepped inside, his heart missed a beat. Red was there too, and he didn't like the uncomfortable, apologetic look on his boss's face.

"Come in, Dale." George held out his hand, giving Dale a too-hearty shake. "Can I get you some water? Coffee?"

"No, sir. Thank you. I just had lunch."

"It is about that time, isn't it? Funny how the day can get away from you. Well, have a seat." He motioned to the chair beside Red.

He settled on the edge of the seat, and George leaned forward, folding his hands on his desk. "When was your last vacation, Dale?"

The question surprised him, and he glanced at Red. His boss's bland demeanor offered no clue about where this conversation was headed.

"Last October. My son was playing in a soccer tournament in Ohio, and Ruth and I went down to watch, then stayed a few days afterward to do a little sightseeing."

"Nice place, Ohio." George picked up a pen and balanced it in his fingers. "Red and I are thinking it might be good if you took a little vacation now, Dale. You've had a lot to deal with these past two or three months. A man needs some time to work through those kinds of losses."

"I've taken a few days off here and there."

"But it might be good to have an extended stretch off. You can't regroup in a day or two."

"I'm doing okay, Mr. Aiken. I don't need any time off."

Turning to Red, George passed him the baton with a slight dip of his head.

Red shifted in his seat, and his complexion grew ruddier. "The thing is, Dale, there've been a couple of mistakes recently. I've worked with you long enough to know they weren't caused by carelessness or negligence. I just figure you've got a lot of stuff to work through. Taking a little vacation might help you do that."

"What kind of mistakes?" Dale sent the foreman a skeptical look. He was always careful. He didn't make mistakes.

"One of your trucks had a bad batch of concrete two weeks ago. Too much water in the mix. We were lucky the driver caught it at the site when he checked the slump, or we'd have had a mess."

"Are you certain it was one of my trucks?"

"Yeah." Red looked at George and shoved his stubby fingers through his thick white hair. "Like I said, I know you have a lot to deal with. Losing your wife and son in a matter of weeks . . . that's a tough thing, pal. So I cut you some slack. You've been a great worker all these years. And a man's entitled to a few mistakes. But the thing is, it happened again on Monday."

Shocked, Dale stared at his boss. Was it possible he'd messed up twice? He knew he was a little distracted. He had a lot on his mind, a mission to plan and carry out. But he'd thought he'd been focused on his job when he was at work.

Yet he'd made mistakes.

And if he'd made mistakes here, had he made others as well?

The thought chilled him.

"Anyway, we think it might be a good idea for you to take some time off," Red continued.

"And it might help to talk things out with someone too," George added. "We'd like you to stop in and see Marla in HR after we're finished here. She can recommend someone to you."

A psychologist. That's what George meant. They'd decided he needed a shrink.

That stunned him more than anything else they'd said.

He didn't believe in shrinks. Never had. All that psychobabble confused people more than it helped them. And in light of what had happened with Bryan, it added insult to injury to suggest he see one.

When Dale didn't respond, Red exchanged another look with George.

"You know about our EAP program, Dale. We've sent plenty of materials to employees, and we've discussed it in meetings here," George said.

That was true. But Dale had tuned out in the meetings and thrown out the material unopened. It was the one thing on which he and Ruthie had disagreed. She'd been convinced the program might help Bryan. He'd been adamant they could solve their own problems.

In the end, he'd won. Or he thought he had. But his son's best friend had confided to him at the funeral that Bryan had found a way around his father's directive. And he'd discovered Ruthie had known about it. The ensuing argument had been the most stressful and prolonged in their marriage. Three weeks after they buried their son, she'd suffered a fatal heart attack.

"Anyway, Marla will give you the name of the counselor at the EAP office. Set up an appointment, Dale. It might help you over the hump. Okay?"

It wasn't a request. Dale knew that. He was backed into a corner because of two stupid mistakes. At least the guy was just a "counselor" versus a shrink, he consoled himself. And if he played it right, Dale was certain he could convince him he was okay and end the charade in one visit.

As for taking a few days off, that might not be a bad thing. He needed to complete his mission. This would give him the opportunity to get focused and finish the job.

"Sure. I'll talk to him."

"Good, good. I told George you'd be okay with this." Red slapped him on the back and stood. "Everything will be fine. And you let us know if you need anything while you're off, okay?"

"I will."

Standing, Dale took the hand George extended.

"You're a good man, Dale. But life can take a toll on the best of us. And you've had more than your share of setbacks recently. We understand. Our main concern is that you take care of yourself."

It was an effort, but Dale managed to maintain an impassive expression. They didn't care about him. All they cared about was satisfying their customers and avoiding lawsuits. A worker who made mistakes was a liability. They might over-look two mishaps after twenty years of stellar service. But three strikes and he could very well be out. Unless he played their game.

"I appreciate that, Mr. Aiken." The words left a bitter taste in his mouth.

Red walked him down the hall straight to Marla's office, leaving him at the threshold. As if he didn't think Dale would follow through on his own. "Take care, pal. Call me if you need anything, okay?"

"Sure."

As Red walked away, Dale stuck his hands in his pockets. In all fairness, this wasn't Red's fault. He almost felt sorry for the man. Red wasn't the type to put any more stock in the mumbo jumbo of psychologists and counselors than he did. His boss was doing what all bosses did: following orders.

And that's what Dale had to do too.

Gritting his teeth, he pushed through the door to Marla's office.

• • •

"Did you hear? Kyle called back."

As Emily entered the control booth after her Thursday radio program, Mark smiled. "I heard. He sounds steadier this week."

"He is. I talked to him during the station break. He said the counselor at school has been 'awesome,' to use his term. I wish more of them were that responsive. And available. And empathetic." She grinned at him. "I don't want much, do I?"

"Just the best for everyone. That's why you're good at what you do."

A soft flush warmed her cheeks. "Either your lines are getting better or I'm getting used to them. I like that one. What do you think, Coop?" she asked as the other agent entered.

"Not bad." Coop's lips twitched into a smile. "I'll let you two discuss it while I check out the parking lot. Meet me at the door in five minutes."

Andy had headed down the hall to secure the facility for the night, leaving Mark and Emily in the control booth. As she fiddled with the simple gold cross that hung on a slender chain around her neck, she tried to summon up the courage to issue the invitation she'd dragged her feet on all week. But with Saturday a mere two days away, she was running out of time.

Mark gave her a swift appraisal and took a step closer, lifting a hand to touch her cheek. "What's up?"

"You don't miss much, do you?" She shook her head and plunged in. "Are you available Saturday night?"

"That depends." Mark gave her a lazy smile. "What did you have in mind?"

"I'm going to a renewal of vows and wondered if you'd like to come as my guest instead of lurking in the shadows as my bodyguard."

"A renewal of vows." His expression was puzzled. "Want to explain that?"

"I've been seeing a patient for a few months, trying to help her sort through some problems in her marriage stemming from a childhood trauma. Anyway, thanks to a lot of courage and hard work on her part, she's finally gotten past it. Her marriage is stronger than ever, and she and her husband are going to renew their vows for their twenty-fifth anniversary. She invited me to attend. I was very touched."

"I have a feeling you should be the guest of honor. I've seen you in action. She may have done her part, but I have a strong suspicion that without your guidance, this renewal might never have happened. And yes, I'd be happy to go with you."

"Just so you know, the ceremony's at a church."

Grinning, he held her jacket as she slipped her arms inside. "Church, huh? Do I detect some subterfuge here? A subversive plan to guide a fallen-away believer back to the straight and narrow?"

"Nope. I'm a great believer in that old adage

about leading a horse to water. It doesn't do any good if he's not thirsty." She flipped her hair outside of her jacket collar, wincing as the fabric tightened across her arm.

"Are you okay?" Mark reached out a steadying hand, a slight frown marring his brow.

"Yes. Now that the stitches are out, I tend to forget about the injury. Then all of a sudden I'll try to use my arm, and wham! I'm reminded I still have quite a lot of healing to do. But forgetting is a good sign, I guess. I must be improving."

Mark took her good arm and guided her out of the control booth toward the door. "If the shrinking size of the bandage is any indication, I'd say that's true. And I never said I wasn't thirsty, by the way."

His comment caught her off guard. She'd expected him to sidestep a discussion of faith.

At her surprised look, he gave a rueful shrug. "I'll admit I haven't thought much about God in the past few years. In a positive sense, anyway. But I also know there's a void in my life. Nothing I've tried has filled it. Thanks to some of the conversations we've been having, though, I'm thinking God may be what's missing. I guess you could say I'm a seeker. Who knows? Maybe I'll find some answers in church, at that renewal ceremony."

As far as she was concerned, Mark's attitude was a huge step forward from the skeptical reception her faith-related comments had generated two weeks ago.

"I hope so, Mark. And it should be a lovely evening."

"Any evening with you would be lovely." He reached out to play with a few strands of her hair. As he leaned toward her, two sharp raps sounded on the door, followed by a pause and a third knock.

"Mark. We're clear."

His lips hovered close to hers, his breath a warm whisper against her mouth, his regret obvious. "I'm going to have to talk to my partner about his timing." With a resigned sigh, he straightened and touched her cheek. "We'll pick this up another time, okay?"

Without waiting for her to respond, Mark turned away and swung the door open.

Was it okay? Emily wondered as she followed him out. She wasn't sure. About that—and a lot of things.

But as she walked toward the car, Mark's hand in the small of her back, she was sure about one thing.

When all this was over, she didn't want the man at her side to disappear from her life again as he had twenty years before.

14

Hope House surprised Mark.

"This is it?" He inspected the large, well-maintained home as Coop pulled into the driveway and followed it to the small parking lot in the rear of the residential property. The shelter was nothing like the institutional-looking structure in a less-than-desirable district that he'd imagined. And Nick hadn't enlightened him after he'd escorted Emily here the week before. He'd simply commented that security was good.

"Yes. What did you expect?" Emily settled the strap of her purse on her shoulder and picked up her briefcase.

"Something more . . . official looking."

"Some of the shelters do look like that. But this is a safe house—an emergency haven for women and children in need of immediate refuge. It can accommodate eight women, or four women and their children. Women only stay here a few days, until they decide what they want to do next."

While Emily was speaking, Coop had exited the car and done a sweep of the area. At his nod, Mark helped Emily out, taking the briefcase from her hand.

"Nick said it was secure." Mark looked around as they strode toward the back entrance. The small yard was enclosed by a six-foot privacy fence, and there was a peephole in the steel door. Prominent stickers on the windows and a sign stuck in the ground near the entrance alerted visitors that the building was equipped with an alarm system.

"It has to be. You'd understand why if you heard some of the stories these women tell."

She rang the back bell. Sixty seconds ticked by before the door was opened by a gray-haired woman with a merry smile.

"Hello, Emily. Sorry for the delay. I'm still adjusting to your new schedule. It's odd to see you here on a Friday."

"It feels odd to me too. You know what a creature of habit I am. Margaret, this is Mark Sanders and Coop . . . Evan Cooper. Margaret Adams."

"My, you do have good taste in men." The older woman shook their hands, her eyes twinkling. "I liked the one you brought last week too. So handsome and well-mannered."

Mark raised an eyebrow, and Emily grinned as she dropped her purse on the large table in the cheery kitchen. "Yes. Nick's quite a guy. But these two aren't bad, either."

"Thanks a lot," Mark said.

Margaret chuckled. "You two feel free to help yourselves to cake and coffee while you wait." She gestured toward the counter.

"Anyone lined up for me today, Margaret? Or am I doing a walk-through?"

"Two of our guests signed up to speak with you.

I'll let them know you're here. Make yourselves comfortable, gentlemen." As she pushed through the door toward the front of the house, she came close to colliding with a woman carrying a baby. The young mother's black eye and split lip identified her as a Hope House guest.

"Oh, Denise. I'm sorry, dear, I didn't see you." Margaret looked back at Mark and Coop as she put an arm around the young woman's shoulders. "I'll alert the rest of the guests that we have visitors. You won't be disturbed." Turning, she cooed at the baby. "Now come along, dear, and let's get this little one down for his nap."

The woman took one nervous look at the two powerful men who dominated the kitchen and hastily backed through the door, followed by Emily.

For several moments, only the hum of the refrigerator broke the silence.

"Guys who do that should be behind bars." A muscle clenched in Mark's jaw.

"Yeah." Coop let out a slow breath. "I bet Emily gets an earful. I don't know how she does it. She talks to people with problems all day at her office, and instead of having fun in her free time, she puts herself through those emotional sessions with teens and listens to the stories these women have to tell. And we think we have a tough job." He shook his head. "How does she do it?"

The question was rhetorical, and Coop didn't

wait for an answer. Instead, he moved to the counter and poured himself a cup of coffee.

Yet the comment lingered in Mark's mind. While Emily's faith gave her obvious spiritual comfort, he suspected her emotional needs went unmet. He was no psychologist, but it seemed to him she filled the empty places in her life with a lot of stuff that tapped her emotional reservoir dry. As a result, she had nothing left to give at the end of the day. Which was probably a good thing from her viewpoint. If she had nothing left to give, she wouldn't notice there was no one to give anything to.

He also suspected that his reappearance had upset the delicate balance she'd created in her life. Forced her to acknowledge that she did have unaddressed emotional needs, just as her discussions of faith had forced him to acknowledge the spiritual vacuum in his life. It hadn't been a comfortable experience for him, and he suspected the same was true for her. Pleasant as their reunion had been, it had also highlighted the fact that they both had issues to grapple with and fears to address.

In some ways, life had been easier for both of them before their paths had crossed in the park. Yet he didn't regret their reunion. And he hoped Emily felt the same way.

But it didn't really matter.

Because there was no turning back.

"Where's Nick?" Mark stepped into his host's home gym, the one room in the house mercifully free of drywall dust. He'd figured his partner would be in here. Tossing a towel on the treadmill, he headed toward the elliptical machine.

"At the office." Coop grunted from his spot on the combo bench and lowered the weights he was hefting. "I don't know why he went to the expense of putting in a home gym when there's a well-equipped facility at the office."

"Convenience. At least that's what he told me."

"He's down there all the time, anyway." Coop wiped a towel down his face as he watched Mark warm up. "The leg's looking good."

"I'd say it's at 98 percent."

"That may be as good as it gets."

"I'll take it. Did Nick say what he was working on? It's Friday night."

"Nope. But between you and me, I think he's brown nosing."

"Nick?" Mark snorted and shook his head. "That's the last thing he'd do. He doesn't play office politics."

"He might join in the game if he's angling for the SWAT team job."

Mark stopped warming up and turned to Coop. "You know about that?"

"We work for an intelligence organization. Our job is uncovering information. How long did you think Dave's retirement would stay a secret?"

"True." Mark propped a fist on his hip. "To be honest, I've known about it for a while. And there's more to the story."

When he paused, Coop swung his leg over the bench and faced his partner. "Okay. You have my undivided attention."

"Steve offered me the job."

Silence descended as Coop scrutinized Mark. "I didn't think you were planning to leave the HRT yet."

"I wasn't. The offer came out of the blue. My first inclination was to turn it down immediately, but for some reason I didn't." He raked his fingers through his hair, puzzled. "I've been trying to sort through it myself before I said anything, but I'm not any closer to understanding my reaction now than I was when Steve brought it up. You know me as well as anyone. Any insights?"

"You want the truth?"

"Yeah."

"You may not like it."

"Has that ever stopped you before?"

"Can't say that it has." Coop chuckled and draped the towel around his shoulders. "If you didn't say no, my guess is the HRT is beginning to lose some of its luster for you. That's what happened to me. It was a great gig, but I've done everything I wanted to do on the team. Plus, my priorities have shifted now that I have Monica and a baby on the way. I don't need the excitement of high-risk missions like I once did. Nor do I feel the need to prove myself by pushing my body to the edge of human endurance in training. I have something better to fill my days."

He leaned forward and rested his forearms on his thighs, clasping his hands between his knees. "I still love the work, which is why I'm staying with the Bureau in a teaching role. But I'm ready for a life where I know I can go home at night instead of wondering whether I'll be called up without warning and sent thousands of miles away for a mission of unknown duration."

"In other words, you want a more predictable life." The kind Emily preferred, Mark thought.

"Bingo."

A feeling of melancholy washed over Mark. As Coop had said, the HRT had been a good gig. But he'd always known it wouldn't last forever. That at some point his partnership with Coop would come to an end. Situations changed. People changed. Sometimes by choice, sometimes by circumstance. Coop had made his choice. Now the ball was in his court.

"Why do I suddenly feel old?"

"I prefer to think of it as maturity," Coop countered with a grin.

"Emily might agree with you on that."

"Speaking of the good doctor—I suspect she has a lot to do with your response to Steve too.

Quantico is a long way from St. Louis. And you've put in enough years to get an office-of-preference transfer."

"That's a one-time shot." Mark had always expected, near the end of his career, to use the discretionary, permanent relocation option available to senior agents and settle in Tennessee. "What if things don't work out with Emily?"

"It is a bit of a gamble, I'll grant you that. But if you want my opinion, the lady seems worth it." Rising, Coop grabbed the ends of the towel around his shoulders in a tight grip. "You know, if you're looking for better guidance than I can give, you might try praying."

That advice from his partner shocked Mark. He knew Coop had made his peace with God when he and Monica were dating. But as with all subjects that involved the heart, Coop had avoided talking about it. This was the first time he'd ever mentioned prayer in Mark's presence.

"I wish I had a picture of your face." Coop grinned at him.

"I can't believe you're suggesting that I pray."

"Like I said, maturity." He snapped the towel at him, as if to dispel any such notion. "You better get moving or we'll be late picking up your lovely date for that anniversary thing."

As Coop exited, Mark wandered over to the window and stared through the slanted mini-blinds, overwhelmed by the sudden complexity of his life. A year ago, he'd been content to train hard and carry out missions. The HRT had been the center of his existence.

Then Coop had gotten married, and the dynamics had changed. The two of them still hung out in off hours on occasion, but it was usually just long enough to grab a quick pizza rather than an evening at a local bar perusing the eligible women. And more often than not when they got together, it was a threesome. Not that Mark minded. He liked Monica. A lot. She called them the three musketeers and did her best to keep Mark from feeling like the odd man out. Yet as inclusive as she and Coop were, they shared such a powerful bond that Mark felt more alone in their presence than he did when he was by himself.

The convenience store tragedy had messed with his head too. Caused him to question his judgment and his abilities, introduced uncertainty where once absolute conviction and confidence had reigned. And needed to reign. In his line of work, a nanosecond of hesitation could mean the difference between life and death. He'd lost that confidence for a while, but in the past few weeks it had returned as he'd come to accept that his decisions that day had been sound. That his tactical response had been appropriate and necessary. In terms of decisiveness, he felt ready to rejoin the HRT.

As for the guilt . . . that wasn't as easy to deal with. Despite his exoneration by the review board, a heavy sense of culpability weighed down his soul. It was what had driven him to write a letter to the boy's parents, against the advice of the Bureau's attorneys. What clawed at his gut every day as he slid his gun into the holster on his belt. What kept him awake at night, yearning for absolution. And he suspected it was also one of the factors driving his search for God.

And if all that wasn't enough, the past two weeks had been fraught with challenges and complications. He'd reconnected with Emily after twenty years. She'd been shot and almost died. An assassin was still after one of them. Coop was leaving the HRT. Steve had offered him a job. He was falling in love all over again with his teenage sweetheart.

Suddenly weary, Mark propped one shoulder against the wall and took a long, slow breath. There was too much on his plate. He'd been taught to handle volatile situations, had run close-quarter-battle routes day after day. But the survival skills he'd mastered in the field were of little use in personal decisions or matters of the heart. Those situations weren't covered in CQB training.

Mark could think of only one source to turn to for help. The same source he'd considered turning to in the park as Emily lay bleeding in his arms.

He hadn't asked for God's help that day. But a lot had changed since then. He'd changed. It was time to reach out to the Almighty. Test the waters. As he'd done with Emily.

Bypassing formal prayer, he simply spoke from the heart in a silent plea.

Lord, I need guidance. And forgiveness. If you can help me out with either of those, I'd be grateful. And thank you for the gift of Emily's presence in my life. I don't know where that will lead, but I know she puts her trust in you. Please help me do the same.

The renewal of vows had been far more moving than Mark expected. The couple had appeared serene and happy, and the sermon by the minister had been inspiring.

As the service concluded with an instrumental meditation piece on the harp, Mark glanced at Emily. She looked gorgeous tonight, in a short-sleeved, peach-colored silk suit that was simple but elegant. Her hair took on a burnished luster in the candlelight, and a faint smile hovered at her soft lips as she looked toward the couple being honored.

After two weeks, she bore little physical evidence of the trauma that had nearly taken her life, Mark noted in relief. The bruise on her temple was gone, the remnants of the abrasion on her cheek masked by makeup. While the bandage on her arm remained, peeking below the edge of her sleeve, the bulk had been reduced to Band-

Aid thickness. In another few days it would be gone.

And in two weeks, so would he. For good. Unless he chose to stay.

Tonight, the minister had talked of courage and commitment. Mark had always thought he possessed those qualities in abundance. In fact, he was called upon to use them every day in the HRT.

But they took on a whole different meaning when applied to his personal life. And in that realm, he wasn't at all certain his supply was adequate.

"Mark? It's over."

At Emily's soft comment, he looked up. She had risen, and the other guests were moving toward the exit. Standing, he took her arm as they left the pew. "Sorry. I was lost in thought."

She smiled and tucked her arm in his. "That's what a meditation is for."

Coop was waiting for them in the vestibule. "Nice service."

"I'm sorry you couldn't sit with us," Emily told him.

"I had a better view of the interior from the back."

At the subtle reminder of the reason for his presence, Emily's brightness dimmed a bit. "This has to be getting old for you. Not to mention boring."

"Boring is good in this case," Mark interjected.

"You know, considering how quiet it's been, you

guys are going to have to let me start going places alone again soon," Emily told them.

"We'll talk about that in a few days," Mark said.

"Is that a stall tactic?" Emily directed her question to Coop.

"I'm afraid I'm not at liberty to discuss tactical issues." He winked at her.

"I should have known you two would stick together. Okay, I'll let it go for tonight. But this subject isn't closed. Will you join us for dinner, Coop? Mary said you'd be welcome."

"I appreciate that. But after sitting through that ceremony, I'm in the mood to call Monica. It reminded me of our wedding. I think I'll hover in the background and chat with my wife."

"That's right. Your first anniversary is coming up, isn't it?" With all that had happened, the date had slipped Mark's mind.

"Next Sunday."

"You need to be there."

"Tell that to Les." As Mark frowned, Coop laid his hand on his partner's shoulder. "It's okay. Monica knew the odds were good I'd be away on some assignment. And she'd rather have me here than in a lot of places I could be." He looked around the vestibule and motioned to a side door. "Wait there and I'll bring the car up."

As Coop disappeared, Emily touched Mark's arm. "It's not your fault about the anniversary. There's no reason to feel guilty."

Looking down at her slender fingers resting against his sleeve, he smiled. "You know, I could get used to having a psychologist around. I think it's good for my mental health."

"You don't strike me as the type to need a psychologist except on rare occasion. You project a great sense of self and purpose. Not to mention confidence. I suspect you work too hard, but that's a common problem these days."

"Yeah. I know someone who does that too."

"Guilty as charged." She gave a sheepish shrug.

"Sometimes I think people who work too hard are trying to avoid addressing an issue."

"Now who's being the psychologist?"

Her tone was teasing, but he heard a wary note in the background. "Am I wrong?"

"We all have our coping mechanisms, I guess." She shifted her purse on her shoulder, avoiding his question. "Besides, I do lots of other things besides work."

"I know. You don't leave a spare hour in the day."

"Look who's talking. Coop told me you're very involved with a basketball team for at-risk kids when you're home."

"Coop has a big mouth."

"I'm glad he shared that. I think it's great. But I don't see that you have a lot of downtime, either."

"I don't. But I'm beginning to understand why I

maintain a hectic schedule. And to search for a way to fill up the empty places in my life that busyness masks."

A flash of headlights interrupted them, and Emily looked toward the door. "You're on the right track in your faith journey, Mark. The presence of God in your life will fill that spiritual void."

"That's not the only part of my life that's empty."

She turned, clearly taken aback by his admission.

He was no less surprised. He hadn't intended to be that candid. Nor imply that he was looking to her to fill the void in his life. He didn't think she was ready to hear that. And her suddenly uneasy expression confirmed his conclusion.

The door to the vestibule opened, and out of the corner of his eye Mark saw Coop step inside.

So did Emily. And she latched on to him as an escape route.

"Looks like our chauffeur is ready." Adopting an artificially bright tone, she turned away from Mark and walked toward the door.

She didn't look back as she joined his partner. When he hesitated, Coop sent him a questioning look.

Prodding himself into action, Mark moved forward, aware that Emily had just sent him a powerful message: She wasn't ready to get serious about their relationship.

Truth be told, he wasn't sure he was, either.

But he was sure about one thing.

Before his assignment in St. Louis ended, he intended to do some serious thinking about his life—and to figure out where Emily Lawson fit into it.

15

As Mark slipped his arms into the sleeves of his jacket on Sunday morning, his BlackBerry began to vibrate.

"Sanders."

"Mark, it's Steve. We've got a lead on the shooting."

Signaling to Coop, who was heading toward the door, Mark drew the notepad on Nick's kitchen counter toward him and pulled a pen out of his pocket. "It's about time. What do you have?"

"Oakdale got a call from a guy who lives near the church. He left on a two-week vacation the morning of the shooting and just found out about it from a neighbor. He thinks he saw the shooter's car pull out of the church parking lot. Carl's sending a detective over to get his statement and thought you might want to join him."

"We're on our way. What's the address?" Mark jotted down the information as Steve recited it. "Can you let Oakdale know we're coming?"

"That will be my next call. Fill me in afterward."

"Will do. Thanks." As Mark reholstered his BlackBerry, he looked at Coop. "We may have a witness to the shooter leaving the scene. An Oakdale detective is heading out to take a statement now. He'll wait for us to join him."

"What about Emily?"

They'd been on their way out the door to escort her to church, Mark suddenly recalled. Frustrated, he checked his watch. "Where's Nick?"

"He had a call on another bank robbery lead. That case sounds as if it's heating up."

Raking his fingers through his hair, Mark shoved the bottom of his jacket aside and propped a fist on his hip. "I need to be there for this interview. You want to take Emily?"

"And risk Les's wrath for letting you out of my sight? Not a chance."

"Emily's not going to give up Sunday services."

"She has to go out by herself eventually, Mark."

At his partner's quiet reminder, Mark tilted his head and regarded him. "You think I'm being overprotective?"

Coop lifted a shoulder. "I understand your concern. But we've already given her a lot more coverage than normal policy would dictate. And based on her comment last night, I suspect she's about to revolt, anyway. She doesn't strike me as a lady who likes to be smothered."

Smothered. Mark hadn't thought of it that way. But he could see where Emily might view their protective efforts in that light. And Coop was right. She was beginning to get antsy. Maybe he needed to ease off a bit. Especially if there was a break in the case.

"Okay. But I'm going to suggest she attend a different church today, just to keep our shooter off balance in case he's watching her."

"She might buy that."

Five minutes later, after a quick call to Emily, Mark joined Coop in the car.

As Coop put the car in gear, he glanced at his partner. "Was she okay with the revised plan?"

"I don't think she was thrilled with the suggestion to go to a different church, and I picked up a little nervousness about being turned loose with no warning, but she was happy about the break in the case. She's going to page me when she gets there." Mark buckled his seat belt and checked the address Steve had given him. "This guy must live across the street from the church."

"Did Steve have any details?"

After passing on what little he knew, Mark directed him to the house. Fifteen minutes later, they pulled up in front of a two-story brick home one house down and across the street from the exit at the far end of the church lot. An unmarked car was parked in front, and as they rolled up behind it, Sergeant Bill Montgomery stepped out.

"Carl called to let me know you were coming," the detective said. "This could turn out to be a wild goose chase, but the guy sounded legit and the timing's about right." He withdrew a notebook from his pocket and flipped it open. "Name's Frank Purnell. He's waiting for us."

Mark nodded. "Let's see what we've got."

A man in his late thirties, with sandy-colored hair still damp from the shower and dressed in shorts and a golf shirt, answered the door seconds after they rang the bell.

"Mr. Purnell?" The detective took the lead.

"Yes. You're from Oakdale?"

Montgomery introduced himself and flashed his badge. "This is Mark Sanders and Evan Cooper with the FBI."

The man did a double take. "I'm not sure the information I have merits this kind of attention."

"Mark has a vested interest in the case," Montgomery told him. "He was one of the shooter's targets."

"Oh. I'm sorry to hear that. Come in, gentlemen."

As he stepped aside to usher them in, Mark caught sight of a youngster hovering in the background. About nine, he had the same sandy-hued hair as his father. And he looked awed.

No surprise there, Mark reflected, suppressing a smile. The presence of detectives and FBI agents in his home would have impressed him as a nine-year-old too. The kid would have stories to tell his friends for months to come, depending on how long he could milk it.

Montgomery flipped his notebook open again

and took down the basics, then asked Frank to run through the events of that morning.

"We were leaving on vacation, and as we backed down our driveway, a car pulled out of the church lot," he said.

"Can you give me an approximate time?"

"I can do better than that. We never leave on schedule for vacation, but this year everything went smoothly. I remember looking at the clock on my dash and thinking we were only thirteen minutes late. It was 8:13."

"That fits," Mark said. "Did you see the driver?"

The man gave a regretful shake of his head. "No. I'm sorry. I didn't pay any attention to him."

"He was wearing a baseball cap."

The men in the room turned to look at the boy hovering in the doorway, the soft uncertainty in his voice betraying his nervousness.

"Come on in, David." Frank motioned for him, and the youngster moved into the room. "This is my son. To be honest, he's the one you have to thank if this information turns out to be helpful. I was so busy wondering whether we'd forgotten anything I doubt I would have noticed the car if he hadn't pointed it out. It caught his attention because it was exactly like ours. Same make, model, color. It might even have been the same year. It was like looking in a mirror. A silver Toyota Camry LE."

A midsized car. That fit the tire impression the

ERT had found, Mark noted. A surge of adrenaline shot through him, and he leaned forward. "Did you happen to get a look at the license plate?"

"No. I'm sorry."

"I did. I had my binoculars out. But it was muddy."

Once again, all eyes turned toward David.

"Did you see any of the numbers or letters, son?" the detective asked.

"There was an eight. I remember, because that's how old I am."

"Good work, buddy." Mark smiled at him, and the kid fairly glowed. "Could you tell if it was a Missouri plate?"

"Uh-huh. It was white at the top and kind of faded to blue near the bottom."

"Do you remember where the eight was? Near the edge or more toward the middle?"

He scrunched up his face in concentration. "No. I'm sorry."

"That's okay. You did good. Was there anyone in the car except the driver?"

"No."

"Was there anything else unusual about the car? Did it have a special antenna or any damage?"

"I don't think so."

"I take it this isn't a car you remember seeing before or since?" Montgomery's question encompassed father and son.

"No. It was new to us," Frank replied.

"You guys need anything else?" The detective turned to Mark and Coop.

They exchanged a look. "We're good," Mark said.

The three men rose to shake hands with both Frank and David.

"You've got good observation skills," Mark told the youngster, resting a hand on his shoulder as they prepared to exit. "That's important for an FBI agent. Think about that when you get older. We're always looking for good men."

"Yes, sir. I will."

As they stepped outside, Coop grinned at Mark. "You made that kid's day."

"Never hurts to begin recruiting young. And we have him to thank for our most solid lead to date."

"No argument there."

They regrouped around Montgomery's trunk.

"I suggest running a check for registrations containing the number eight for zip codes within a hundred-mile radius of St. Louis," Montgomery said. "Considering our shooter hangs around cows, he could be in an outlying area."

"Sounds reasonable," Mark concurred. "How much detail are we likely to get?"

"With the computer search, not much beyond license plates containing the number eight. A lot of the registration information isn't in the database. It will take a hand search to drill down on the records."

Things hadn't changed much since his field agent days, Mark reflected. Computerized record-keeping at the state level was still archaic. And there were often frustrating gaps in the paper records.

"That could take days," Coop noted.

"If we're overwhelmed with matches, we could always pare down to a fifty-mile radius," the detective said. "I'll get this in the works right away. We won't make much headway with the Department of Revenue folks on a Sunday, but a call from Carl and your boss might speed things along."

"We'll work our end," Mark promised. "Thanks for taking the lead on this."

As he and Coop headed toward their respective sides of the car, Coop tossed a question over the hood. "I saw you checking your BlackBerry during the interview. Emily get there okay?"

"Yes. I also got a page from Nick. He could use our help on the bank robbery case. You up for that?"

"Are you?"

"To be honest, I'd rather spend the day with Emily. But considering Nick's been picking up some escort duty for me, and with Steve cutting me some slack at the office to work the shooting, I haven't been around to help on the bank case as much as I should have. I owe him."

"Okay." Coop slid into the car. "At least it gets me out of the construction zone for a while."

"Feel like some company?"

At the sound of Mark's voice on the other end of the phone, Emily smiled. "That would be nice. Are you sending Nick over?"

"Cute. What did you do all day?"

"Caught up on case files."

"Sounds exciting."

"Necessary."

"Boring."

"Your word, not mine. Besides, I kept hoping you'd call to tell me about the latest on the shooter and I wanted to stay close to the phone. Or is it top secret?"

"I would have called sooner, but Coop and I were out all day tracking down new leads for Nick on a bank robbery case. And no, it's not top secret. But I'd rather tell you about it in person."

"It's kind of late. And tomorrow is a work day."

"I won't stay long."

"Is this just an excuse to come over?"

"Yep. I'll bring ice cream."

"Sounds like a bribe to me. But make it double chocolate anything and you've got a date."

"Look for me in fifteen minutes."

"Buy some for Coop too. That's the least you can do, considering all the chauffeuring he's done."

He chuckled. "Duly noted. See you soon."

Long after the line went dead, Emily's smile lingered as she sat on a stool at her kitchen island, elbow on counter, chin propped in hand. Mark had that effect on her. He always had. The warm, husky cadence of his voice alone was enough to brighten her day.

And today it needed brightening. Her solo trip to church this morning had left her on edge. While she'd told Mark and Coop last night that it was time they cut her loose, she'd found herself looking over her shoulder and hurrying to and from her car, her pulse hammering with every step. Although she knew she was vulnerable even with Nick or Mark and Coop by her side, she'd felt far more exposed and at risk on her own.

The experience had left her unsettled and fidgety, and working on boring case files, as Mark had called them, had been her best antidote to that jitteriness. Not that she'd admit that to Mark. If she told him her excursion had freaked her out, he'd insist on continuing the escort service. But she needed to get used to going out alone. Besides, whatever lead had surfaced today might put them on track to solving the case. She knew Mark was hoping for a resolution before he had to return to Quantico.

Thoughts of his departure in less than two weeks erased the last remnants of her smile. She'd like to stay in touch, but after their kiss, and after Mark's revelation last night following the renewal ceremony, she knew his intentions were serious. How he expected to explore their relationship when he was a thousand miles away at best—and often much farther on far-flung missions—she had no idea. Nor had she asked him to share his thoughts on that subject. If she did, he would take that as encouragement. And she wasn't ready to consider offering that to another man in a high-risk profession.

How could she, after losing Grant?

While the pain of his death had diminished, the memory of the night the chief had arrived at her door, soot-stained and choked with emotion, was as vivid as if it had happened yesterday. Even now, five years later, there were nights she reached for Grant sleepily in the pre-dawn darkness, only to touch cold, empty sheets and be reminded that abject loneliness was the price to be paid for loving too much.

All at once, tears pricked her eyes. She'd never been a weepy person. But considering all that had happened in the past two weeks, she supposed she was entitled to a good cry.

This wasn't the time, however, she reminded herself as the doorbell rang. Mark would take one look at her red eyes and pull her into a comforting hug. Which would do nothing to help her regain her emotional equilibrium.

Sliding off the stool, she grabbed a tissue out of the box on the counter, dabbed at her eyes, and composed her face. A quick check in the hall mirror as she passed reassured her she'd erased all evidence of her momentary loss of control.

After a quick look through the peephole, she flipped the lock and opened the door.

"Ice cream delivery." He held up a white sack as he stepped inside and secured the lock behind him. "Chocolate chocolate chip for the lady. Butter pecan for me."

Before she could greet him, he leaned down and kissed her. Not a casual brush of welcome, but a coaxing, caressing, lingering melding of lips, held in place with a firm hand at the nape of her neck.

When at last he drew back, she tightened her grip on the edge of the door. "What was that all about?"

"Wasn't it obvious? I'm glad to see you." He waved the sack at her. "Let's eat this before it melts. After that kiss, my guess is it's already starting to drip." With a wink, he stroked the back of his hand down her cheek.

Confused, Emily watched his broad back as he disappeared into her kitchen. Last night, he'd hinted that he might be looking for a serious relationship with her. While she suspected he didn't have all the answers about how to make that work in their situation, she had a feeling he was determined to find them if she gave him the green light to try.

At best, she'd flashed a yellow light his way. In truth, it had been closer to red. And she'd expected him to back off.

Instead, he was acting as if she'd signaled green. Something in her training should be kicking in about now to give her an insight into his strategy. But nothing was clicking. Had he missed her signal? Or was he ignoring it?

He stuck his head out the kitchen door. "Everything okay?"

"I don't know."

"Come on in and we'll talk about it. Your ice cream is turning to soup."

Not certain she wanted to have this conversation, Emily joined him at the kitchen table, noting he'd already put a hefty dent in his double serving.

When she sat motionless, he tapped the edge of her cardboard cup with his spoon. "You'll have to drink that if you wait much longer."

Figuring it was safer to eat than to talk, she dug in, spooning the creamy treat into her mouth, trying to tamp down the emotions his kiss had kindled in her. And to ignore the way Mark's presence filled the room. But she couldn't manage the latter. He looked too good tonight, dressed in well-broken-in jeans that molded his muscular thighs and a chest-hugging T-shirt that displayed the logo from a charitable run he must have participated in. It was the most casual attire she'd seen him in— yet it enhanced his masculinity every bit as much as the distinguished suits he usually sported. Maybe more.

"You didn't like the kiss?"

She almost choked on the ice cream sliding down her throat.

He passed her a glass of water and waited in silence while she took a gulp.

"You don't beat around the bush, do you?"

"Nope. I like to know what I'm up against."

Toying with her spoon, she scraped up some of the melting ice cream from the bottom of her cardboard cup as she considered how to respond. She respected honesty. She counseled patients not to be afraid of it. And she was a great advocate of open communication. In her professional life.

In her personal life, however, she was finding her advice hard to follow. Mark was forcing her to confront issues she didn't want to deal with. Deep inside, she knew her problem with the man across from her was rooted in fear. She liked Mark. Enough that she could fall in love with him if she let herself. But that would put her heart at risk. Again. And she couldn't live with the terror of not knowing when he left in the morning if she'd ever see him alive again. Been there, done that. Once was enough.

"I think it may be too soon to have this conversation, Mark." She chose her words with care. "We only reconnected a couple of weeks ago."

"I'm not asking you to marry me, Em. I'm not that rash. But I do think we were brought together again for a reason. And I have a feeling it might lead to a serious relationship, if we decide to explore it. The vibes are still there, twenty years later. And as much as I liked the teenage Emily, I like the grown-up version even better."

She felt the same about him. But it didn't erase her fears. Or solve the logistical problem. "I'm not sure I see the point in pursuing this. Your life is in Quantico and mine is here."

"That could change. My temporary boss here has offered me a permanent job."

It took her a few moments to find her voice. "You'd move to St. Louis?"

"If I had a reason to."

His meaning was clear. And that was even more scary. Her expression must have reflected that, because he reached for her cold hand and interlaced his fingers with hers.

"I'm not asking for a commitment, Emily. Just a chance."

"I thought you loved your job."

"The HRT has been great. But I always knew it wouldn't last forever. I found out not long ago that Coop's leaving in a few weeks. And much as I hate to admit it, I'm getting a little old for the rigors of the job. I'd be moving on anyway in a year or two. Coop's decision may have pushed me to consider it sooner rather than later, but it was coming. And after running into you again, I have an added reason to give Steve's offer serious consideration."

"What would you do here?"

"I'd be on the reactive squad, and I'd head up the SWAT team."

Another dicey job, she reflected in dismay.

As if reading her mind, he gave her a measured look. "It's not as dangerous as the HRT."

His comment jolted her. She'd known the HRT was a high-risk job; apparently it was more perilous than she'd ever imagined. She also heard his unspoken message: while he was trading down on the risk scale, risk remained.

More of it than she felt capable of handling.

"With my background, there are very few jobs that would be risk-free, Em." His quiet voice held a hint of apology . . . and regret.

"I know."

"That's the problem, isn't it?"

Since he'd been honest with her, she decided she owed him the same in return. "Yes. When I lost Grant, I came close to losing myself. I might have, if Maria and Evelyn hadn't helped me pick up the pieces, and if I hadn't had my faith to cling to. I survived, but I wouldn't want to travel that road again."

"Loss is part of life, Emily. Whether it happens unexpectedly, as it did with Grant, or later in life, with disease or old age. It's inevitable. The best we can do is consider each day a gift and embrace it fully. Otherwise, we exist rather than live."

Once again, moisture clouded her vision. He was right, and she knew it. But she wasn't yet ready to accept what that implied.

"I need some time to sort things out, Mark."

"I understand. I don't have to give Steve an answer until I leave."

"So I get two whole weeks to figure this out?"

"Other jobs in St. Louis will come along down the road if I pass on this one."

"Not as well suited to your skills."

"We don't know that. Whatever is supposed to happen, will happen." He picked up their empty ice cream containers and deposited the cardboard cups in her trash can. After rinsing his hands at the sink, he rejoined her. "Let's switch gears. I have some news."

"Good, I hope."

"Helpful, anyway. A man who lives near the church where the shooter parked spotted the car leaving. We got a good description and one digit of the license number, thanks to his observant eight-year-old son. We're pulling the registrations that match for a hundred-mile radius."

"How many cars are we talking about?"

"Hard to say. It's a common color and a popular car. But the odds are our shooter is on the list somewhere. We'll track down every registration if we have to." He folded his hands on the table and gave her an appraising look. "Coop thinks you're feeling smothered by our escort service."

"A little." His changes of subject were beginning to throw her off balance.

"Okay. You know the drill. Vary your routine, as well as your arrival and departure at the office.

Don't wander into secluded places. Avoid going out at night. Call if there's the slightest indication of trouble. If you promise me you'll follow those rules, we'll ease up on the security. But I'd like you to have an escort to the radio station. It's a predictable time and place, plus it's dark when you leave."

"Okay. That sounds sensible."

"All of this, however, does not mean I intend to stop seeing you. Unless you tell me to back off."

She'd known he'd get back to personal issues.

It would be safer if she did tell him to keep his distance, Emily knew. But also lonelier. Mark's reappearance in her world had forced her to acknowledge how much she missed the sharing and laughter and closeness of having someone special in her life. For five years, she'd shoved those memories, and the needs they awakened, to a far corner of her heart where she could pretend they didn't exist.

But the pretending was over, thanks to the man sitting across from her.

Her gaze fell on the blinds at her windows, and she was struck by the symbolism. As Nick had closed the blinds to protect her from physical danger, she had shuttered her heart to protect herself from emotional peril. And just as she yearned to open the blinds and let the warmth of the sunlight fill her condo, so, too, did her heart yearn for the healing touch of love.

One of these days, the physical danger would be past and she could let the sunlight back in to her home. But if she let Mark get too close, the emotional danger would never go away. Closing her eyes, she drew a shuddering, uncertain breath.

When the silence lengthened, Mark took her hand in a warm clasp. "Do you want to sleep on it?"

Did she? As Emily opened her eyes and looked down at his long, lean fingers, gentle yet strong, she suddenly couldn't imagine letting Mark walk out of her life again. Whatever her future held, she sensed this man was part of it. In what exact capacity, she wasn't certain. But as he'd reminded her, he wasn't proposing. He was simply asking her to give their relationship a chance. To let him continue to see her. She didn't need to sleep on it to know she wanted that as much as he did. Whatever the risk.

"I don't want you to back off. But I can't give you any promises, either."

Her reward was a smile that warmed her all the way to her toes. "I'm not asking for any, Em. For now, seeing you is enough." He checked his watch and stood, tugging her to her feet. "Coop's waiting. I need to go."

"He's been outside all this time?"

"Yes. He's talking to Monica on his BlackBerry. And he prefers your porch to Nick's construction site any day."

She walked with him to the door, where he turned and pulled her into the circle of his arms. "When I said seeing you was enough, I hope you understood it includes this."

Once more he bent to claim her lips in a lingering kiss.

"Sleep well," he murmured, drawing back just enough so his warm breath whispered at her lips as he spoke the words. And then, with a smile and a touch to her cheek, he was gone.

Emily watched through the peephole as Coop materialized out of the shadows and fell into step beside Mark. And as she pressed her fingers against lips that continued to tingle from his touch, his strategy became clear.

He figured if he hung around a lot and gave her enough of those amazing kisses, he'd wear down her defenses.

And she had to admit his plan was already starting to work.

16

The guy was an idiot.

Dale had just suffered through one of the longest half hours of his life, thanks to . . . he checked the EAP counselor's card . . . Randy Miller. Dale had wanted to throw up as the man ran through his polished, fake, "I'm concerned" routine. But if Red and George wanted him to play this game, he had to go along or his job would be on the line. That meant he was beginning his Monday by meeting with a moron. And hoping it would end here.

Unfortunately, Mr. Sensitivity had other ideas.

As Miller leaned forward in a practiced posture of caring, looking like an older version of nerdy Clark Kent in his black-rimmed glasses, it took every ounce of Dale's self-control to stifle his revulsion and maintain a neutral expression.

"I think it would be good if you talked with someone who has more expertise in counseling people who've faced the kind of trauma you're dealing with, Mr. Edwards."

It was the sentence Dale had been dreading. The clown wanted him to talk with a shrink.

"I don't think that's necessary, Mr. . . . ." He consulted the card again. "Miller. I'm used to handling my own problems."

"Sometimes it's difficult for us to see our personal situations clearly, Mr. Edwards." The man's patronizing manner made Dale want to gag. "And there's nothing wrong with admitting an occasional need for help to sort things out."

This had nothing to do with helping him, Dale thought, trying to swallow past his disgust. It was all about passing on responsibility. He knew how the system worked. He'd seen plenty of examples in his own job. Everything these days had to be double-checked and signed in triplicate or the attorneys could eat you alive if you were unlucky enough to find yourself facing a lawsuit. It was all about dotting the i's and crossing the t's and covering yourself. This spineless twit didn't want to sign off on Dale without a second opinion.

Going in, Dale had known there was a possibility the guy would pass the buck to a shrink. And he was prepared to argue against it, if necessary. In a polite, rational way, of course. It was important to convince Miller he was coping, that he had his act together, that the time off mandated by Red and George was all that was needed. Two weeks of breathing space to rest and regroup. That was the case he planned to make.

Until Miller threw him a curve.

Jotting down a name and phone number on a pad of paper, he handed it to Dale. "I'd like to set up an appointment for you with Dr. Emily Lawson. She sees referrals from EAP programs for some of the largest companies in St. Louis. I've sent a number of people to her, and the feedback has been excellent."

As Miller went on to sing her praises, Dale tried to process the bizarre turn of events.

He'd been referred to the very person he'd had in his crosshairs two weeks ago.

Coincidence couldn't account for this twist of fate, he was certain of that. It had to be a sign. The Lord wanted him to see her. Their meeting must be the key to whatever plan the Almighty wanted Dale to implement. Somehow, during that face-to-face encounter, God would show him how he wanted his vengeance to be exacted.

There was one problem, however. While Dale didn't thinkthe cops had a clue about his identity, his on-the-job slipups worried him. He couldn't afford mistakes . . . there, or in his mission. There could be no connection between him and Emily Lawson. He had to protect his identity.

"All right, Mr. Miller. I'll talk to her. But I'd like to keep this anonymous."

"That's not a problem. No one but you, me, and Dr. Lawson will know about your appointment with her, and only the two of you will know what was discussed."

"I appreciate that. But information can leak. And a lot of people think there's kind of a stigma attached to seeing a psychologist. I'd be more comfortable if I could see her anonymously."

The man frowned. "You mean, keep your identity confidential?"

"Yes. I think it would help me, you know . . . open up." He tried to convey an earnest, cooperative attitude.

"I must admit, I've never had that request before." Miller leaned back in his leather chair. "In today's world, there isn't a stigma associated with counseling, Mr. Edwards."

"The thing is, I had a buddy once who went to a counselor for a drinking problem. Somehow that information got into his records, and when he tried to change jobs they found out about it. Even though he'd licked the problem, they didn't hire him. I'd rather not put myself in that position." Dale hoped the Lord would forgive him for that fabrication.

The man considered him for a few seconds, then nodded. "Okay. I think we can do this. The important thing is for you to see Dr. Lawson. What name shall I set it up under?"

"Joe Smith?"

"You can't get much more anonymous than that." The ingratiating smile the man flashed him grated on his nerves. "I'll be in touch later today to let you know what slots she has available. Would tomorrow or Wednesday be okay, if I can get you in that soon?"

"Sure." The sooner the better.

Standing, the EAP counselor held out his hand. "I do appreciate your coming today, Mr. Edwards. All of us want to help you through this difficult period. I know Dr. Lawson will be of great assistance as well. And I want you to feel free to call me if there's anything else I can do for you."

"Thank you." Dale took the man's hand in a brief grip before exiting.

As he headed down the hall toward the elevator, he pulled the idiot's card out of his pocket. The tremor in his hand surprised him, but treating a jerk with respect took a lot out of a man.

The elevator pinged, and as the door slid open he

ripped the card into a dozen small pieces with more force than necessary.

And before he stepped inside, he deposited them where they belonged.

In the trash can beside the door.

Two hundred and eighty-nine possible matches on the car.

It had taken two days to cull them from the thousands of plates containing the number eight. And the final result was far from perfect. As Mark had suspected, incomplete information had inflated the list. Fifty of the names were there because the hand search revealed the registration had not included either a model or a color.

Tuesday was not beginning on a high note.

Handing the list he'd paged through to Coop, Mark looked at Steve as the squad supervisor spoke.

"We ran the names through NCIC. Other than two people who showed up with reports of stolen property, everyone was clean."

Discouraged, Mark leaned back in his chair. The National Crime Information Center was the most comprehensive listing of crime-related data in the United States. He'd hoped it would identify some suspicious characters on the list. But if that database didn't raise a red flag, there wasn't one to be raised. On the owner of record, anyway. But a friend or relative could have used the car too.

There was no way to determine that without con-
tacting every owner. And then hoping he or she
would be honest about who had driven the car.

"How are we going to handle this?" he asked.

"I already discussed it with Carl. They'll take
care of the interviews in their own jurisdiction, but
there are only a few in the Oakdale zip code. We
inherit the rest by default."

"A good cluster of them are in close proximity to
St. Louis metro. The others are scattered." Coop
scanned the pages. "We'll have to pull in some of
the region offices to assist in tracking these people
down."

"They'll love that." From his field agent days,
Mark recalled his own distaste for requests for
assistance from other offices. In most instances,
they were a nuisance . . . dead-end interviews or
wild goose chases that took him away from his
own cases and produced nothing.

"You have any other suggestions?" Steve
prompted.

"Unfortunately, no. But this could take more
time than we have if the guy is going to try again."

"We've got ninety agents here. We can spread
the interviews in our jurisdiction around. But first
you and Dr. Lawson need to review that list. If
either of you recognizes a name, that could expedite things."

Mark checked his watch. It was approaching six.
"We'll stop by Emily's on our way home and give

her a copy. I'll review it tonight too. By tomorrow morning, we should know if there's anyone we should focus on."

"We'll hold off on the interviews until you both have a chance to look it over. And hope this guy is in no hurry to finish the job."

"I'm sorry, Mark. I don't recognize any of the names. I wish I did." Emily tossed the multi-page document onto her coffee table, leaned back on the sofa, and tucked her legs under her with a frustrated sigh.

For the past half hour they'd been scrutinizing the license plate list. Mark had finished a few minutes earlier, with the same result, and he wasn't any happier than she was.

"I guess we'll be hitting the pavement." Mark directed his comment to Coop, who sat in a side chair, ankle crossed over knee, nursing a soda.

"Tracking all these people down will be a massive job." Emily looked from Coop to Mark. "Isn't there any other option?"

"Not unless our guy sends us another clue that helps us narrow down the list," Mark responded. "But I'm not complaining. This is a big step forward. If he's in here, we'll find him." He tried to sound more confident than he felt.

"He's been quiet for the past week. Maybe he's giving up, despite that note he sent you."

"It's possible. But I'm not counting on it." His

gaze sharpened. "You're not getting complacent about security precautions, are you?"

"No. Anything but."

"Good. The arm's looking better, by the way." He examined the jagged wound, visible now that the stitches had come out and the bandage was off.

She brushed her fingers over the scar. "The doctor says I'm a quick healer."

"That seems to be true. Physically, at least."

When Mark's loaded comment was met with silence, Coop looked from one to the other and rose. "I think I'll step outside and give Monica a call. Let me know when you're ready to head out," he told Mark.

As the door opened, then shut with a quiet click, Mark moved over to sit beside Emily. "I need to leave in a minute."

She sighed. "I know."

"You look tired."

"Must be catching. Have you checked a mirror lately?"

He wiped a hand down his face. There was no sense disputing the obvious. "I'll be glad when all this is over and we can focus on more pleasant things. Like this." He rubbed his chin against her hair, enjoying the feel of her soft curves pressed against him.

"What you said to Coop a minute ago . . . it's true, Mark."

Her soft comment surprised him. Knowing how

skittish she was about the subject, he'd expected her to let his implication about psychological and emotional healing pass.

"You've got a lot to overcome, Em. I understand that."

"You'd think with all of my training and experience, I'd be able to deal with my own fears. I know *why* I'm afraid to get close to people. I just can't manage to apply in my own life the remedies I give to everyone else." She huffed out an annoyed breath. "If nothing else, though, this whole thing has given me a better understanding of what some of my patients go through as they try to put their own histories behind them. And speaking of histories . . . how are you doing with the convenience store incident? With everything that's been happening, have you had a chance to work through that at all?"

"Believe it or not, yes. I've accepted that I did what I had to do. The guilt, however, is another story. It's still there, and I suspect it always will be, to some extent. I'm hoping God will help me find a way to manage it. That's what I'm praying for, anyway."

"You're praying?" She turned to give him a curious look.

Shifting toward her, he framed her face with his hands, brushing his thumbs lightly over her cheeks. "Thanks to you. If our paths hadn't crossed, I doubt I'd have factored God into the healing equation. I'm glad you got me started on that journey, Em."

He stroked her hair, letting the silky strands drift through his fingers, signaling his intent a heartbeat before he claimed her lips in a gentle kiss.

"I hate to go." His voice was husky as he rested his forehead against hers.

"The feeling is mutual." She whispered the words, and her breath was like a warm caress against his face. "I figured out your plan, by the way."

"What plan?"

"The plan to break down my defenses with kisses."

"Is it working?"

"I don't think I better answer that."

A chuckle rumbled deep in his chest. "I'll take that as a very positive sign. Walk me to the door?"

He rose and pulled her to her feet in one smooth motion, keeping her hand in his as they moved toward the small foyer.

At the door, he turned to her. "Be careful."

"Always. You too."

"Sleep well."

He reached for the handle, but when she touched his shoulder he turned back. To his surprise, she stood on tiptoe and brushed her lips over his.

The significance of the gesture wasn't lost on him. Until now, he'd initiated every romantic encounter. Tonight, she'd taken the lead.

A slow, warm smile began at his lips and spread to his eyes. "Good night, Em."

As he stepped outside and waited for the lock to click behind him, Coop materialized out of the shadows in the corner of the porch.

"Everything okay in there?"

"Yes. Thanks for that timely exit."

"Hey, I'm a sensitive guy. I can pick up vibes."

"Right. Like the night we went out for pizza after running that killer CQB training route and you forgot you'd promised to take Monica to dinner. You didn't exactly handle your phone call to her with a lot of finesse."

He winced. "You would remember that."

"She does too."

"Okay, it was a mistake. A big one. But I'm getting better. I just need a little more practice. Which is hard to get when I'm gone for weeks at a stretch." He gave Mark a pointed look.

"Tell Les about it. He's the one who decided you should be my shadow."

"Yeah. Like that'll do a lot of good." He waited while Mark slid into the passenger seat, then walked around the car and took his position behind the wheel. "Did you give any more thought to Steve's offer?"

"Lots of thought. No action."

"Does she know about it?" Coop nodded toward Emily's condo as he backed out of the parking space.

"Yes. But she's running scared. After her experience with Grant, guys in high-risk professions aren't on her top ten list of favorite people."

"Like I said before, love changes everything."

Coop was right, Mark acknowledged. In his case, anyway. While he didn't think he was head over heels yet, he was rapidly falling. He wouldn't be considering a permanent move to St. Louis if he wasn't.

As for Emily . . . more and more, he was convinced she felt the same way. If he was an accountant or a doctor or a salesman, the risk factor wouldn't be a barrier, and he suspected she'd have given him a green light long ago. But he couldn't change who he was. He might be able to find a way to use his skills in a less risky position, but law enforcement wasn't just a job for him; it helped define him as a person—in the same way Emily's work helped define her.

He had a feeling she understood that.

But he wasn't confident she could accept it . . . even if their future together hinged on it.

17

On Wednesday morning, Dale flipped through the magazine in Emily's waiting room, trying not to appear nervous. The Lord had brought him here for a reason, he was sure of it. During the next hour, God would show him his next steps in righting the wrongs.

"Can I get you some coffee, Mr. Smith?"

He raised his head. The Mexican-looking receptionist was smiling at him. That radio talk show guy he'd begun listening to at night was right. The U.S. was being taken over by foreigners.

"No, thank you." He buried his nose back in the magazine, hoping she'd leave him alone.

To his relief, she got the hint. Lowering the magazine a bit, he gave the headline of the story a disinterested scan . . . then read it again.

"Immobilization Drug: Attacker's Best Friend."

As he scanned the first few paragraphs, Dale's heart began to thud. According to the article, the powerful, fast-acting drug was tasteless, odorless, and colorless. Soluble in liquid, a couple of teaspoons were enough to wreak havoc on the central nervous system. It immobilized without loss of consciousness, leaving victims responsive but passive and incapable of thinking clearly.

While the drug was illegal, the article suggested it could be made with common, available ingredients—and that the recipe was easy to find. The drug could also be sourced on the Net or easily purchased on the black market.

How that information fit in with Dale's mission was a mystery. But somehow he knew it did.

Emily looked over the notes she'd taken during her phone conversation with Randy Miller as she prepared for her first meeting with Joe Smith. Age fifty-nine, employed by Aiken Concrete for twenty-four years, he had been considered a solid, dependable employee until the past month or so, when he'd become distracted and distant.

The cause was no secret. Two months ago, his sixteen-year-old son—an only child—had hung himself in the barn. Three weeks later, his wife had suffered a fatal heart attack. In total, Mr. Smith had taken five days off work for the two funerals. His stoic fortitude had amazed his supervisor and co-workers—until he'd begun making mistakes on the job.

The mistakes were a given, Emily reflected. A person didn't suffer those kinds of blows without major fallout. She knew that firsthand. Fear was the legacy of her tragic loss. But now that Mark had entered her life, she'd faced her issues and was trying to work through them.

Based on the preliminary information Randy had given her—and his top-line assessment—Mr. Smith wasn't even close to that stage yet. Meaning he could be on a direct path to a major breakdown.

Laying down her notes, Emily took a final sip of her coffee, set the cup aside, and headed toward the door to the reception area. A man with thinning gray hair looked up as she stepped into the waiting room.

"Mr. Smith? Emily Lawson. It's nice to meet you." She moved forward and extended her hand.

The man rose as she approached, folding his

magazine in half as he tucked it under his arm.

He took her hand in an almost too-firm grip. About five-foot-nine, he had a lean but muscular build, suggesting he was accustomed to physical labor. Up close, his tanned, weathered face spoke of long hours in the wind and sun, while the lines radiating from the corners of his eyes and mouth conveyed prolonged strain. He wore jeans and a cotton work shirt, the sleeves rolled up to reveal sinewy muscles in his forearms. Penetrating brown eyes, rather unnerving in their intensity, were fixed on her as he shook her hand.

"How do you do?"

"Please, come in." She stepped aside and ushered him into her office, indicating the sitting area off to the side.

He chose one of the striped chairs and sat stiffly on the edge, twisting the magazine in his hands as he surveyed the room.

Considering his comment to Randy about the stigma of counseling, his nervousness didn't surprise Emily. Her first order of business was to put him at ease.

Picking up her pen and notepad, she chose the chair at right angles to him. "Did Maria offer you something to drink?"

"Yes." He gestured toward the Starbuck's cup on her desk. "I hope I didn't interrupt your morning coffee."

"I must confess, today it was a double chocolate

chip frappuccino. And it's long gone. Are you sure you wouldn't like a beverage? Water, perhaps?"

"No thank you." He twisted the magazine tighter in his hands.

"If you change your mind, let me know." She crossed her legs and settled her notebook on her lap. "I spoke with Randy Miller about your situation. I'm very sorry for your losses, Mr. Smith."

"Thank you."

"It's not surprising for that kind of trauma to have a negative impact on your work performance. Why don't we talk about what's been happening at your job?"

"I made a couple of mistakes."

"I imagine you've been distracted."

She waited for him to comment, but he remained silent, wary and watching. After several more queries about his problems on the job met with monosyllabic answers, she tried asking a few questions about his wife. Same result.

Consulting her notes, Emily took a few moments to regroup. Joe Smith wasn't the first resistant EAP referral she'd had, but she couldn't remember too many who had been as tightly strung as this man. His rigid body posture, the mangled magazine in his hands, his intent but guarded gaze . . . no wonder his boss had been worried about him.

If he wouldn't talk about his wife or his job, she doubted he'd open up about his son. The death of a child was always hard on a parent. And suicides were devastating. But she could try.

"Would you like to tell me a little about your son, Mr. Smith?" she asked gently.

"He was a good boy. He shouldn't have died." The man's gaze bored into her. "It was wrong that he died."

"The loss of such a young life is always a tragedy. I do some work with young people, and I've discovered that depression is often a very serious problem for teens. Do you think that might have been an issue with your son?"

His shoulders stiffened. "He had his blue days now and then, like we all do. But he was a strong boy. He would have been fine if he'd gotten out in the fresh air and enjoyed God's creation, or read the Good Book, instead of holing up in his room."

Denial. Emily ran into it frequently. "Depression can often be helped by treatment, in much the same way antibiotics heal an infection." She strove to maintain a relaxed, conversational tone. "And it often runs in families. Is there a history of depression in your family, Mr. Smith?"

"No, ma'am." He stared at her, his face expressionless. "And my son wasn't depressed. Just a little down."

Now she was picking up another emotion. Anger, perhaps. Possibly self-directed. Deep inside, he might be questioning his beliefs about the value of counseling and wondering if he could have averted the tragedy by seeking professional help for his son. If that was the case, a sense of blame and a familial propensity to depression could lead to serious guilt and self-loathing—a dangerous combination.

The picture that emerged troubled her. While Mr. Smith hadn't offered her any direct insights into his thoughts or feelings, she'd gleaned a fair amount from body language and what was left unsaid. The bottom line was that he appeared to be poised on the verge of meltdown, his tension palpable. Some of it could be attributed to the counseling situation, which he clearly found uncomfortable. But she sensed it went far deeper than that and was sourced in roiling emotions buried inside. Anger, guilt, grief, confusion. As far as she could see, none of those emotions had found an outlet. And they needed to. Or the pressure would build until it burst.

Today, however, was a wash. The best that could be said was that he'd shown up. All she could do was hope that Mr. Smith, like Jack Hanley, would recognize sooner rather than later that he needed help. Until he was ready to talk to her, however, there was little she could do except be available.

Rising, Emily moved to her desk, picked up one of her cards, and held it out to him. "I understand this situation is awkward for you, Mr. Smith. But I'd like to see you again. Now that we've met, I hope you'll feel more comfortable in the future. In the meantime, if you'd like to talk, don't hesitate to call me at any hour of the day or night. My exchange can reach me within minutes."

"Thank you." He took the card and slid it into his shirt pocket as he stood, tucking the magazine under his arm.

"May I set up another appointment for you? How about Friday or Monday?" She didn't want to wait a week to see him again.

"Monday is okay."

"Give me a minute."

Rising, Emily flashed him a pleasant smile. But his expression remained impassive. Closed. Verging on hostile. This wasn't going to be an easy case, she reflected. But as she slipped through the door to the reception area, closing it behind her, she was glad he'd come.

Because Joe Smith needed help.

Badly.

Dale stared at the closed door as Emily exited. She was smooth, he'd give her that. With her gentle, caring tone, she oozed empathy. He could see how his son would have been sucked in by her.

But her comments about depression had disgusted him. She made the blues sound like an inherited disease, like high blood pressure or diabetes. But it wasn't a sickness. It was a weakness. And no one could help you overcome weaknesses except yourself. And God.

That's what he'd told Bryan.

And John.

All at once he was propelled back four years to his last phone conversation with his older brother. Two days before Christmas. The day before John had walked out into his garage, turned on the car, and waited for the deadly fumes to end the grief that had plagued him after he'd lost his wife to cancer the prior summer.

Dale had tried to stand by him through his anguish, had pushed him to talk to the Lord, but John had sought "professional" help instead of seeking it from God—just as Bryan had. And like Bryan, he'd been misled. As Dale had reminded both of them on numerous occasions, the Lord said, "Come unto me, all ye that labour and are heavy laden, and I will give you rest." Come to *me*. Not some shrink.

But John had gone to the wrong place for help. Dale had tried to protect his son from falling into that same trap, but Bryan hadn't listened. Instead, he'd talked to this woman. On the radio, no less. And he'd ended up dead too.

He couldn't bring Bryan or John back. But he could at least eliminate the woman who'd caused his son's death.

And God would be pleased.

The door to the reception area opened again, and Emily crossed the room to hand him an appointment card. He pocketed that too.

"We're all set for Monday. But feel free to call me sooner if you'd like to talk."

"I will."

The door that led from her office to the hall had a peephole in it, as had the one from the hall to the reception room, he noted, waiting while she checked the corridor. She was being careful. That meant he would have to be too.

"Sorry about the cloak and dagger stuff." She twisted the lock and opened the door. "I had a little problem recently and I'm being cautious. Take care, Mr. Smith."

Stepping outside, he waited as the door closed behind him. Then he headed toward the exit.

Once out of sight of her peephole, he withdrew the two cards from his pocket. Tearing up the one with the appointment on it, he discarded it in a trash can near the door. The other one he fingered thoughtfully.

A plan was forming in his mind. Through his conversation with Emily Lawson, the Lord had reminded him he wasn't avenging just one death. His brother, too, had died as a result of a shrink. Not the one who had ruined Bryan's life. But they were all alike. Equally dangerous—and liable.

He'd also been reminded that John and Bryan hadn't died instantly. They'd had time to think about their life coming to an end, John as he drifted into unconsciousness, Bryan as he'd gasped his final, choking breaths. That's why his first plan had failed, Dale concluded. Emily Lawson needed to die more slowly. And she needed to know her death was a punishment for the wrongs she and others like her had done.

Tucking the magazine more securely under his arm, Dale looked at the card Emily had given him as she'd told him to call her. Any time.

That one he kept.

"Mark, Steve wanted me to check with you about . . ."

As the woman's words trailed off, Mark slipped his Glock into his holster and turned to find Allison Schwartz, one of the professional support people in the St. Louis office, staring at the copy of the shooter's note on his desk.

"Allison? What is it?" He and Coop had been preparing to spend their Wednesday afternoon following up on the names they'd been assigned to investigate from what had become known as the Eight List. But her expression stopped him cold.

"It's nothing, I'm sure." She shook her head, but her attention remained riveted on the piece of paper on his desk. "It's just that . . . the handwriting on that note reminds me of my brother-in-law's."

"Take a closer look." He picked up the sheet of paper and passed it to her.

Frowning, she studied the script. "See how the t's are crossed with a slanted line? That's what caught my attention. My brother-in-law does that."

It was probably nothing, Mark told himself. An odd coincidence. But he could remember several cases from his investigative days when such a coincidence had provided the key to solving a crime.

"This is from the shooter, isn't it?" Allison gave him a concerned look.

The existence of the note was common knowledge in the office, but few had seen it.

"Yes."

"In that case, it can't have anything to do with my brother-inlaw. He's a straight arrow. A hard-working, churchgoing family man."

"Quantico believes the note was forged, Allison. If you think the resemblance to your brother-in-law's writing is that strong, we need to talk to him. What's his name, and how can we reach him?" He pulled a small notebook out of his pocket.

"Mike Evans. He's a residential builder. Evans Construction. They handle a lot of higher-end housing developments. I'll call my sister and get his cell number."

"Thanks."

As she exited, Mark motioned to Coop, who was chatting with an agent on the far side of the bull pen, an open room that was honeycombed with cubes. When Coop walked over, Mark filled him in. As he finished, his desk phone rang and he scribbled down the number Allison recited.

"Let's stop in and see Steve before we leave," Mark said.

Five minutes later, Steve had Paul Sheehan in Quantico on the speaker phone.

"We need to get some original handwriting samples," Paul said. "As we speak I'm emailing Steve some suggested text to have him write. And have him use two different pens. I'll need the originals to do a thorough analysis, but if you fax me a copy of the samples you get I can give you a preliminary opinion on whether I think it's a match."

"We'll do that right away, Paul. Thanks." Steve ended the call, checked his email, and printed out the text Paul had sent. "Do you two want to track this guy down or focus on the Eight List?"

"Both. It shouldn't take long to deal with Mr. Evans. We'll courier the samples back here from his office."

"Good enough." Steve pulled the text from Paul off his printer and handed it over. "I'll have copies faxed to Quantico and overnight the originals. You'll hear from me as soon as he gives us a preliminary read. And I'll get some intelligence analysts working on Evans."

As Mark and Coop headed to the car, Coop looked at his partner. "You realize this is a long shot."

"Yeah." Mark pulled out his BlackBerry to call Evans and set up a meeting. "But stranger things have happened. Keep your fingers crossed."

• • •

Mike Evans met them in the construction trailer at Windsor Hills, his latest West County development project. Midforties, with salt-and-pepper hair and a face tanned from long hours in the sun, he was dressed in khaki slacks and a blue dress shirt that was rolled to the elbows. A hard hat sat on the corner of his cluttered desk in the cramped office.

"Sorry for the heat, gentlemen." He shook their hands as they introduced themselves and motioned them to seats across from his desk. "These trailers aren't equipped with the best air conditioners, and they sure can't keep up with this sweltering weather."

"No problem, Mr. Evans." Not quite true, but Mark resisted the urge to loosen his tie. After years on the HRT, neither he nor Coop were used to wearing suits. And the humid heat of St. Louis wasn't conducive to the FBI dress code for agents. But they'd manage.

"How can I help you today? It isn't often I get a visit from the FBI."

The man appeared more curious than nervous, Mark assessed. If he had anything to hide, he was doing a masterful job masking it.

"We received a note about a week ago that appears to be forged. Allison Swartz was in my office today and saw it. She remarked that it looked a lot like your handwriting. We'd like to get an original sample of your writing to send to our experts in Quantico."

"I'm more than happy to cooperate, gentlemen. But even if my handwriting was forged, I doubt that will help you much. A lot of people have memos and notes from me."

"We understand that, but we're trying to follow up on every lead," Coop said.

"Of course. What specifically do you need from me?"

"Several handwriting samples." Coop handed over the text Paul had suggested. "If you could write those paragraphs on different sheets of paper, switching pens each time, we'd appreciate it."

"No problem." The man took the proffered document, extracted a pen from the chaos on his desk, and began to write.

Ten minutes later, he gathered up the samples, tapped them into a neat pile, and handed them over with an apologetic grin. "I'm afraid my penmanship deteriorated as I went along. Sister Mary Elizabeth, who taught me cursive, would have a fit. But I hope this gives you what you need."

Taking the stack of paper, Mark scanned the top sheet, angling it to allow Coop to do the same. The writing looked like a match to him, and a quick glance confirmed his partner felt the same way.

"This will work," Mark assured the contractor.

"Can you tell us where you were on the morning of Saturday, August 3, about eight o'clock?" Coop asked the question as Mark slid the handwriting samples into a folder.

Pulling out his PalmPilot, the builder scanned back to the date in question. "On a plane returning from Chicago. I was at a conference the prior Thursday and Friday." He gave them the flight number without prompting, as well as the location of the conference.

"Thank you." Mark jotted down the information. "Proceeding on the assumption the handwriting sample is a match to the forgery, we'd like you to put together a list of everyone employed here in the past six months—tagging anyone who was fired or may have been disgruntled—along with a list of subcontractors you've used during the same period. We'll also need the names of anyone who has access to this office, plus anyone you can think of in the St. Louis area who might have a sample of your handwriting."

"The employee and contractor rosters I can have to you within an hour or two. I'll jot down the names of anyone else I can think of who might have a document with my handwriting on it, but that will be an extensive list and will take longer to put together."

"We'll start with whatever we have. If you could fax the information to Steve Preston at our office as soon as possible, we'd appreciate it." Mark wrote the number on a slip of paper and handed it to the builder. He looked at Coop, and the other agent gave a slight nod. "That's all we need for now, Mr. Evans." They rose and shook his hand. "Thanks for your help. We may be back in touch."

Once settled in their car, Coop glanced at Mark as he turned the key in the ignition. "Looks like a match to me."

"Me too. And considering our shooter had fresh concrete on his boots, the link to Mike Evans fits. But given the size of this operation and the number of contacts the man has, I don't know how much that will help us."

"Look at it this way. Everything we learn gets us one step closer to finding this guy. We can always hope a name Evans supplies matches one on our Eight List."

"That would be too easy." Mark stared out the window as the late August sun beat down on the parched landscape. Despite the new leads, that's how this case felt to him. Parched. They needed a big break, a connection among the loose threads they'd assembled that would tie them together. And they needed it soon.

Because in his gut, Mark felt certain about two things.

First, the note he'd received hadn't been a hoax or an idle threat.

Second, they were running out of time.

18

At seven o'clock that night, Mark's BlackBerry began to vibrate. Pulling it off his belt, he pressed it to his ear. "Sanders."

"Mark, it's Steve. I heard from Paul Sheehan. He won't commit to a match without seeing the hard copy, but he's 95 percent certain Evans's writing was forged for your note."

"Coop and I came to the same conclusion from eyeballing it." Mark looked over at Coop as his partner parked the car in front of Emily's condo and mouthed, "It matches."

"We also did some checking on Evans. His alibi is solid and his record is spotless. The man's a boy scout."

"That's what Allison said."

"His employees all check out too. We ran them through the NCIC and looked for matches against the Eight List. Nothing."

"Any other leads from the Eight List investigation?"

"Lots of alibis that need to be checked. Nothing promising."

"Same on our end." He and Coop had spent a frustrating day traversing the city's South Side with nothing to show for their efforts.

"Evans also sent over a list of contractors he uses. I talked to Carl, and Oakdale is going to work on getting their employee rosters and running a preliminary check against the Eight List and NCIC. Let's touch base in the morning."

"Okay. Thanks."

As Mark slid the device back into the holder on his belt, Coop opened the driver-side door. "Hang tight while I take a look around."

"Trust me. I have the drill down by now."

Three minutes later, Coop opened Mark's door. "We're clear."

"You know, I'm getting kind of used to this service."

"Enjoy it while it lasts, pal, because it's never going to happen again. When do you want me back?" He scanned the area again as he walked with Mark to Emily's door.

"Nine. I'd stay later, but Emily needs her sleep."

Mark pressed the bell, and Emily answered a few seconds later.

"Hi." She stepped aside. "Are you coming in, Coop?"

"No." The two men answered in unison as Mark entered.

"You know you're always welcome," she told him with a grin.

"Good night, Coop." Mark reached around Emily and closed the door in his friend's face.

"That wasn't very nice."

"He'll live. Besides, if he hangs around I can't do this." Stepping close, he claimed her lips in a kiss of welcome thorough enough to leave no doubt in her mind about how much he'd missed her. "Is my plan still working?" he murmured when at last he eased back.

"No comment." But her breathless response gave him his answer.

Chuckling, he draped an arm around her shoulders and guided her toward the living room. "What's on our agenda tonight?"

"How about a movie?"

"Sounds good."

"Did you have dinner?"

"We stopped at a fast food place."

"Not very healthy."

"True. But as the name says, fast. We had a busy day."

"Any news?"

"Some. If you can spare a soda, I'll give you an update."

"Go ahead and get comfortable. I'll be back in a minute."

When she returned, Mark had shed his jacket and tie and was rolling up the sleeves of his dress shirt.

"I hope you don't mind. But in the HRT I rarely wear a suit, and the field office dress code is requiring some adjustment. The heat isn't helping, either. It was ninety-five again today."

"And no end in sight, according to the weather people." She handed him a soda and watched as he consumed half of it in one long gulp.

"At least you look cool. And I mean that in every sense of the word." He gave her white shorts and sleeveless red knit top an appreciative perusal. "Come sit next to me."

She settled beside him, tucking her legs under her. "Tell me the news."

"Someone in our office recognized the handwriting on the follow-up note the shooter sent."

She angled toward him, her expression startled. "You're kidding!"

"No. We do get odd breaks like that once in a while. Our handwriting expert in Quantico will confirm the match tomorrow after he gets our original sample, but he's 99 percent certain already from the fax we sent." He told her about their visit with Mike Evans, and the follow-up lists that was generating.

"Meaning more leads but no solution." Frowning, Emily ran a finger around the rim of her soda can.

"Hey, don't get discouraged." Mark lifted her chin with a finger. "The pieces are beginning to fall into place. And we're working our way through the Eight List. We're going to find a match somewhere, Emily. Trust me. Now tell me about your day."

The parallel creases in her brow deepened. "Not so good."

"Is your arm bothering you?" He leaned around her in concern to examine the healing wound.

"No. I was speaking in a professional sense. I had a new patient—an EAP referral. He lost his only son to suicide a couple of months ago, and his wife to a heart attack three weeks later. Now he's having problems on the job."

Mark entwined his fingers with hers. "Wow. Those are tough breaks."

"Very. And he's not handling them well. Part of the problem is he's keeping everything bottled up inside. I didn't get very far with him, and I'm not optimistic about his next visit on Monday, either. But he needs help."

"What was it you once told me about leading a horse to water?"

She conceded the point with a shrug. "I know. I just didn't like the vibes I was getting. There has to be a way to reach him."

"At least you got him to agree to come back."

"He could always cancel."

"Don't look for trouble."

"I don't have to. It's finding me all by itself." Her shoulders drooped and she sighed.

The strain of the past three weeks was getting to her, Mark realized. There was a gauntness to her face that reflected both fatigue and weight loss. The strain around her mouth and eyes was also new since their first conversation in the park. And he'd added to it by putting pressure on her about their relationship. Perhaps he should back off on that front until things settled down. She knew how he felt. Pushing would do nothing except increase her stress.

Pulling her close, Mark pressed his lips to her hair. "Hang in there, Em. This will be over soon. I promise."

"I hope so."

"What do you say we put on one of those zany Marx Brothers movies I spotted in your DVD rack? I think we're both due for some laughter."

"Okay."

He eased away from her and stood to retrieve the movie, hoping it would help both of them forget for a little while the cloud that had been hanging over them since the day in the park.

But once the movie ended, they'd be back where they were before it began.

Hunted by an unknown assailant.

And while he'd been quiet for a while, Mark had a growing sense of unease that he was getting ready to make another move.

They were keeping an eye on her.

Dale hunched down in his Ford Taurus rental car and watched as the guy who'd dropped off the FBI agent earlier at Emily Lawson's condo returned. Considering the thorough scan he gave the parking lot before he headed for the door, Dale figured he was either an agent or a cop too.

Parking his car in the long-term lot at the airport and picking up a rental car for the next few days had been a smart move, Dale decided. He was too close to completing his mission to take any risks. Considering how he'd muddied up the license plate on his car the day of the shooting, he was confident no one could have read the number. But after the mistakes at work, he needed to take extra precautions, just to be safe.

His plan was almost finished, and it was a good one. A righteous one. God approved. He could tell.

Now it was a matter of deciding when to implement it. That's why he was watching her place. Why he planned to follow her for the next couple of days. He needed to find out if the cops or the feds were guarding her round the clock. He hoped not. She needed to be alone for his plan to work.

Dale watched as the two men returned to the car and drove away. The shades were drawn in the shrink's condo, but she was there.

Two hours later, she was still there. Alone.

Good.

It was time for him to take the next step.

"I just had a call from Les."

Turning from the coffeemaker, Mark watched his partner enter Nick's kitchen, setting aside his pleasant thoughts about the previous evening with Emily. "A call from the boss. Interesting way to start the day."

"He wants me back in Quantico for the weekend. For a little R & R, as he put it."

"Sounds reasonable. You've worked three weeks straight without a break."

"He's never cared about that in the past when we were in the middle of a mission. None of us got a break until the job was finished." Coop leaned back against the counter and folded his arms across his chest as he sized up his friend. "And the job here isn't finished."

"I'll stick close to Nick while you're gone. Besides, my schedule is impossible to pin down these days. The shooter has no idea where I'll be, except at night when I'm here sleeping. And Nick's got a state-of-the-art security system."

"Les wouldn't know that. Unless someone told him."

Grinning, Mark poured a cup of coffee and handed it to Coop. "Happy anniversary."

"What I want to know is how you managed to pull this off."

"Trade secret."

"Especially since things are beginning to get interesting here." Coop continued as if Mark hadn't spoken.

"More interesting than spending the weekend with Monica?"

A slow smile tugged at Coop's lips. "Good point. Forget I said that."

"It's forgotten. I had a call this morning too. From Steve. Paul confirmed the match."

"We expected that."

"He also said they're beginning to get employee names from Evans's contractors. He's passing them on to Oakdale. They'll run them through NCIC and check the names against the Eight List as they come in while we hit the streets again. But we're operating with reduced manpower today. Nick's closing in on the last bank robbery suspect and Steve's had to pull quite a few agents in to assist. The arrests may go down this weekend."

"See all the fun I'll be missing?" Coop grinned and refilled his cup.

"Yeah. You look real upset."

"Hey, I'll be thinking about all of you."

"Right."

"Unless Monica distracts me too much."

"Why do I think that's a given?"

Chuckling, Coop drained his cup and set it on the counter. But as he turned back to Mark, his expression grew more serious. "Listen, whatever you did . . . whatever strings you pulled . . . thanks. I owe you."

"I'll keep that in mind."

"I bet you will. Just do me a favor, okay? Stay out of trouble while I'm gone."

"Don't I always?"

Rolling his eyes, Coop snagged the car keys. "Let's hit the road. We've got a shooter to catch."

Emily took off her headphones and rose from the chair in the studio as Andy gave her a thumbs-up from the glass window in the control booth.

The program had gone well tonight, she concluded. Kyle had called back, sounding much more upbeat since he'd begun talking to a counselor at school, and the rest of the teens she had chatted with had been receptive to her suggestions. These were the kinds of sessions she most enjoyed.

As she gathered up her notes, she saw Mark and Coop rise from their seats in the booth. After a brief discussion, Coop exited and Mark turned toward her. The warmth of his smile was like the thawing, life-generating caress of the spring sun.

That was an apt analogy, Emily reflected as she moved to join him. After Grant's death, she'd been convinced she could never again take the risk of loving. Not even someone in a "safe" profession, let alone an FBI agent. Yet a mere three weeks into their reunion, she was finding it harder and harder to imagine life without Mark. The twenty-year gap in their relationship had melted away as her memory of the teenage Mark with grand plans and high ideals melded with the reality of the grown man who'd brought them to fruition with integrity, discipline, and an admirable sense of honor and justice.

She'd loved Mark back in those Wren Lake days, when young passions were high. Yet she'd gotten over him after life had set them on different paths.

This time, however, she didn't think she'd emerge unscathed if she let him walk out of her life.

And that would happen in nine days, when he returned to Quantico. For always, if she let fear stop her from following her heart. Or temporarily, if she was willing to give their relationship a fair chance. But unless she was, she couldn't let him take the job here. His sole tie to St. Louis was her. If she didn't think their relationship had a future, she had to be honest with him. And she had to decide soon. Mark's boss wouldn't dally about filling the job in St. Louis.

"Good program." Mark squeezed her hand as she entered the booth.

"Thanks."

"Ready to call it a night?"

"Yes. See you next week, Andy."

"I'll be here." With a wave, the long-haired technician set off down the hall to lock up.

Mark put his hand in the small of her back and guided her toward the door. When Coop gave a soft, patterned knock, signaling the all-clear, he stepped out first and motioned Emily to follow.

"You know, I'm starting to consider this clandestine stuff routine," she commented as they walked toward the car. "That's pretty sad."

"A temporary inconvenience." Coop opened the door for them as they slid into the backseat.

"I hear you've been given a reprieve for your

anniversary, though," Emily said as he took his place behind the wheel.

"Also temporary, unfortunately. But I'll take it."

"Your wife must be thrilled that you'll be home to celebrate the big day."

"That's putting it mildly." Grinning, he glanced at his two passengers in the rearview mirror. "By the way, Mark, she says thanks. And to tell you you're invited for dinner as soon as you get back. Steak, no less."

Curious, Emily looked at Mark. His face was hard to read in the dim light, but she thought she detected a flush on his cheeks.

"You had something to do with this?"

"Not much."

"Don't believe him, Emily. Somehow he convinced our boss—who doesn't have a sentimental bone in his body—to give me a weekend pass. I always suspected my partner was a romantic at heart, although he keeps it well hidden. But being around you seems to bring it out in him."

"Knock it off, Coop." Mark's comment came out as a low growl.

"Sorry, buddy. I didn't mean to embarrass you."

"Sure."

"Hey, Emily deals with feelings all day, every day. I'm sure she understands."

Mark threw a quick, speculative glance her way, clearly not comfortable with his partner's revelation about his softer side. But she was glad Coop had passed on that bit of information. It gave her yet another insight into the man who'd stolen her heart so many years ago on the shores of Wren Lake.

And it also reinforced her growing sense that her youthful crush hadn't been misguided. Mark Sanders had been worthy of her affection years ago. And he was worthy of her love now.

If only she could find the courage to risk her heart again.

Dale had never been able to fathom why some men enjoyed frequenting sleazy, dark, smoky bars in questionable areas of town.

The ready availability of alcohol was one reason, he supposed. He'd noticed the staff wasn't too diligent about checking IDs, and a lot of the guys sitting around the tables had to be borderline minimum age.

The waitresses could be the attraction too. Most of the patrons were blatantly ogling the young women in their skin-tight jeans and low-cut tops.

It was possible the music was a draw, but he doubted it. Most of the customers were ignoring the small band that was playing some loud rock tune. For all he knew, it was the same song they'd been playing when he'd arrived forty-five minutes ago. They all sounded alike to him.

He'd picked the same, shadowed corner table two nights in a row. It gave him a good view of the bar, and he'd already spotted some repeat customers from Wednesday night. The regulars were the ones he watched tonight. And it didn't take long to pick out the one he needed to contact. The twenty-something guy with shaggy blond hair and several days' growth of beard sat on the stool he'd occupied at the bar last night, and as the evening went on he conducted a series of discreet transactions.

That was the other reason to come to a place like this. For a price, in relative anonymity, you could get anything you wanted. Cash was passed one way, goods the other. The exchange took seconds; eye contact was rarely made.

Several years ago, before his cop buddy had retired to Florida, he'd talked one night about the ease of doing business on the black market. Dale had half listened, never expecting to need the information. Now he wished he'd paid more attention. But he remembered a fair amount and had observed enough over the past two nights to do this.

He'd have preferred to make his own drug, but the recipe on the Internet was too complicated for his limited chemistry background. And he didn't want to leave a trail by ordering the drug online via one of the products masquerading as a "health supplement." There was no completely anonymous way to get it; this was the best he could do. Still, it bothered him. He didn't like relying on other people. Never had. For anything. But he didn't have any better options in this situation.

Pulling the brim of his baseball cap lower, he adjusted the cheap, black-rimmed reading glasses he'd bought at Walgreens in an attempt to alter his appearance. Reaching into his pocket, he withdrew the note written in the same style he'd used for his recent communication to the FBI agent and scanned it.

Liquid ecstasy. Tomorrow night?

He'd found the street slang for the drug on the Internet too. There were a bunch of names for it, but this one appeared most often. The perverted use suggested by the name turned his stomach, but if the drug served its purpose, he could live with the term.

Two tables away, some guy yelled to the waitress to bring another round. This was the third for that table in the past half hour. The excess filled him with disgust. He didn't drink alcohol, but he'd ordered a beer so he wouldn't stand out. The untouched bottle sat on his table, the label dotted with beads of sweat. Like the ones forming on his forehead.

Signaling to the waitress, he folded the note into quarters. When she approached, he kept his chin down and handed it to her, along with a five-dollar bill. "Please give this to the blond guy at the bar."

She took it without a word, pocketing the money. After she delivered it, cocking her head his direction, Dale watched from under the brim of his cap as the man unfolded it. Sixty seconds later, the guy turned his direction and scrutinized him. Then he scribbled on the paper, refolded it, and gave it back to the waitress. She dropped it on his table as she passed.

Slowly Dale unfolded it. The amount the guy had jotted down was higher than it should be. He knew that from his research on the Net. But he wasn't going to quibble about a few dollars. It was a small price to pay for vengeance.

Lifting his chin, he gave a slight nod. The man turned back to the bar.

As Dale stood and threw some bills down next to his now-flat beer, relief flooded through him. His plans were falling into place. Tomorrow he'd have the drug in hand.

After that, it was just a matter of picking the right time and place.

19

As Nick pulled up in front of the American Airlines entrance at Lambert International Airport on Friday at noon, Coop leaned forward from the backseat and addressed Mark. "Watch yourself."

"I will. Besides, your replacement is excellent." He shot Nick a grin.

"I'm under strict orders to keep him in sight whenever he ventures out of the house," Nick told

Coop. "Since my focus is the bank robbery case, that means I get an extra body for the weekend. A good deal, if you ask me. I can use all the help I can get."

Grimacing, Mark turned back to Coop. "Are you sure you don't want some company on this trip?"

"Forget it, pal. Two's company and all that. Nick, thanks for the accommodations."

"Sorry about the drywall dust."

"I survived." Reaching for his duffel bag, he looked back at Mark. "Depending on how things go, I'll either see you early next week here or in Quantico in a week."

Per Mark's conversation with Les, they were going to regroup on Monday morning via conference call to discuss the status of the case and decide if Coop's presence was still needed in St. Louis.

"Okay. Thanks for all your help. Have a good flight."

With a nod, Coop got out of the car and slung his duffel bag over his shoulder. Lifting his hand in farewell, he disappeared inside the terminal.

While Mark was glad Coop would be able to spend his anniversary with Monica, his partner's absence meant he'd have less opportunity to focus on the shooting. For the weekend, at least, the bank robbery took precedence, so he'd have to stick close to Nick. The pieces in that case were falling rapidly into place, as they often did near the end.

Prior to the shooting, Mark had worked closely

with his academy buddy to track down leads on the perpetrators. They'd discovered that the series of robberies, which had taken place in rapid succession over a four-day period, were the work of three men. Two had been identified and located during the past week and were being tailed. Nick was on the verge of locating the third. They knew he'd been in touch with his girlfriend, and they'd put round-the-clock surveillance on her, expecting she'd lead them to him. Once she did, they'd move in on all three simultaneously. They'd been holding back on arresting the first two, afraid their capture would tip off the third suspect that they were closing in on him too, and he'd flee.

A few agents would continue to track down the names on the Eight List, but progress would be slow. Nor did Mark expect that Oakdale would do much work on the contractor employee lists this weekend.

He understood why resources were being diverted to the bank case. It was hot and breaking. And he knew the clerical nature of list-checking wouldn't have much appeal to the Oakdale detectives, or be a weekend priority.

But he didn't have to like it.

Emily Lawson had been unaccompanied all day. Dale knew, because he'd been following her. Better yet, no one had stopped by to see her all evening.

Settling back in his car, he checked his watch. He needed to leave for the bar soon to pick up his "order," but he'd hang around and watch her condo for a few more minutes in case that FBI agent decided to pay a late call.

His plan was ready to implement. Everything he needed was in a tote bag in the backseat, triple checked against his list. The last picture he'd taken of Ruthie and Bryan. A cordless drill. A screwdriver. A twelve-inch length of metal pipe, one inch in diameter. Duct tape. Latex gloves. Eight feet of flexible garden hose. Baseball cap. Glasses. Later tonight he'd add the drug to his cache.

And sometime in the next seventy-two hours, Emily Lawson would die.

The blond guy was sitting at the bar, in the same place he'd been the previous two nights. Dale scanned the dim room, heavy with smoke, as he settled his glasses on his nose and pulled his cap lower. No one took any notice of him as he paused inside the front door, and he eased over to the bar. Sliding onto the empty stool beside the man, he focused on the bartender and ordered a beer.

When it was delivered, he took out his wallet and paid for it. As the bartender took the cash, Dale slid out another bill, folded it in thirds, and laid it on the counter by his elbow with the denomination showing.

Five minutes dragged by while the guy next to

him ignored the bill and smoked his cigarette.

Dale began to sweat. Had he misread the man's message? Maybe this was some kind of sting operation, and the guy was an undercover cop. Although securing the drug this way had seemed the least traceable option, he was suddenly afraid he'd made a disastrous mistake.

Just as he was about to snatch back the money and abort the sale, the man repositioned his arm on the bar, covering the bill. With his other hand, he reached under and palmed the cash. Pulling a pack of cigarettes from his shirt pocket, he laid it on the bar next to Dale.

Out of the corner of his eye, Dale could see the pack was open. And it contained a small bottle, not cigarettes.

The man had come through.

Following his neighbor's lead, Dale waited several minutes. Then he casually picked up the cigarette pack and pocketed it. As he rose, the man spoke in a low, amused voice.

"Have fun, Pop."

Revolted, Dale turned away. The thought of using the drug for the purpose the man implied sickened him. Those who hurt or exploited innocent people were scum.

For him, the drug would serve a righteous purpose.

And it would do so soon.

Very soon.

The doorbell chimed as Mark came up the basement stairs in Nick's house at noon on Saturday, and he took the last few two at a time. Wiping his hands on his paint-splattered jeans, he strode across the foyer and checked the peephole.

Now there was a pretty picture, he thought, his lips tipping into an appreciative smile.

Emily stood on the other side, juggling two large white sacks in her arms.

Flipping the deadbolt, Mark pulled the door open and grinned at her. "This is a surprise."

Relief flooded her face. "I was about to give up. That was my third ring."

"Sorry. I was in the basement cleaning a roller and I didn't hear the bell. Welcome to the construction zone." He stepped aside and ushered her in.

She took three steps in and came to an abrupt halt, her eyes widening as she surveyed the interior. "Wow! While I was waiting on the porch, I came to the conclusion you'd been exaggerating about the condition of Nick's house."

He could understand why. From the outside, the stately, two-story, Federal-style brick structure was in pristine condition, with new tuck-pointing and freshly painted shutters. Set on an acre of ground amid towering oak and maple trees, it was an impressive edifice.

The inside was another story, as Emily had discovered. All of the rooms were in various states of rehab. The smell of fresh paint predominated, and a fine haze of drywall dust was suspended in the air.

"Nope." He shut and locked the door. "The exterior is deceptive. Designed to lure in the unsuspecting."

"No wonder Coop had trouble with his allergies."

"It's not that bad once you get used to it. So what brings you over?"

"Curiosity, for one thing. After all the talk about Nick's house, I was dying to see it." She winced and gave him a rueful look. "Oops. Pardon the expression. Anyway, he told me to stop by anytime. When you called this morning to say the two of you would be painting the dining room today, I thought I might be able to bribe a tour out of him if I brought lunch." She held up the two white bags. "If all else failed, I came prepared to barter some manual labor for a tour. I wield a mean paint-brush."

He eyed her paint-smudged jeans and T-shirt. "They look like they've already done a tour of duty."

"Yes. I . . . Grant and I did a lot of work at our house."

Sensing she didn't want to talk about that, he let the comment pass. "Unfortunately, Nick got called in a couple of hours ago. The bank robbery case is about to break. But you can bribe me. For the price of a sandwich and the offer of help, I'll show you every nook and cranny in this place. And trust me, I know my way around. Nick's had me crawling under stairwells, wedged into closets, and hanging from the rafters."

Twenty minutes later, after a thorough tour, they sat down to enjoy their turkey sandwiches in the kitchen. As Mark unwrapped his, the back door rattled, and a second later Nick appeared.

"I'm convinced he can smell food ten miles away." Mark spared his host a quick, amused glance and bit into his sandwich.

"Very funny. Hi, Emily. I saw your car. What's up?"

"I stopped by for a tour. Mark obliged. And I brought food."

"Healthy food too, I see," he remarked as he checked out the sandwiches.

"It beats that tofu thing you concocted the other night that Coop almost gagged on." Mark shook his head and turned to Emily. "We had to make an emergency pizza run."

"You guys don't know what's good for you," Nick countered.

"We know what we like."

"They're not always the same thing. Don't let this bottomless pit eat all the sandwiches, Emily. I want to run upstairs and change. And I have to return a few calls." He tossed a UPS envelope on the table. "Steve asked me to deliver this to you. It came late yesterday afternoon from Quantico."

Swiping a napkin across his mouth, Mark picked up the envelope as Nick headed toward the stairs, noting that it was marked personal and confidential. Les's name was on the return address. Odd. His boss rarely communicated in writing.

"Do you mind if I open this?" he asked Emily.

"Not at all."

Pushing his chair back from the table, Mark pulled the tab on the envelope and reached inside. A note from Les was clipped to the top of two sheets of stationery.

"Mark—this came to your attention two days ago. In light of present circumstances, I asked Christy to look at it. Sorry for the intrusion. Les."

Puzzled, Mark removed Les's note and glanced at the unfamiliar script. Flipping to the second page, he sought out the signature.

Adam and Barbara Wheeler.

The parents of the boy he'd killed.

Mark sucked in a sharp breath, and his heart gave an odd jolt.

"Mark?"

He heard the concern in Emily's voice above the sudden rushing in his ears. Raking unsteady fingers through his hair, he lifted his head and looked at her. Apprehension tightened her features, and she'd stopped eating.

"It's a letter from Jason Wheeler's parents." The words came out hoarse and uneven.

She set down her sandwich. "Is this the first contact you've had from them since the shooting?"

"Yes." He looked at the letter and turned it facedown on his lap. "I thought I was doing okay, that I'd dealt with the situation. But I have a feeling this is going to tear me up all over again." The words came out choked, and he wiped a hand down his face.

"You don't have to read it."

"Yes, I do." He clenched his napkin into a tight ball and rose. "Would you excuse me for a few minutes?"

"Of course."

Gripping the sheets of paper, Mark stepped onto the back porch. Coop would have had a fit if he was here, Mark knew, sparing a quick glance toward the wooded common ground behind Nick's property. As a concession to safety he moved into the corner, where clematis vines climbed right-angle trellises and afforded a degree of privacy and concealment.

He sat down in an antique wicker chair Nick had scrounged up at some garage sale, the fibers creaking as they accommodated his weight. Oblivious to the oppressive heat, he drew a deep breath, turned the pages over, and began to read.

Dear Mr. Sanders: Please forgive our long delay in responding to the letter you sent following Jason's death. As you can imagine, this has been a very difficult time.

Your letter, however, touched us deeply. Until we received it, we had allowed anger to consume us. Anger at you, anger at the FBI, anger at the junkie who chose to rob the convenience store that morning, anger at God. It has taken us weeks to work through that. But with much prayer and reflection, we have found some measure of peace.

From your letter, it was clear to us you carry a heavy burden of grief and guilt. We, too, grieve. We cannot offer you a reprieve from that, for the loss of a young life filled with promise is, indeed, a sadness of immeasurable depth. But we hope we can ease your guilt by letting you know we don't blame you for the death of our son. From all we have learned, you acted in an appropriate, even heroic, manner. You did your best to stop the thief and preserve the lives in that store. Our son's sudden, unexpected move could not have been predicted. Had you not acted, there is a good chance our son would have died anyway—and perhaps others, as well.

We have found great comfort in two Bible verses, and we pass them on to you in the hope you, too, will find them consoling. We also take comfort in knowing that while Jason's life on earth was short, he lives on in a better place, with the Lord.

From Romans, "We glory in tribulations

also: knowing that tribulation worketh patience; and patience, experience; and experience, hope."

And from the thirty-third Psalm, "Many are the afflictions of the righteous: but the Lord delivereth him out of them all."

May hope and solace ease the burden in your heart. Our prayers are with you, and we ask for yours in return as we continue our journey toward healing.

The signatures blurred. Leaning forward, Mark rested his elbows on his knees and bowed his head, letting the letter dangle from his clasped hands.

It had been years since he'd been overcome by tears. His work on the HRT demanded rigid emotional control, and he'd learned to turn an impassive face to the world. Whatever feelings he experienced as a result of the horror he saw remained contained. Even after the shooting incident, when he'd been raw and bleeding inside as well as out, he hadn't shed a tear. The feelings were there, yet they'd gone unexpressed.

But the letter from Jason's parents had done him in.

He knew people needed to find outlets for their emotions. That's why he and Coop had always pushed themselves to the limit in training. Physical exertion had been a release valve for the tension and stress and trauma of their job. And it had worked for many years. But after the shooting it had failed him. The intense effort he'd put into rehab hadn't given him release from the emotional baggage of the shooting. Like the new patient Emily was worried about, Mark hadn't found an adequate way to deal with the loss of an innocent life. His recent, tentative foray into prayer had provided some relief. But the understanding—and absolution—of the boy's parents had been the missing piece.

The tears flowed down his cheeks unchecked. Tears of cleansing and gratitude and liberation. Thanks to the generosity and compassion of Jason Wheeler's parents, he at last felt able to put that chapter of his life to rest and move on.

"Mark?"

The worried query filtered into his mind as if from a distance. Without looking up, he handed Emily the letter in silence, not trusting his voice. Not wanting her to see his tears. He was grateful when she took it in silence and gave him the time—and space—to regroup.

Several minutes passed before she dropped down to his level and laid her hand on his knee. "They must be very special people." Her voice caught on the last word.

He wiped an eye on each sleeve of his T-shirt before he raised his head. Moisture clung to Emily's eyelids too, he noted.

"I never expected anything like this." His words

came out hoarse. And ragged. "I thought they'd hate me."

"You did your best, Mark. It's obvious they recognize that."

"I don't know if I could have been as generous in their place." As the full measure of their benevolence began to register, it awed—and humbled—him.

"Faith can give people incredible strength."

"I'm beginning to realize that."

She touched his cheek, still damp from tears. "Could you use a hug?"

Instead of responding, he stood and drew her to her feet in one smooth motion, enfolding her in his arms. And as he clung to her, he gave thanks for the gifts he'd been given. Absolution from two strangers who owed him nothing, and the comfort of this extraordinary woman's arms. Both imbued him with a strength that had nothing to do with bench presses or elliptical machines. The latter gave him the muscles to endure physical trials. Today's gifts gave him a far superior strength: to simply endure.

"I wondered where you two had wandered . . . oops."

As Nick stuck his head out the door, Emily started to twist free of Mark's embrace. But he tugged her back, holding her firmly within the circle of his arms, her back pressed against his chest, his hands looped around her waist.

"Sorry," Nick apologized. "I need to talk to you when you're . . . when you have a minute, Mark." Sandwich in hand, he beat a hasty retreat, letting the screen door bang behind him.

"Why do I always pick friends whose timing stinks?"

Emily turned her head to look up at him, a whisper of a smile hovering at her lips. "At least he made a discreet exit."

"True. But something's up. He never changed clothes." He sighed and tightened his hold on her, bending his head to nuzzle her neck. "I have a feeling duty is about to call."

He could feel the sudden tension in her body and knew what she was thinking. He'd studied a bit of psychology, himself. He was aware that an emotional download could leave a person shaky and off balance. That driving a car in that condition was risky. And that going into a volatile situation requiring sharp reflexes and absolute focus could be dangerous.

"I'm okay, Em." He stroked her arms in a soothing, rhythmic motion, his tone gentle. "I've had a lot of practice compartmentalizing emotion. You don't need to worry."

"Okay." She gave a stilted nod.

Stepping beside her, he draped an arm around her shoulders and led her toward the door. "Let's find out what's going on."

As they entered the kitchen, Nick was standing

by the sink wolfing down the last of his sandwich, his BlackBerry on the counter beside him.

"What's up?" Mark asked.

"We've got some suspicious activity on the South Side, and we need to beef up surveillance there. I volunteered us."

There was a lot Nick wasn't saying. Mark could read it in his eyes. But Emily didn't need to know any more. She was already spooked enough.

"No problem. Gets me off the painting detail, anyway." He turned to Emily. "I'll walk you out."

"Thanks for the lunch, Emily. I may take you up on your painting offer another time." Nick washed down the last bite of sandwich with a long swallow of soda. "Let me take a look around before you head out to the car."

Mark helped Emily gather up the remnants of their lunch, and three minutes later Nick stepped back inside.

"You're clear."

Taking her arm, Mark went out the door first. Nick followed, waiting on the porch as he scanned the parklike setting.

"I don't want to linger in the open," Mark said as they reached her car. Pulling her close once again in a brief embrace, he brushed his lips over her forehead. "I'll call you later about church."

They'd planned to attend services together tomorrow, with Nick in tow, but Mark had a feeling that wasn't going to happen.

"Don't worry about it, Mark. It sounds like things are hopping on Nick's case. Just promise me you'll be careful."

"Always."

She hesitated for an instant, searching his face, before sliding into the car.

Once she was out of sight, Mark turned back to the house. He hadn't given her that promise lightly. Nor had he lied when he'd told her he was good at switching focus.

Or he had been, until a certain Emily Lawson had reentered his life.

His guilt over Jason's death, Coop's announcement about leaving the HRT, the job offer from Steve, the letter he'd received today—even the threat of their unknown sniper. He could temporarily forget all those things when the job demanded it.

Emily, however, wasn't as easy to put out of his mind.

And there wasn't a thing he could do about it.

20

The organ swelled, and Emily opened her hymnbook for the final song. If things continued like this, she and Mark would never end up attending services together.

He'd sounded exhausted when they talked on the phone earlier. He and Nick hadn't gotten home until after two in the morning, and when he'd called her at eight they were heading out again. He'd had no idea how long they'd be gone, but it sounded like he had another grueling day ahead of him. If all went well, Nick's suspects would be arrested sometime in the next twelve hours. Mark wouldn't be home until it was over.

Once that case was closed, more agents would be available to track down the shooter, Mark had told her. He'd assured her they were making progress, but she saw little evidence of that. As if there weren't already enough loose ends to tie up on the shooting case itself, she knew he also owed Steve an answer on the job offer before he returned to Quantico next weekend.

To her surprise, he hadn't pressed her about their relationship in the past few days. Just the opposite. He'd backed off a bit, keeping his displays of affection low key. A hug, a touch, a brush of the lips across her forehead. Perhaps he thought she had enough on her plate and was giving her space, she mused. He'd even downplayed her concerns about the job decision, assuring her other offers would come along if he passed on this one.

But this opportunity was a perfect fit for his skills, and they both knew it. She owed him an answer to his question. Was she willing to give their relationship a chance to develop into a serious commitment?

She'd been singing the final hymn by rote, her

attention focused inward, but all at once certain parts of the lyrics began to resonate with her.

"You shall wander far in safety though you do not know the way . . . If you stand before the pow'r of hell and death is at your side, know that I am with you through it all . . . Be not afraid, I go before you always. Come follow me, and I will give you rest."

The words were inspiring. Hope-filled. And she wanted to believe them. Wanted to tell Mark she'd subdued her fears. That she would put her trust in God and take her chances, enjoying whatever time they had together. That she could handle it if their relationship turned out to be short-lived, as hers and Grant's had been.

But she wasn't there yet. The fear of loss was still too great for her faith to overcome. Closing her eyes, she bowed her head and let the comforting, familiar melody soothe her soul as she prayed.

Lord, please give me the courage to turn my fears over to you—before I pass up what may be the chance of a lifetime.

The girlfriend had led them straight to the third bank robbery suspect. They'd caught only a quick glimpse of him from their car as he'd cracked the door to let her in, but it had been enough to make a positive ID.

There was just one little problem.

The woman had brought her three young children with her.

Now four people, minimum, were in the duplex. Meaning the suspect had potential hostages. And he wouldn't be afraid to use them, Mark concluded as Nick spoke to Steve by phone. The man had killed a bank guard in one of the robberies and had a rap sheet a mile long. There was no question he was armed and dangerous. And no matter what the woman meant to him, when the chips were down Mark suspected he'd trade her life—or the lives of her children—for his freedom.

That left them with no good options. If they stormed the front door, there was a high probability someone would be killed. On the other hand, alerting the suspect to their presence and demanding a surrender could lead to a standoff.

As he rang off, Nick gave Mark a rueful look. "Steve wants an ops plan. Like I really have time to put one together. This guy could bolt at any minute."

Mark grinned in sympathy. It wasn't easy being the case agent in a situation like this. "Is he on the way?"

"Yes. So is Luke."

That didn't surprise Mark. For a potentially volatile arrest situation of this magnitude, one of the senior special agents in charge would typically show up. And Luke Garavaglia was a hands-on kind of guy.

"You want to do a drive-by?" Mark perused the neighborhood.

"Yeah. Then we'll head over to the firehouse. Steve wants to set up the command post there. And he put the SWAT team on standby."

The drive-by confirmed that the neighborhood was a typical South Side setup: a block of brick two-story duplexes, garages in back accessed via an alley, narrow walks leading to the porches. The unit under surveillance was rented by a Wray Samuels, according to the intelligence Nick had run after they'd arrived. No obvious connection to the suspect, but he'd had his share of brushes with the law too.

As they cruised by, Mark knew agents would already be moving in to watch the exits, and that unmarked units were surrounding the block. Local law enforcement would be tapped to set up a deep perimeter. The guy wouldn't be able to go any-where without being spotted. In fact, it would be better if he did try to leave. Agents would have him surrounded in seconds, and they could make a quick, clean arrest.

Within twenty minutes, the team had convened at the firehouse two blocks away. Nick laid out a preliminary ops plan. In the end, inspired by the setting, they decided to have two agents dressed as firefighters try to evacuate the duplex on the premise of a gas leak.

If that went bad, they'd bring in a negotiator.

The SWAT team would be the last resort.

Stepping outside into the relentless late-afternoon sun, Mark pulled his sunglasses out of his pocket and slipped them on. At least he and Nick had ditched their suits. They'd dressed in jeans and cotton shirts to better blend in with the neighborhood, as had the other agents who'd been called in. They paused outside to hammer out a few last details, and he shifted from one foot to the other as heat from the concrete pavement warmed the soles of his shoes.

Nearby, the black-clad SWAT team was suiting up in body armor and Kevlar helmets. He could relate to their discomfort, though they masked it well. He'd worn gear like that in even hotter conditions more often than he cared to remember.

"Okay, let's move."

As Luke gave the signal to take their positions, Mark checked his watch. Five o'clock. If they were lucky, this would be over in fifteen minutes and he could spend part of the day with Emily.

If they weren't, it was going to be a very long evening.

"Steve, Carl Owens, Oakdale. Sorry to bother you on Sunday."

"No problem. The arrests on our bank robbery case are about to go down and I'm working anyway. What's up?"

"I found a match between the Eight List and one of the contractor lists."

Keeping one eye on the duplex, Steve shifted the phone as he pulled a pen and notebook out of his pocket. "Who is it?"

"Guy named Dale Edwards. Works for Aiken Concrete in Fenton."

"That fits."

"So does his residence. He lives in Labadie."

The rural community about forty miles from St. Louis was home to some new, high-end housing developments as the relentless urban sprawl continued, but it was also populated by small farms that could accommodate cattle, Steve knew.

Another piece fell into place.

"What else do we know about him?"

"Not much. I just found the match a few minutes ago. I did run him through NCIC, but he's clean. You want us to contact Franklin County and pay him a visit, or would you rather have your people handle it?"

"Why don't you coordinate the preliminary contact? Our agents are spread out on the bank arrests today. In the interim, we'll do a background check on this guy."

"Sounds good."

"How did you end up with list duty at 5:30 on a Sunday, anyway?"

"I was in the office working on a homicide and found the latest contractor roster on my desk.

While I waited for a call, I went through a few pages. And got lucky."

"We were about due for another break. Keep me in the loop."

As the line went dead, Steve considered passing on the news to Mark. But distracting an agent at a critical point in an arrest sequence wasn't a good idea. He could brief him once Carl reported back and after they had some background on Edwards.

Besides, the match could be a coincidence. There was no guarantee Edwards was their man. At the moment, the tenuous links between him and the shooting were circumstantial. They would need a lot more evidence to connect him to the crime before any charges could be brought. And since neither Mark nor Dr. Lawson had recognized the man's name when they'd reviewed the Eight List, there didn't appear to be any direct connection to suggest he'd targeted one of them.

For now, Steve decided to hold off on alerting Mark. But he did put in a call to the office to initiate a background check on Dale Edwards.

This was the day.

Dale flexed his hands on the wheel and took another sip of the soda from the cooler he'd filled with cold drinks hours ago at home. He'd needed every one of them too. Sitting in the parking lot outside his quarry's condo had been a hot job. His only break had been when he'd followed her to church earlier in the morning.

The hypocrisy of that excursion had repulsed him. Watching her smile and greet people as she'd headed toward the doors of the brick structure with the white steeple had been sickening. How could she spend her life leading people away from the Lord, take his place as the supreme counselor, and have the gall to put in an appearance at Sunday services?

Well, she'd need all the prayers she could get before this day was over, he thought in satisfaction. His hand tightened on the soda can, denting the flimsy aluminum, and he forced himself to relax his grip. In less than two hours, she'd be meeting her maker. And facing heat far more intense than what he'd suffered as he'd sat in his stifling car all day.

From his spot in a far corner of the parking lot, he had a clear view of her porch and her car. She hadn't taken one step out the door after her trip to church. Nor had she had any visitors. Good.

He patted his pocket, verifying he'd transferred the photo of Ruthie and Bryan from the tote bag. Then he checked his watch. Six o'clock. If no one showed up in the next hour, he'd implement his plan.

And this time, he'd finish the job.

"Steve? Carl again. We checked out Edwards's place. He lives on about ten acres of land, and the guys did spot a couple of cows in a pasture. No one answered the door, and the garage was empty."

From his concealed position, Steve shifted the BlackBerry against his ear and squinted toward the duplex where the suspect was holed up. "That doesn't help us a whole lot."

"No. But this might. They also talked to a neighbor, who said Edwards recently lost both his wife and teenage son. The son committed suicide and the wife died a few weeks later of a heart attack. They've seen him around the house at odd hours in the past week or so, and wondered if he'd lost his job on top of everything else. And they mentioned seeing a strange car turn in his driveway a few nights ago."

"Those kinds of losses could precipitate a breakdown. But that wouldn't give him a motive for attacking Mark or Dr. Lawson."

"There could be pieces we haven't discovered yet that would complete the picture."

"True. One of our agents called me with some basic background on Edwards." He pulled a notebook out of his pocket and flipped it open, keeping one eye on the apartment building. "He's a long-term employee at Aiken Concrete. If he's been let go, it's a very recent development. Wife, Ruth, son, Bryan. Age fifty-nine. No brushes with the law. He's lived in Labadie for twenty-plus years. Excellent credit rating, pays his taxes on schedule, churchgoing. He sounds like a model citizen."

"Put enough stress on anyone, and they can break. You know, it could come down to Mark and Dr. Lawson being in the wrong place at the wrong time. They might have been random targets after all."

"My gut tells me that's not the case."

Carl's sigh came over the line. "Mine does too."

As the agents dressed as firefighters stepped into sight in front of the duplex, Steve shifted position for a better view. "Carl, I'll be in touch. We're about to move on the arrest."

At seven o'clock, Dale called Emily Lawson's exchange. Less than five minutes later she returned the call.

"Mr. Smith, Dr. Lawson. How can I be of help?"

"You said I could call if I wanted to talk. I was wondering if you might be able to meet me somewhere. Maybe a Starbucks? I was going to wait to call you until tomorrow, but I . . . I need to talk to someone tonight. That is, if you don't have other plans."

There was a brief moment of silence. "I don't usually meet patients on Sunday . . . but I can make an exception today. Which Starbucks would be convenient?"

He'd already scoped out a small mall near her condo. The large parking lot would serve his purposes very well, and it was only about a mile from the church where he'd parked on his first attempt. And where he intended to finish the job tonight. It would be easy to walk back to the mall when he was done. He gave her the address.

"Believe it or not, that's very close to me. When would you like to get together?"

"Would fifteen minutes be okay?"

"Fine. I'll meet you there."

As she severed the connection, Dale smiled.

Things were going exactly as he'd planned.

The arrest of the third suspect hadn't gone as smoothly as they'd hoped, but at least it was over, Mark thought in relief. The woman and two of her kids had come out after agents masquerading as firefighters warned that the gas leak might cause an explosion, but at the last minute the suspect had gotten suspicious, grabbed the third kid, and slammed the door shut. However, once he realized the place was swarming with police and federal agents, he'd agreed to talk to a negotiator. An hour later, he'd surrendered.

As the SWAT team members stripped off their stifling gear, Steve touched his shoulder.

"Let's find some shade." The supervisor tipped his head toward a scraggly, lone maple tree as the suspect was led out of the house in handcuffs while police officers tried to manage a growing crowd of spectators.

As Steve told him about the match and Oakdale's

unsuccessful attempt to contact Dale Edwards, Mark frowned. "The name doesn't ring a bell. Did you run it by Emily again?"

"Not yet."

"I'll call her. Do we have any intel on Edwards?"

"He's clean. But he's had some recent trauma that could be making him unstable. Neighbors think he may have lost his job. And his wife and son died recently."

"An accident?"

"No. The teenage son committed suicide and the wife died of a heart attack soon after."

Despite the oppressive heat, a cold knot formed in Mark's stomach and he felt some of the color drain from his face.

"What's wrong?" Steve's eyes narrowed.

"Emily told me about a new patient she saw this week with the same background. An EAP referral. But she'd have recognized the name if it was on the Eight List."

"Maybe not. There were almost three hundred people on there."

Mark raked his fingers through his hair. "Look, I need to call her. Can someone track Edwards's boss and find out if he was referred to his company's EAP?"

"I'll take care of it."

"What are the names of the wife and son? I'll run them by Emily."

"Ruth and Bryan."

"Bryan." Mark repeated the name. It was familiar, but he couldn't place where he'd heard it.

"Does that mean something to you?"

"Maybe. It will come to me. But first let me call Emily." He punched in her number. After four rings, the answering machine kicked in. "Emily, if you're there, pick up." He waited, but when there was no response, a flicker of panic licked at his gut.

"I'm heading out there." He slid the phone back in its holder. "Who can you spare?"

As the lead case agent, Nick needed to deal with follow-up interviews as soon as possible and coordinate the scene search. Mark knew he wouldn't be available.

Scanning the crowd, Steve motioned for Kevin Shaughnessy, one of the senior agents, to join them. Mark apprised him of the situation as they headed for his car at a trot.

Once they were underway, Mark tried Emily's number again. Still no answer. On a whim, he punched in directory assistance. At the prompt, he gave the name Evelyn Martelli, praying Emily's neighbor didn't have an unlisted number. He breathed a sigh of relief as the call went through— and a bigger one when she answered.

"Mrs. Martelli, this is Mark Sanders with the FBI. We met on a few occasions when I was visiting Emily."

"I remember you very well, young man. What can I do for you?"

"Put my mind at rest, I hope. I've been trying to call Emily, and there's been no answer. I assume she's gone out, and wondered if you might have seen her leave."

"As a matter of fact, I did. About half an hour ago. I was watering my begonias on the front porch, and we chatted for a minute."

"Did she by any chance say where she was going?"

"No, I'm afraid not. All she said was that she had to meet a patient. I teased her about breaking her no-work-on-Sunday rule, but she smiled and said there are always exceptions."

The knot in Mark's stomach tightened, and he had to struggle to keep his tone neutral. "Thank you, Mrs. Martelli. You've been very helpful."

Mark punched in Steve's number, noting the tremor in his hand. When his boss answered, he dispensed with a greeting. "According to Emily's neighbor, she left a few minutes ago to meet a patient. Steve, it's got to be Dale Edwards."

"Let's slow down a little. Assuming Edwards is the shooter, we know he's a good marksman. If he wanted to take her out, why not use the rifle again, from a distance, and keep it anonymous? He was careful on the first attempt . . . why would he take chances now?"

"I don't know. But stress can do strange things to

people. And he's had more than his share. He could be starting to crack, to make mistakes."

"Okay. I'll put out an alert on both their cars. But Edwards's neighbors said they saw an unfamiliar car pulling into his place the other night, so he may be driving a different vehicle."

"We can only go with what we have. Let me know as soon as you reach Edwards's boss. I'm going to track down Emily's office manager and find out the name of her new EAP patient."

Once again, Mark severed the connection and punched in directory assistance. Maria's last name was Fernandez, but he had no idea what her husband's first name was. And according to the live operator who eventually came on the line, there were more than a hundred listings in the St. Louis area for Fernandez. Two minutes later, he was back on the phone with Evelyn.

"Raul," she supplied. "Nice man. Emily has Maria and Raul and me over to dinner on occasion. And that young man from the radio station, Andy."

At the mention of the radio station, the name Bryan fell into place with an ominous click.

The distraught young man who had called Emily several times, the one she'd told him she'd worried about, had been named Bryan.

Edwards's son, Bryan, had committed suicide.

Was Bryan the link between Emily and Edwards?

But if he was, it still didn't explain why Edwards would go after Emily.

"Mr. Sanders, is Emily all right?"

With an effort, he pulled himself back to the conversation. "I hope so, Mrs. Martelli. Another agent and I are about ten minutes away. Do you have a key to Emily's condo?"

"Yes."

"We'd like to take a look around. She may have left some clue about where she was going."

"Of course. I'll be waiting for you. And I believe I'll say a few prayers."

A good idea, Mark thought somberly as he slipped the BlackBerry back onto his belt. A very good idea.

"Joe Smith. But that is not his real name."

Maria's response to Mark's question confirmed his growing suspicion. Dale Edwards had seen Emily as a patient, using an assumed name.

Closing his eyes, Mark tightened his grip on his BlackBerry and tried to rein in his escalating panic as Kevin sped toward Emily's condo. "Are you sure, Maria?"

"Yes. Randy Miller, the EAP rep, told me. He said the guy didn't want anyone to know he was going to counseling. Loco, huh?" There was a brief pause, followed by a worried question. "Emily . . . she is in trouble, sí?"

"I hope not. We're checking it out now. What companies does Miller represent?"

She reeled off several—including Aiken Concrete.

326

Suspicion became probability.

"Maria, I've got another call coming in. I'll be in touch later." Without giving her a chance to respond, he switched lines. "Sanders."

"It's Steve. We reached Aiken, and through him the EAP rep. Edwards saw Dr. Lawson last week under the name Joe Smith."

Probability became certainty.

"We're pulling up in front of her condo now. I'll get back to you."

"I'll put some agents on standby. And I'll alert Carl. We'll find her, Mark."

"Yeah. I know."

There was no question in his mind about that.

He only hoped it wouldn't be too late.

21

The light was fading quickly, but Emily spotted Joe Smith as soon as she pulled into the parking lot. He was leaning against his car, a drink in each hand. He lifted one cup in greeting when he saw her, and she swung into the empty space beside him.

As she gathered up her purse, she was glad she'd exchanged the dress she'd worn to church for a jean skirt and knit top. She hoped the casual attire would be less intimidating to her skittish patient than her typical office garb had been a few days ago. But the change of clothes had left her rushing to get to their rendezvous in the allotted fifteen minutes, and she'd forgotten to retrieve her cell phone from the recharger. She knew Mark would worry if he called and got no answer, considering she hadn't ventured out alone in the evening since the shooting incident.

But he was tied up with the bank robbery arrests. In all likelihood, she'd be back long before he had a chance to call. Besides, she didn't need to bother him with this. He had enough on his mind. And the situation was straightforward. She was meeting a patient, in a public place, with lots of people around. What could be safer?

With the setting of the sun, the heat was dissipating, but the steamy weather had taken a toll on the older man, Emily concluded as she joined him beside his car. His cotton shirt was limp, his slacks wrinkled, his hair matted down with sweat.

"Thank you for coming. The place is crowded, though, and I'd rather not talk about personal things in there. So I got us each a drink and hoped we could visit in your car. Double chocolate chip frappuccino, right?" He held up one of the cups.

"That's right." She'd never conducted a counseling session in her car, but if it put her patient at ease, she was willing to give it a try. "Sure, we can talk out here." She reached for the cup, but he withdrew his hand.

"I'll hold it until you get in."

Acceding with a nod, she moved to the passenger side of her car and opened the door for him. Once he was seated, she closed it, circled the hood, and slid behind the wheel. Flipping up the covers on the cup holders, she took her frappuccino.

"A perfect drink for a hot night." She took a sip and opened her notebook. "I'm glad you called, Mr. Smith. I've been thinking about you. When people experience a great deal of stress, it's easy for them to lose perspective. Often talking to friends, or a third party, can be very helpful. Have you talked about what happened with anyone?"

"No. It's hard to find the words."

"I understand." She took another sip of the cold drink and set it in the holder. "When bad things happen, our feelings are often confused and muddled. It can be difficult to sort them out. That's why counselors can help. We're able to look at the situation more impartially and can offer guidance to help people work through their feelings and get their life back on track. I'd like to help you do that, if you'll let me."

"I think that's what Mr. Miller had in mind when he recommended you. He said you were very good at what you do." He glanced down at her cup. "Your frappuccino is melting."

"If you do the talking, it will give me a chance to drink it." She smiled at him and picked up her cup again.

"Deal." He waited while she took a sip. "I thought I might tell you about my brother, John."

"Okay."

"You asked me if there was any history of depression in our family. Well, my older brother lost his wife four years ago. After that, he wasn't the same. He lived down in Arkansas. I always wished he was closer, but I called him two, three times a week. And I tried to get him to go to church, to read the Bible. But he kept slipping further and further away."

"Did he seek any professional help?" She kept sipping, keeping up her end of the bargain.

"Yes, ma'am. He went to a psychologist. Things got worse after that."

"I'm sorry to hear that. Was he on any medication?"

"Yes. It didn't help. I told him he should put everything in the hands of the Lord, but he didn't listen. He was a strong believer before his wife died. After that, he kind of fell away. Looked to the world for answers, instead of to the Lord. Like Bryan did."

"Bryan?"

"My son." He pulled a photo out of his pocket and held it out for her to see. "This is a picture of him with my wife, Ruth."

That was an odd coincidence, Emily reflected as she peered at the photo in the fading light, trying to focus. The troubled young caller on her teen show a couple of months ago had also been named Bryan.

"He was a very handsome young man, Mr. Smith. And your wife was lovely."

"Thank you."

Without prompting, he launched into a lengthy story about how he and his wife had met. Considering his reticence during their first session, she was surprised—but pleased. Perhaps, now that he seemed more willing to talk, he'd open up about deeper issues too.

As he finished his story, she drained the last of her drink and set the cup in the holder. Or tried to. She missed on the firstattempt, blinking in surprise. Must be the twilight shadows, she decided, taking more care with her aim on the second attempt.

"You mentioned your brother earlier, Mr. Smith. What happened to him?"

"He took his own life."

Jolted, she stared at him. Two suicides in one family. That could indicate a pattern. Couldn't it? For some reason, she was having difficulty organizing her thoughts.

"I told Bryan to give it to the Lord, but he didn't listen, either."

"Is that what you think you should do too?" The last few words came out slurred. Frowning, she took a deep breath. Maybe the heat was affecting her.

"I know the Lord is with me."

A wave of dizziness took her by surprise, and she

grabbed the wheel, curling her fingers around the rim as her pen dropped, unnoticed and soundless, to the floor.

"Are you all right?"

"I . . . I don't know." She tried to fight down a sudden surge of nausea.

"You don't look very well. Why don't you let me drive you home? I can take a taxi back here to pick up my car."

Before she could respond, he stepped out of the car. A few seconds later, he pulled her door open and extended a hand.

"Look . . . I'll just . . . call someone." She frowned. Why were her words garbled?

"No need. I'm happy to help." He tugged her from the car.

Despite his assistance, she staggered when she tried to stand and had to lean on him heavily as he propelled her around to the passenger side of his vehicle.

She wanted to protest as he eased her into the seat and shut the door, but she couldn't get the words out. Letting her head drop back against the seat, she heard the back door open. Shut. Then the driver side door opened and he slid behind the wheel. The engine rumbled to life, and he put the car in gear.

"I need to . . . give you . . . my address."

"We're not going there."

His response sounded distorted to Emily, but she

understood its meaning. Or she thought she did. Confused, she turned to him, trying hard to focus on his blurry profile. Hadn't he said he was going to take her home?

In truth, however, she was beginning to think she needed to go to an emergency room. There was something very wrong with her. Her muscles weren't responding to her brain's commands. And she was having difficulty processing information.

"Bryan should never have called you."

She tried to concentrate. Bryan was his son. No, wait, that was wrong. Bryan was the name of the distressed teen she'd spoken with several times. The one she'd worried about, who had stopped calling. But wasn't Bryan also the name of Joe's son?

"I told him not to," Joe continued as she tried to keep up. "But I found out later, after he hung himself, that he kept calling you anyway. He wouldn't have died if he'd listened to me instead of going behind my back. You misled him, Emily. The same way that therapist misled John. And you're responsible for Ruthie's death too. She wouldn't have had that heart attack if Bryan hadn't killed himself."

He flipped his signal and stopped speaking long enough to complete a turn and switch on his lights in the deepening dusk.

"I made a mistake with you in the park. Shooting was too quick. God wants you to know why you're going to die. So he showed me a better way. A slower way. He wants you to think about dying, like John and Bryan did as the life slipped out of their bodies. You go to church. You might know that passagefrom Psalms: 'The Lord is known by the judgment which he executeth: the wicked is snared in the work of his own hands.' It's time for your sentence to be carried out, Emily. An eye for an eye, like it says in Exodus. A life for a life. Except it's just one life for three. Not exactly a fair trade. But it will have to do."

As Emily fought a losing battle to hang on to awareness, his words registered in her mind. Followed by a horrifying realization.

Joe Smith—her newest client—was the shooter.

Even under the best conditions, she knew reasoning with a sick, delusional person wasn't likely to have much effect. And she was at a distinct disadvantage. There was no strength in her body, thanks to whatever he must have slipped into her drink. Her muscles had simply stopped responding to her brain's commands. And what little control she could still exert on her mind was slipping fast. But she had to try.

"The Lord said that . . . vengeance was his." Her whispered words were barely audible.

He turned to her. "And I am his instrument."

His steady calmness, and the absolute conviction in his tone, told her with terrifying certainty she wasn't going to be able to dissuade him from his mission.

As her brain began to succumb to the fog swirling around it, Emily's thoughts turned to Mark. All along, she'd been afraid to consider a commitment to him, fearing he would leave her alone, as Grant had.

Now, she was about to leave him.

The irony of it cut deep.

Regret pooled in her heart. If she had it to do over again, she'd make a different choice. She'd acknowledge that everyone's hold on life was tenuous, at best. That each day was a gift to be cherished and fully lived, without fear, as Mark had told her not long ago. She'd remind herself often of a saying she'd once read: "Yesterday's the past, tomorrow's the future, but today is a gift. That's why it's called the present."

Lord, I've been foolish. I should have embraced the gift Mark was offering. I can't help myself now. I put my life in your hands. But if it's your will, please give me another chance. And if today is the day you call me home, please give Mark the courage to accept it without turning away from you.

"Hey, David, look at that!"

The excitement in his friend's whispered comment caught David's attention. Ever since those FBI agents and that detective had visited his house, his friend Eric had been a whole lot less bossy. And when David had recruited him for surveillance, Eric hadn't argued about who was going to be in charge, using his six-month age advantage as rationale, the way he usually did. They both knew the optimal place to keep an eye on the street was from David's tree house—now known as their command post. Besides, it was logical for David to be in charge of this mission.

He'd talked to the FBI.

"What do you have?" David scooted over to Eric and peered into the darkness.

"Look at that car. The driver turned off the lights as soon as he came around the corner."

Lifting his binoculars, David studied the car, wondering if it might be the same one the FBI agents and detective had asked about. But no. This was a different make. And it was a dark color. There weren't any eights in the license plate, either. Shoot. He'd been hoping to spot the car the police were looking for.

Still . . . it was kind of weird that the guy would turn his lights off. At least, he was pretty sure it was a guy. It was kind of hard to tell in the dark. And there was someone with him. He couldn't see the person's face, but from the longer hair he figured it was a lady. Her head was twisted kind of funny, though. Like she might be using the corner of the seat to prop it up, the same way he did when he wanted to sleep on long car trips.

"What do you think?"

Eric was asking his opinion, he realized. Way cool!

Instead of answering, David watched as the car turned into the church parking lot and disappeared. It might not be the same car he'd seen that Saturday they left on vacation, but it had some connection with the church. Like that other car did. Goose bumps broke out on his arm despite the heat. Something was going on here. Maybe something big.

"David! Did you see that? He turned in at the church! What should we do?" Eric was growing more agitated by the second.

It was time for an executive decision, David decided. He'd heard his dad use that term at dinner, when he was telling David's mom about something he'd decided at work. David figured it meant he'd taken charge. And that's what he was going to do.

"We wait."

"Wait?" Eric sounded confused. "What for?"

He had no idea. But he wasn't about to let Eric know that. Swatting at a mosquito, he propped his elbows on the wooden railing of the rustic tree house and glued the binoculars to his eyes. "We'll know when we see it."

"Huh?"

"Just keep watching, Eric. You cover the far exit; I'll watch the one where the guy turned in."

"What are we watching for?"

"Anything that looks weird."

"But what if we actually see something weird?" Eric sounded nervous now.

"I'll tell my dad."

"Okay. Yeah. That's a good idea."

David knew that would appease Eric. Passing the buck to adults was always the easy way out of a sticky situation. All they had to do was become kids again and leave problems to the grown-ups to sort out.

But if the information they uncovered helped those FBI guys, they might pay David another visit.

And if they did, he might even invite Eric to come over and meet them.

Maybe.

If he felt really generous.

Getting Emily from the mall parking lot to the church had been a piece of cake. The ease of it convinced Dale that God looked with favor on his plan.

He glanced at Emily. Her eyes were open, but she was slumped in the corner of the front seat, unmoving. The drug had worked exactly as the article had said it would. Once it had taken effect, she'd offered no resistance. And she'd understood why she was being punished. Her comment about vengeance had told him that. He hoped there was enough awareness left in her brain that she'd know she was dying. And that she couldn't do a thing to stop it. That was important.

Ashe turned into the parking lot he'd visited three weeks ago, he scanned the street. It was a stifling night. None of the residents were sitting on their front porches witnessing his clandestine visit. That was a sad thing, how no one sat on front porches anymore. When he was a boy, the family had congregated there every night in the summer. He and Ruthie had followed that practice too, when they were first married.

But then things changed. People had gotten soft with air-conditioning. Nobody wanted to sweat anymore. The boob tube had replaced porch-sitting and conversation. That was one of the reasons he and Ruthie had moved to the country. They might not have had any close neighbors, but the air was fresh and clean, and they'd had each other to sit with on the front porch each night. It had been a good life.

Until a couple of months ago.

His face hardened as he drove toward the far corner of the lot and backed the car into the shadows of the surrounding woods, up against the underbrush. If he was lucky, no one would notice the car until morning. But he didn't need that long. It would all be over in an hour, perhaps much less. By the time anyone got suspicious, Emily Lawson would be dead.

Reaching up, he flipped off the dome light, then released the trunk. The latex gloves he'd pulled on when he'd retrieved his tote bag from his car back at the mall would preserve his identity this time, just as they had on his first visit here, he thought in satisfaction.

After removing the tote bag from the backseat, he withdrew the screwdriver and punched out the trunk light.

Dale had walked through the steps dozens of times at home, much as he'd done for the shooting. He knew exactly what he needed to do, and he knew precisely how long it would take. He laid his bag in the trunk and went to work, his movements careful and methodical.

First, he used the cordless drill to create a hole in the bottom of the trunk, on the right side. Quickly. The less noise the better. After that, he worked the pipe through the hole and twisted it until he had a smooth opening. Next, he inserted one end of the hose into the tailpipe and secured it with duct tape, taking care to ensure a tight seal. Finally, he threaded the hose through the hole he'd created in the trunk and taped it down inside, sealing the hole with more tape. He replaced all of the tools in the bag and set it beside the car, leaving the duct tape on top.

Pushing past the low-hanging branches of the trees, he opened the passenger side door. The good doctor almost fell out, and he bent to catch her. Hoisting her in his arms, he eased the door shut with his hip, making as little noise as possible.

She didn't weigh much, he discovered as her head lolled against his shoulder. Or maybe he was stronger than he knew. Living in the country, working the land, reading the Good Book—those all created strong muscles and a strong mind. He wished he could have convinced Bryan of that. And John.

All at once his vision blurred, and he stumbled. But this wasn't the time for tears, he reminded himself. Later, when the job was done, when justice had been meted out, he could grieve. It would be appropriate then. The grief of the just. And the avenged.

He lowered Emily into the trunk, positioning her head away from the hose. He didn't want this to be over too fast. She watched him, her eyes glazed and confused, her body limp. Amazing. The drug had rendered her completely helpless. But on the off chance she figured out what was going on and tried to yank the hose free, he pulled her hands behind her back and crossed them at the wrists, binding them with duct tape.

Depositing the roll of tape in his bag, he took out the baseball cap and glasses and put them on. As he grasped the trunk lid, he regarded his quarry. The woman who had ruined his life. Who had pretended to be God, thinking she could save troubled souls when only the Almighty could do that. But she'd inflict no more damage.

"Good-bye, Dr. Lawson." The title came out in a sneer. "I now commend you to the righteous wrath of the Lord."

He lowered the trunk lid, exerting pressure until the lock caught with a quiet click. Returning to the driver's seat, he slipped inside and took the remote locking mechanism off her key ring. After ripping out the notebook pages she'd written in during their conversation, he inserted the key in the ignition. Once the engine purred to life, he got out, locked the door, and stripped off his gloves. Stuffing them into the tote bag along with the notes and locking mechanism he would dispose of later, he set off across the parking lot without a backward look.

It was done.

"Somebody's coming from behind the church!"

"I can see that." David kept his binoculars fixed on the solitary figure carrying a small bag. He was as keyed up as Eric, but he didn't think it was good to let that show. FBI agents and detectives would always stay cool on the outside even if they were nervous on the inside.

The eight-year-olds watched in silence as the man turned away from them and strode down the street.

Lowering his binoculars, Eric turned to David. "That's weird. Where's his car? And that lady?"

"She didn't drive out the other end of the parking

342

lot, did she? You were supposed to be watching that side."

"I was." Eric bristled, his tone defensive. "Nobody came out down there. I just happened to look away for a minute. That's why I saw the guy. So whaddya wanna do?"

David turned around and sat with his back against the railing to ponder the situation. It was good to think things through. That's what the cops and FBI agents always did in the books he'd read.

Okay. Let's see. He and Eric could go over to the church parking lot and see if the car was still there. But if his father found out he'd left the yard at night without permission, he'd be grounded for, like, forever.

Besides, not that he'd tell Eric this, but he wasn't all that thrilled about the idea of wandering around the back of that church at night. All those dark woods would be spooky.

He could tell his dad. But what if it was nothing? What if he and Eric made a big deal out of this and found out it was just some guy dropping his wife or daughter off, and she was in the church at some quilting meeting or something? They'd feel like idiots.

Except . . . they hadn't seen any other cars turn into the lot, and they'd been watching the place for an hour. There were no lights on in the church, or in the basement, as far as he could tell. And why had the guy turned his lights off as he drove down their street?

"David." Eric prodded him with his elbow. "What are we gonna do?"

With sudden decision, he stood. "We're going to tell my dad."

22

Nothing.

Emily had left nothing in her condo to indicate where she was going. There were no voice mail messages on her answering machine, no jotted notes, no address book lying open that might offer a clue about her destination.

His anxiety mushrooming, Mark propped his fists on his hips and took one more look around her kitchen. Short of aimlessly trolling the streets and hoping to spot her car somewhere, there was little he could do to track her down. Except pray some law enforcement officer somewhere would spot her car and link it to the alert.

But the odds diminished as the minutes passed and the field of search broadened. According to Evelyn, she'd left—he checked his watch—an hour ago. She could already be fifty miles away.

Or gone forever.

He didn't want to think about that possibility. Tried not to. But it was there, and he couldn't ignore it. Edwards had tried to kill her once. And come very, very close. A second attempt would be carried out with as much care as the first—if not more—to ensure he didn't fail again.

As a result, there was a high likelihood he would succeed.

Intellectually, Mark knew that. You couldn't deal with the dregs of society for as many years as he had without knowing the odds in a situation like this. Realism turned to pessimism fast in the world he inhabited. If she'd been missing for an hour,

the chances of finding her alive weren't good.

But his heart wouldn't accept that.

What kind of cruel twist of fate would allow him to reconnect with her after all these years, then snatch her away? God wouldn't let that happen.

Would he?

Mark's BlackBerry began to vibrate, and he whipped it out, trying to steady the tremor in his hands. "Yes?"

"We've got her car." It was Steve.

The terse statement slammed him like a body punch. "Where?" A single word was all he could manage. He was already moving toward the door as he spoke, gesturing to Kevin.

"The same church parking lot he used as a staging area for the first attempt."

He sucked in a sharp breath at the frightening, perverted logic of the location. The guy was finishing the job where he'd started it. A rising swell of panic threatened to swamp him, and he broke into a sprint.

"We're on our way. Is Emily there?" It was the hardest question he'd ever had to ask—and he braced for Steve's response as Kevin slid behind the wheel.

"The car's locked and appears to be empty. But the engine is running. The call came in from Frank Purnell. The same guy whose kid gave us the tip that resulted in the Eight List. His son saw the car turn in with a driver and a female passenger. Ten minutes ago the man walked out alone. The boy told his dad, and Purnell went over to check out the car, then called 911. Oakdale is enroute."

Mark gestured for Kevin to take the next left. "We're two minutes away. I'll call you when we have news."

The next 120 seconds were the longest Mark had ever endured. Far worse than the brief HRT fire training exercise in the three-story tower known as the hot house. Pitch dark, filled with caustic smoke that clawed at his lungs and heat that seared his eyes, the concrete inferno had left a lasting impression on him. Those few minutes had been as close to hell as he'd ever wanted to get.

Until now.

As they turned the corner onto the street where the church was located, he saw an Oakdale police car converging from the other direction. He and

Kevin got there first and swung into the lot, the police close behind.

"In the corner." Mark pointed to the far end. He recognized Emily's car. Frank Purnell stood beside it.

Without waiting for the car to come to a complete stop, Mark pushed open the door and hit the ground running.

"Tell me what you know." Mark grabbed the man's flashlight and clicked it on as he swung the beam around the interior, then began to circle the car, Frank on his heels.

"Ever since you and your colleagues came to the house, David's been into this surveillance thing. He and a friend have been watching the street from his tree house, hoping to spot that car we saw the day we left on vacation. I told him it was a long shot, but that didn't stop him. Anyway, that's why they were up there tonight and noticed that the driver turned off his lights when he pulled onto our street. At first, I thought it was their overactive imagination, but when they kept pushing I decided to come over and check it out. I'm still not convinced that—"

Mark's sudden, explosive oath cut Frank off midsentence. Kevin was beside him in two strides, pushing past the undergrowth around the rear of the car. Mark tossed him the flashlight as he bent down to yank at the hose that had been fed into the floor of the trunk.

"Either get a door open in the next ten seconds or smash a window," Mark snapped at the cop who'd followed Kevin over. "And radio for an ambulance."

Two more police cars arrived, but Mark didn't even notice. He was focused on the trunk. "Emily? Can you hear me?" He leaned close, willing her to answer. But there was only silence.

The sound of shattering glass suddenly sliced through the darkness. A few seconds later, the trunk release clicked.

Mark yanked up the lid—and fought down a wave of panic as he caught his first glimpse of Emily.

Her hands were bound behind her with duct tape, her eyes were closed—and she didn't seem to be breathing.

Fear coursing through his veins, Mark pressed his fingers against her neck, as he'd done three weeks ago just a few hundred yards from this spot. Her pulse that day had been steady, if a bit faint. Now, in addition to being faint, it was rapid and irregular. But at least it was there.

Sliding his arms under her knees and shoulders, he lifted her gently out of the trunk. One of the cops had already retrieved a blanket from his car and had spread it on the ground. Another produced a pair of scissors from his first aid kit. Mark reached for them, but Kevin intervened.

"Let me."

Mark didn't argue. Considering how badly his hands were shaking, he'd do more harm than good if he tried to use them.

Dropping to one knee, Kevin carefully cut through the tape, freeing Emily as the ambulance turned into the parking lot and pulled to the rear of the building.

Mark knelt beside her and took her hand, brushing the hair back from her forehead. "Hang in there, Em." The hoarse entreaty was all he could manage.

"What do we have?"

The paramedics joined him, and he moved aside to give them room to work.

"Carbon monoxide poisoning."

The two technicians went into action.

"Put her on 100 percent oxygen while I get her vitals." The first technician pulled on a pair of latex gloves as he talked. "Then get a blood sample. Let's be prepared to intubate. And start a drip."

A hand settled on Mark's shoulder, and he looked up to find Steve at his side.

"What are you doing here?"

"I'm the boss. I don't have to do cleanup duty after an arrest." He dropped down beside him to balance on the balls of his feet. "How is she?"

"Alive. Beyond that, I have no idea."

"We'd better be ready for seizures." The first technician pulled the stethoscope out of his ears. "And let's get an EKG."

"Is she going to be okay?"

At Mark's question, the man turned. "Carbon monoxide poisoning is tricky. Any idea how long she was in the car?"

"Ten or fifteen minutes. In the trunk."

The man winced as he turned back to prep Emily for the EKG. "High levels of CO can be fatal within minutes. I'm guessing you got to her just in time. Is there any chance this was a suicide attempt?"

"No."

At Mark's cold tone, the man shot an apologetic look over his shoulder. "Sorry. Most of these cases are."

With an effort, Mark curbed his anger. The guy didn't know Emily. Otherwise, he'd understand that suicide would be the last thing she'd ever contemplate. No matter how bad things got.

"Her wrists were bound," Mark told him.

"But not her feet?"

"No."

The paramedic glanced down at her hands, lifting one to examine it. "Odd that there's no chafing on her wrists. You'd expect some if she'd tried to free herself." He laid her hand down and gave the rest of her body a quick scan. "And there's no visible trauma to indicate resistance or struggle. The unbound feet bother me too." He refocused on the EKG. "She may have been drugged."

"Does that complicate things?" The quiet question came from Steve.

"It can. It would help if we knew what was used." He looked over at his partner. "Get some blood samples for toxicology."

"Is that Frank Purnell?" Steve touched Mark's shoulder again and inclined his head toward the man standing in the shadows nearby.

"Yes."

"I'm going to talk to him. And his son."

He should be doing that, Mark knew. No one wanted the guy who'd done this caught more than he did. And he and Coop had taken the lead on the case up until now. But he couldn't leave Emily. And Steve didn't seem to expect him to.

The paramedic checked the data being generated by the EKG, and Mark watched over his shoulder. It was gibberish to him. "Is her heart okay?"

"So far, so good. I'm more worried about cerebral edema."

"Give me that in English."

"Swelling of the brain. It's a common result of severe carbon monoxide poisoning. They'll monitor for that at the hospital." He looked at his partner. "You ready to transport?"

"Yes."

As they lifted the gurney and wheeled Emily toward the ambulance, Kevin joined Mark.

"I'm going with her." Mark watched as they maneuvered the gurney into the vehicle.

"That's what I figured."

"Tell Steve I want to be there when we bring this guy down."

"I'll pass that on."

Without waiting for a response, Mark headed toward the ambulance. He trusted the other agents to give this case their full attention.

Right now, Emily needed him more.

And once she was awake enough to understand his words, he was going to do his best to convince her she needed him for a lot longer than that.

Like forever.

Dale signed the tab for the rental car, lifted his tote bag, and headed toward the bus at Lambert International Airport that would take him to long-term parking.

His mission was over.

He hoped God was pleased.

But his own emotions were a confusing jumble. He'd expected to feel a sense of righteousness after he'd finished his task. Of completion.

Instead, he felt depleted.

And empty.

Since Ruthie's death, his life had been filled with purpose as he'd focused on the mission God had given him. Now, God was silent, leaving him directionless.

What would fill his days in the weeks and

months and years ahead? His work was meaning-less. The home he'd loved was empty and silent. His family was gone.

Nothing mattered anymore.

All at once, the grief he'd held at bay for the past two months struck with sudden, sharp force. It was like a physical blow, and he stumbled as he boarded the bus. He'd have fallen if someone hadn't reached from behind and grasped his arm to steady him.

"Careful there. That's a tricky step. You okay?"

He looked over his shoulder at the thirtysome-thing man in a business suit, briefcase in his hand. Perhaps a hotshot salesman returning after a long day of travel, anxious to get home to his wife and family. There'd probably be a light left on for him, welcoming him back, and maybe a plate of food warming in the oven.

Ruthie had done that for him, on the nights he'd worked late.

But there was no one waiting for him now. The two people he loved most in the world were buried six feet under the parched ground. There'd be no light on for him, no plate set aside. The house would be dark and empty and silent. Tonight, and for all the nights to come.

Resuming his ascent, he shuffled down the narrow aisle and chose a seat in the back of the bus. The young man who'd assisted him sent a concerned look his direction, but he averted his head. He didn't want the man's sympathy. He wanted Ruthie and Bryan.

The bus jolted forward, and he gripped the bag in his lap as he stared out into the darkness, wiping his sleeve across his eyes. He couldn't go back to the house yet. He needed to be with Ruthie and Bryan.

It was time to say a proper good-bye.

"How's she doing?"

Lifting his head out of his hands, Mark raised bleary eyes to find Nick standing above him. "Holding her own. That's what they tell me, anyway. They've been working on her ever since we got here. They've only let me stick my head in twice." He checked his watch, surprised to find it wasn't quite eleven o'clock yet. He felt as if he'd been in the ER waiting room for ten hours. "Why aren't you home sleeping?"

"The adrenaline's still pumping from the arrests." Nick dropped into the chair beside Mark.

That was a lie. Nick had to be dead on his feet, considering all the hours he'd been putting in on the bank case. It spoke volumes about their friendship that he'd shown up to offer moral support.

"Thanks." The word came out hoarse and barely there.

"No problem."

"Any news on Edwards?"

"No."

That was the answer he'd expected. Steve would have called if there were any breaks.

"Mr. Sanders?"

A nurse stood on the threshold of the waiting room, and Mark vaulted to his feet, his heart thudding against his ribcage. "Yes?"

"Dr. Lawson is beginning to say a few words. Would you like to go in?"

"Yes." He turned toward Nick. "I'll be back."

"I'll be here."

When they reached Emily's curtained cubicle, the nurse turned to him. "The doctor will be by in a few minutes. He'd like to speak with you." She held the curtain aside for him to enter.

From his youngest days, Mark had never liked hospitals. And his distaste for them had grown through the years. They were too often the source of bad news.

But not at the moment. On Mark's last visit, Emily had been awake but unresponsive. This time, as he moved toward the bed and entered her peripheral vision, she turned her head toward him. And somehow managed a sleepy smile. Swallowing past the lump in his throat, he smiled back.

"Hi." He leaned down and brushed his lips over her forehead above the oxygen mask, grasping her cool hand in his.

"Take the job, Mark."

"What?" He frowned and backed up to look at

her face. Her muffled voice was weak, her words slurred, and he wasn't sure he'd heard her correctly.

"Take the job here."

Not quite willing to believe what he thought she was implying, he entwined his fingers with hers. "We can talk about that later."

"I love you." Her eyelids drifted closed as she whispered the words.

There was no doubt about the meaning of *that* statement. But she'd also been drugged and poisoned. He'd have to wait until she was more coherent to accept it as truth. Yet he couldn't stop the surge of hope that filled him with warmth.

"I love you too, Em," he whispered. If he'd had any doubts about the depth of his own feelings, they'd evaporated in the past several hours as he'd faced the possibility he might lose her.

"I hurt," she mumbled, giving no indication she'd heard his declaration.

"Where?"

"Everywhere. My head."

"Mr. Sanders?"

He turned to find a white-coated figure at his elbow. The doctor was dark-haired and fortyish, and the shadows under his eyes spoke of sleep deprivation or dedication. Probably both.

"She says she hurts."

"I'm not surprised. But we'd rather not put any more drugs into her body. May I speak with you for a minute?" He motioned to a spot outside of Emily's curtained alcove.

Relinquishing Emily's fingers, Mark joined the doctor.

"Brendon O'Neal." The man held out his hand, and Mark returned his firm grip. "You came in with Dr. Lawson, correct?"

"Yes."

"Sorry it took me so long to catch up with you. Crazy night. I understand you filled out a lot of the paperwork when she arrived."

"Yes."

"Are you a relative?"

"No."

"Do you have medical power of attorney?"

A wave of panic washed over him. "No. Her pastor does. I can get his name for you. Is there a problem? One of the paramedics mentioned cerebral edema." His voice choked on the last word.

"I see nothing to indicate any major trauma as a result of the CO poisoning, and she's responding well to oxygen therapy. I'm more concerned about the drug that was used to subdue her. We sent the blood samples the paramedics took to toxicology, and at their suggestion we ran some tests for GHB, rohypnol, and ketamine hydrochloride. A good decision, because those drugs only remain in the bloodstream in a measurable amount for a few hours. The test came back positive for GHB."

"GHB." Mark repeated the name. It had been a long day, and his brain wasn't clicking on all cylinders anymore.

"Gamma hydroxy butyrate. On the street it goes by a variety of names, including Easy Lay, Liquid Ecstasy, Clear X, and Liquid X, among others."

Shock rippled through Mark. "He gave Emily a date rape drug?"

"Yes. As you may know, victims of those drugs suffer anterograde amnesia, meaning they have little or no memory of what occurred while the drug was active in their system. Dr. Lawson will never be able to give us a coherent account of what happened. After examining her, I think the drug was used strictly to immobilize her. But it would be prudent to confirm that."

It took a couple of seconds for the doctor's meaning to sink in, and when it did, Mark felt sick to his stomach. Surely Dale Edwards hadn't . . . He tried to swallow past the bile that rose in his throat.

"I realize she's already been through a lot of trauma today," the doctor continued. "But the effects of the drug are just beginning to wear off, and she'll remember little of the next few hours. We'll check her out as quickly and painlessly as possible. If you'll get me the name of her pastor, we'll clear the procedure."

Turning to look at Emily through the gap in the curtain, Mark took a deep breath. If Edwards had touched her, the prosecution would want to know.

And there were health implications to consider as well. "I'll have it for you in five minutes."

The doctor nodded. "Will you be staying around?"

"Yes."

"There's coffee in the waiting room."

"Thanks."

He waited until the doctor left, then returned to Emily's cubicle. She was sleeping again, her long lashes sweeping against her pale cheeks, the rise and fall of her chest reassuring in its steadiness. Beneath the sleeve of her hospital gown, he caught a glimpse of the scar on her left arm, and he reached over to trace it with a gentle finger.

She'd been through so much. Too much.

When this was over, if she'd meant the words she'd said a few minutes ago, he made a silent, fervent vow to do his best to protect her every day for as long as he lived.

Because he could no longer imagine his life without her.

"Mr. Sanders?"

Much to his surprise, Mark had dozed off in the waiting room. Nick had too, he noted with a quick glance. But he came awake instantly when Dr. O'Neal addressed him.

"I have two pieces of good news," the man told him. "First, the drug was used for one purpose. To immobilize. Period. Second, Dr. Lawson is awake and responsive, and she's asking for you. We're about to move her to a regular room."

Mark closed his eyes and drew a long, slow breath. *Thank you, Lord.*

Three minutes later, when Mark stepped into Emily's curtained cube, he was astonished at the change in her. She looked much more alert, and the oxygen mask had been removed. She reached out a hand as he approached, and he drew it to his lips.

"We have to stop meeting like this, you know."

"I think I've heard that line before." His lips quirked into a smile.

"You have. And I hope I never have to use it again."

"Amen to that." Perching on the edge of her bed, he assessed her. Her color was better and her eyes were focused. But he saw the strain in her features. Leaning over, he traced the faint twin furrows on her brow.

"Headache?"

"Yes. Thanks to the drug I was given, the doctor says I could have hangover symptoms for the next two or three days. That will be a new experience for me." She rubbed her thumb over his knuckles and searched his face. "Did you find him?"

"Not yet. But we will." His jaw settled into a determined line.

"Promise me something, Mark." Her grip on his hand tightened.

He hesitated, feeling her urgency, sensing he wasn't going to like her request. "I'll try."

"Don't hurt him."

"Emily, the man tried to kill you. Twice."

"He's very troubled, Mark. And ill. He needs help. Please don't let anyone hurt him."

As far as he was concerned, the world would be better off without Dale Edwards. "If he pulls a gun on us, there's nothing I can do to protect him."

She gave a slow nod. "I understand that. But if he doesn't?"

It was impossible to ignore the plea in her eyes. "I'll do what I can." It was the best he could offer.

"Thank you." She squeezed his hand. "Now go home and get some sleep. You've got to be running on pure adrenaline. It's one o'clock in the morning."

"I'll wait until you're settled in your room."

"That could be hours."

"She's right." O'Neal joined them. "She's out of danger. And the best thing for her to do is rest. I think she'll find that easier to do if she knows you're at home sleeping. You and your friend look dead on your feet."

"Friend?" Emily sent Mark a questioning look.

"Nick's here with me."

Her face softened. "Thank him for me. And take him home."

"Good advice. I'll see you before they move you upstairs," the doctor told her.

As he disappeared, Emily reached for Mark's hand again. "Go home and crash. Just promise you'll come back tomorrow."

"Try and keep me away." Leaning over, he brushed his lips across hers. There really wasn't any reason for him to stay. An Oakdale cop was close by—and would remain that way until Edwards was arrested. Not that Emily needed to know that. She'd had enough stress for one day. For one *lifetime*.

"You can do better than that." She put her arms around his neck as he attempted to pull away. "I know that for a fact."

"Don't tempt me." He chuckled and rubbed his cheek against her temple. Easing back a bit, he framed her face with his hands. "Get well first."

She touched his chin, now sporting a scratchy stubble. "I kind of like this bad-boy look."

He took her hand and kissed her fingertips. "Stop that."

With an exaggerated sigh, she retrieved her hand. "I guess I've lost my woman-in-jeopardy allure."

"Trust me, Em. Your allure hasn't faded." And leaning over, he claimed her lips in a brief but intense kiss designed to erase any doubt from her mind. "Still worried?"

With a contented smile, she shook her head.

"Good. But if you need convincing again tomorrow, I'll be happy to comply."

"I'll hold you to that."

And with that promise echoing in his ears, he knew he would sleep better tonight than he had in weeks.

23

Mark always set his BlackBerry on audible alert at night and left it beside his bed. In general, its piercing beep brought him instantly awake.

But on Monday morning, when it went off in the early dawn hours, he had to struggle back to consciousness. He could function on three hours of sleep for brief periods. And he'd had missions where he hadn't slept more than an hour or two at a stretch for four days. But after the stress of the past forty-eight grueling hours, his body craved rest. And its lethargic response to the rude early morning summons let him know that in no uncertain terms. Must be a sign of age, he conceded as he groped across the top of the nightstand in the dim light.

His fingers closed around the device, and he squinted at the text message.

We've got Edwards under surveillance. Call me.

It was from Steve.

Suddenly wide awake, he swung his legs to the floor and punched in the squad supervisor's number.

"It's Mark. Where is he?"

As Steve relayed the location, Mark's eyebrows rose. "Are you sure?"

"Yes. Someone spotted the car an hour ago and got suspicious, considering few people visit there in the daylight, let alone at night. We've got two agents on surveillance now, and Oakdale is on the way. Franklin County is giving us backup. I heard you want to be on hand for the arrest."

"Yeah." He snagged his jeans off the floor where he'd dropped them the night before. "How long will it take me to get there?"

"Twenty-five or thirty minutes, at best, from Nick's place." Steve paused. "Considering your personal involvement in this case, your presence isn't protocol, Mark."

"I know that. I won't do anything stupid."

Silence.

"Look, I'll keep a low profile, okay?" Mark shoved his second leg into the jeans and held his breath for several eternal seconds before Steve responded.

"Consider that an order. Let me give you the directions."

Relieved, Mark opened the notebook on his night-stand and jotted down cryptic notes as Steve spoke.

"Thanks. I'll be in touch." Ending the call, Mark reached for his Glock and tucked it into the holster on his belt. He'd do his best to see that Emily's wishes were honored, but he wouldn't lose much sleep if Edwards had to be taken down.

When he stepped into the hall, he found Nick waiting.

"I heard your BlackBerry. What's up?"

"They found Edwards."

"Give me three minutes."

"I thought you were taking the day off?"

"Not when there's a job to finish," Nick called over his shoulder as he jogged down the hall.

Before Mark could protest, Nick disappeared through his bedroom door. Once again, Mark was grateful for his support. Last night, during the long hours in the emergency room, Nick hadn't said much. But his presence had spoken volumes then, as it did now.

Two and a half minutes later, Nick joined him in the kitchen. "Let's roll."

Light was just beginning to tinge the sky pink as they headed west. Mark craved a cup of coffee, needing the jolt of caffeine to clear the cobwebs from his brain. He suspected Nick did too. But he didn't want to waste precious minutes with a stop. And since he was behind the wheel this time, he decided for both of them. No coffee.

They drove the first fifteen minutes without talking, the pink-tinged sky giving way to pale blue as the sun rose behind them. Finally Mark broke the silence.

"Believe it or not, Emily's worried about Edwards."

Nick looked toward him. "That doesn't surprise me."

"She thinks he's got major psychological problems. And she made me promise to do my best not to let him get hurt."

"That doesn't surprise me, either."

"Take the lead on this, okay?" Mark flexed his fingers on the wheel, keeping his gaze fixed on the road. "We both know I shouldn't even be there. And I promised Steve I'd stay in the background."

"Okay."

They lapsed into silence again.

Twelve minutes later they joined their fellow agents and a detective from Oakdale, who were parked on a side road in the rural area. Their vantage point atop a small hill offered a good view of the landscape below from behind a thick, concealing screen of foliage.

One of the agents came to meet them while the other kept his binoculars trained on a location out of their sight. Nick stepped forward.

"Morning, Kurt. Where is he?"

"About four hundred yards past the crest of the hill. His car's at the entrance. There's only one road in and out, and deputies from Franklin County have both ends covered." He nodded to a patrol car off to one side.

"Does Edwards know you're here?"

"If he does, he hasn't given any indication of it. And he doesn't appear to be armed."

"Don't count on it." Mark spoke for the first time. "And trust me—the guy's a good shot."

"Understood. You want to take a look?"

"Yes."

When they reached the top of the hill, Mark recognized the other agent as a sniper from the SWAT team. The man handed his binoculars to Mark. "He's in the top right quadrant. Crazy place to make an arrest, isn't it?"

Without responding, Mark lifted the binoculars to his eyes and surveyed the scene below.

Holy Cross Cemetery was tucked into a small, sheltered valley in the rolling landscape and surrounded by a wrought-iron fence. A slight mist hung over the headstones, giving the place an ethereal quality. The two-acre plot was peaceful and serene, the stillness broken only by the morning song of birds as they greeted the new day. A silver four-door Toyota Camry was parked at the entrance gate.

It took Mark mere seconds to spot Dale Edwards. The gray-haired man was sitting with his back against a granite headstone, his head lowered against his raised knees, his shoulders slumped. He was holding something, but it didn't look like a weapon.

"He hasn't moved since we arrived," Kurt told them.

Despite his antipathy toward Edwards, the dejection and defeat in the man's posture as he kept solitary vigil at the grave Mark assumed held the remains of his wife and son almost made him feel sorry for the man.

Almost.

But that didn't mean he was any less committed to bringing him to justice.

Handing the binoculars to Nick, he stepped back and waited for his friend to look the terrain over and call the shots.

"Okay." Nick turned to the SWAT team member. "Brett, pick a spot and alert me once you're in position."

In a case like this, a sniper was only supposed to shoot if a life was threatened. But Mark decided it couldn't hurt to remind him. As the agent turned toward the car to retrieve his rifle, Mark spoke again, honoring his promise to Emily. "We're going to try to do this without taking the guy out."

The other agent gave him a steady look. "Always."

While Brett moved aside to insert the earpiece for his voice activated radio and load his rifle, Nick discussed the ops plan with Mark, Kurt, and Bill Montgomery from Oakdale.

"Bill, let's have you stick close to Edwards's car. Mark, you cover the front entrance. You should be able to get behind that equipment shed near the gate without being seen. And remember . . . you're only there for insurance. If any shots have to be fired, we'll fire them. Kurt, you and I can circle around the back. We can use those larger monuments on either side of Edwards as cover. I'll give you a hand signal before I let him know he has company."

When Brett rejoined them, Nick filled him in on the plan as he worked his own earpiece into position. "Okay, we're set. Let's do it."

With a nod, Brett moved toward a ridge closer to the cemetery while the rest of the group headed down the hill.

Fifteen minutes later, from his position behind the equipment shed, Mark had a good view of Edwards. The man hadn't moved a muscle. He was dressed in a cotton shirt and brown slacks, and if he had a gun it was well-concealed. But Mark's instincts told him the man was unarmed.

He watched as Kurt and Nick silently moved into position, guns drawn. In order to avoid being seen, they'd had to give the cemetery a wide berth as they headed around the fence to approach from behind. Brett would be in position by now too, his crosshairs trained on Edwards.

As Mark drew his gun, he recalled Emily's request. And was beginning to better understand it. It was hard to reconcile the older man thirty yards away with the person who had meticulously planned and executed two murder attempts. This guy didn't look like some cold-blooded killer who placed zero value on life. He looked more like a shattered, grief-stricken husband and father who'd simply reached the end of his emotional endurance and snapped.

All at once, Nick gave the signal.

"Mr. Edwards, FBI. You're under arrest. Stand up and raise your hands above your head." Nick's clipped command reverberated in the quiet air.

Edwards didn't move.

"Mr. Edwards, stand up." Nick tried again, raising his volume.

After several moments of silence, the man slowly lifted his head. His eyes were glazed, and at the utter desolation on his face, an unwanted twinge of sympathy tugged at Mark's heart.

"Stand up," Nick repeated a third time, his tone more forceful.

Edwards rose stiffly, using the top of the rounded headstone for support.

"Raise your hands above your head."

Instead of complying, Edwards turned toward his car and lurched forward, half stumbling as he took a few halting steps. Now that the man was facing him, Mark confirmed that the small flat object in his hand wasn't a weapon. But as Edwards moved unsteadily toward him and reached up to put the item in his shirt pocket, Mark sucked in a sharp breath. The three other agents had only a back view. And from behind, it would appear Edwards was reaching for a weapon. Brett's trigger finger would be poised, ready with a subtle shift in pressure to take him out.

A surge of adrenaline shot through Mark, and he stepped from behind the equipment shed, his Glock aimed at the older man.

"Nick!" The urgency in his voice cut through the quiet air. "Tell Brett to hold his fire! He's not reaching for a gun."

The sharp command startled Edwards, and he looked toward Mark in confusion, his step faltering.

"Mr. Edwards, put your hands above your head." Mark issued the instruction slowly and deliberately as his gaze locked on the older man.

This time, after a brief hesitation, Edwards complied.

Nick and Kurt moved in. Kurt cuffed him and did a pat-down.

"He's clean."

As Nick read Edwards his rights, Mark reached over and withdrew the flat object the man had slipped into his pocket. It was a dog-eared photo of a smiling teen and pleasant-faced, middle-aged woman.

"That was my family."

Edwards's voice, as raw as a festering wound, pierced the professional detachment Mark had been struggling to hold on to. The two people in the photo had represented this man's world. A world that had ended with their deaths.

When Emily had spoken of Edwards with compassion, Mark had been less than sympathetic. But as he looked at the photo and at the shell-shocked husband and father standing two feet away from him and considered how he'd felt last night when he'd been afraid they wouldn't find Emily in time, he began to understand how a man could break when the people he built his life around—the people he loved—were abruptly taken fromhim. And he also understood why Emily had been so reluctant to take a second chance on love—and loss.

"I was doing God's work."

Jolted, Mark stared at Edwards.

"He told me to avenge their deaths. I followed his instructions, just like Abraham did with Isaac. But it doesn't bring them back. Or make the pain go away." Tears began to leak out of the corners of his eyes.

A quick exchange of glances among the agents assured Mark he wasn't the only one feeling off balance. This was like no arrest he'd ever made. Yes, Dale Edwards was homicidal. But he was also misguided. Delusional. Sick. Broken.

All along, Mark had fought to contain a growing hatred for the man who had wreaked havoc on his and Emily's lives for the past three weeks. Who had come close to killing the woman he loved. Twice.

Now, he was shocked to find the hate evaporating, much as the mist in the quiet cemetery was vanishing under the warmth of the rising sun.

Dale Edwards was a man to be pitied, not hated.

Holstering his gun, he leaned over and gently tucked the photo back into the man's shirt pocket.

As Nick and Kurt led him away, Mark followed, weaving his way among the graves while a variation of a familiar phrase echoed in his mind. And in his heart.

Have mercy on him, Father, for he knows not what he did.

"David Purnell and his friend must be thrilled." Emily handed Mark the folded-back Wednesday edition of the Post-Dispatch and sat beside him on her couch.

"I'm sure they are." Taking the paper, Mark examined the photo of Carl and Steve with the two boys, who were proudly displaying honorary badges from the Oakdale PD and letters of commendation from the FBI.

"Who knows? They could be future FBI agents or detectives in the making."

"Or, at the very least, responsible citizens who aren't afraid to get involved." He set the paper aside and angled toward her, dropping an arm around her shoulders as he played with her hair. "How's the hangover?"

"Improving. The headache's fading, I can stand without the room tilting, and my appetite is kicking back in."

He tipped his head and scrutinized her face. "Honest?"

"Cross my heart." She traced an X on her chest. "Since leaving the hospital, I've had thirty-six hours in my own house to recuperate, with the shades up and sunlight spilling in. And didn't I eat more than my share of that gourmet meal you provided tonight?" She tried to tease away the lines of worry on his face.

To her relief, they eased slightly.

"Yeah. You even pilfered part of my dessert."

"All's fair when it comes to chocolate."

Chuckling, he twirled a lock of her hair around his finger. "I talked to Coop again today."

Emily tried not to be distracted by his touch. "Didn't you talk to him on Monday too?"

"Yeah." One corner of his mouth hitched up. "He claimed to be a bit peeved about missing all the excitement."

"Let's see . . ." Emily pretended to give Coop's complaint serious consideration. "Spending your first anniversary with your wife or chasing around in sweltering weather after a murder suspect. Why do I think he wasn't all that upset?"

"I told him the same thing. He didn't argue much."

"Speaking of a murder suspect . . ." Her tone grew serious. "I appreciate whatever you did to see that Dale Edwards was taken unharmed."

"I didn't have to do anything. There was no call

374

for force. You were right, Em. He's a very sick man. At least now he'll get some help."

"I hope so." She was silent for a few moments. Then she forced herself to switch gears. "Why did you talk to Coop today?"

"To tell him I decided to accept Steve's offer."

Happiness bubbled up inside her. "You're staying?"

"Mmm-hmm." He continued to play with her hair, but his intent gaze was fixed on her eyes. "Do you remember anything about that first night in the hospital?"

"Not much." She tried to read his expression. "Why?"

"You told me to take the job."

Her pulse skipped a beat. She had no memory of that exchange. In fact, her total mental shutdown was the most frustrating thing about the whole experience. From the time the full effects of the drug kicked in until the early hours of Monday morning, she could remember nothing.

But she did recall that Mark had dominated her thoughts as she began to lose awareness. And she remembered thinking how ironic it was that she was the one who seemed poised to die when all along she'd worried that Mark might be taken from *her*, as Grant had been.

She also remembered feeling regret. And thinking that if she had it to do over again, she'd live each day fully and without fear.

Those were her last coherent memories.

Over the past couple of days, as she'd rested and regrouped, she'd reflected on her final thoughts as she'd prepared to die. And she'd reaffirmed the decision she'd made Sunday night as consciousness faded—that given another chance, she'd move forward with Mark.

But she hadn't realized she'd voiced it.

Nor had she found a suitable opportunity to bring up the subject. Mark had been busy at the office with paperwork, his visits had been brief, and she'd been feeling out of sorts. And it wasn't a subject she'd wanted to talk about over the phone.

"You were pretty disoriented on Sunday night. I understand you might not have meant what you were implying." Mark took her hand and wove their fingers together, picking up the conversation when she remained silent. "It was the other thing you said that convinced me to take the job."

"What other thing?" She gave him a wary look.

"You said you loved me."

Warmth suffused her cheeks, but before she could respond he continued. "I'm sure you have no memory of that, either. But I hoped it reflected what was in your heart, even if your mind hadn't quite accepted it yet."

"You were willing to take that chance?" A sense of wonder filled her.

"Yes. Because *I* love *you*."

Fireworks began to go off somewhere in the

region of her heart. "I don't remember saying that to you. But your instincts were right."

He went absolutely still. "You want to spell that out for me?"

It was time to take the leap. Time to take the lessons the experience of the past few weeks had taught her and put them into practice.

It was time to let trust replace fear.

"I love you too."

His lips were on hers in an instant, his hands framing her face as he told her in the silent, eloquent language of love how much her declaration meant to him. The kiss played havoc with her pulse, and when he pulled her close, she couldn't tell if the thudding against her chest was his heart or hers. Or both.

"I want to marry you, Emily."

"I think I'd like that." A slow smile curved her lips, and as she pulled back far enough to trace the outline of his strong jaw she felt a muscle twitch beneath her fingertip.

"When?"

"We've been back together for less than a month. We probably shouldn't rush things."

"So next week would be too soon?"

He grinned, but she could tell he was more than half serious.

"Maybe a bit. Besides, you have to go back to Quantico for a while. How about a Christmas wedding?"

"That's four months away."

"It will give us a chance to plan."

"I already have plans." He leaned down and nibbled at her lips.

"If you keep that up, you'll wear me down," she murmured.

"That's the plan. Remember?"

Chuckling, she drew back. "Where is your patience, Agent Sanders?"

"I think I lost is somewhere in those green eyes of yours."

"Look at it this way. We'll have time to arrange a wonderful honeymoon."

"Do you have any place in particular in mind?" He gave her a lazy smile.

"I was kind of thinking about a nice, secluded cabin at Wren Lake."

"How come I already knew that?"

"Because I'm predictable?"

"In a good way."

She wrinkled her nose. "Predictable can also mean boring."

Chuckling, he pulled her close. "Trust me, Em. You are never boring."

"I think I'll make proving that to you a priority at Wren Lake."

She gave him an impish grin, and his eyes deepened in color.

"Then I heartily second the motion for Wren Lake."

His BlackBerry began to vibrate against her hip, and she gave him a questioning look when he hesitated.

Making no attempt to hide his irritation, he finally pulled it off his belt and glanced at the caller ID. Sliding it back into its holder, he reached for her again. "Now where were we?"

"Do you need to take that?"

"No. It was just Coop. I'll call him later."

She snuggled beside him. "Do you think he'll be surprised about our news?"

"Not a chance."

"Why not?"

"He had me pegged two days after the shooting. And a few days after that, he started dropping hints about the two of us. When I explained that our very different lives weren't conducive to romance, he responded with three words."

"Which were . . . ?"

"Love changes things."

"Hmm." She considered that. "I suppose he's right. But it's a good change, isn't it?"

Smiling, Mark drew her into the circle of his arms. And in the instant before his mouth once again claimed hers, his response whispered against her lips.

"The best. For always."

Acknowledgments

Although this is book 2 in my Heroes of Quantico series, it's actually the first one I wrote. And when the idea began to percolate in my mind, I was more than a bit intimidated by the amount of research I would need to do to ensure that my book accurately portrayed police and FBI procedure.

Many people assisted me along the way, and I'd like to offer my thanks to a few who went above and beyond.

To twenty-one-year FBI veteran Tom Becker, now chief of police in Frontenac, Missouri, who offered me great insights—with great patience. Not only did he answer my many questions (and follow-up questions!), he also agreed to read my manuscript. And his diligence in doing so put the final polish of authenticity on this book. What a trouper! *An Eye for an Eye* wouldn't have come together as well as it did without his gracious and generous assistance.

To Captain Ed Nestor from the detective division of the Chesterfield, Missouri, Police Department, who gave me a thorough behind-the-scenes tour (that convinced me I *never* want to be arrested!) and spent hours answering my questions. His input was invaluable.

To Captain Craig Koehler of the Illinois State Police, who read the final manuscript with a fresh eye. His perceptive comments and suggestions greatly enhanced the story.

To fellow author and nurse Patricia Davids, who reviewed and tweaked the medical sections of the book.

To all those who organize and present at the Citizen Police Academy I attended. I came away from that experience with a renewed appreciation for the dedication and courage of police officers.

To the fabulous folks at Revell—Jennifer Leep, Kristin Kornoelje, Twila Bennett, Cheryl Van Andel, Michele Misiak, Carmen Pease, Claudia Marsh, Deonne Beron, Janelle Mahlmann—and so many more who have helped bring this book to market. You are a great team, and I feel blessed to work with you.

And of course, to my agent, Chip MacGregor of MacGregor Literary, who persevered until he found the perfect home for this series.

On a personal note, my love and thanks go to my husband Tom, who has shared in the excitement of my suspense debut every step of the way, and to my mom and dad, whose parenting skills are worthy of the hall of fame.

Finally, a caveat. Readers familiar with the world of law enforcement may notice that in a few cases I took a bit of dramatic license with protocols. But beyond those situations, I have tried to be as true to police and FBI procedure as possible.

Irene Hannon, who writes both romance and romantic suspense, is the bestselling author of more than thirty novels. Her books have been honored with the coveted RITA Award from Romance Writers of America (the "Oscar" of romantic fiction), the HOLT Medallion, and a Reviewer's Choice Award from *Romantic Times BOOKreviews* magazine. A former corporate communications executive with a Fortune 500 company, Irene now writes full time. In her spare time, she enjoys singing, long walks, cooking, gardening, traveling, and spending time with family. She and her husband make their home in Missouri.

To learn more about Irene and her books, visit www.irenehannon.com.

Center Point Publishing
600 Brooks Road ● PO Box 1
Thorndike ME 04986-0001 USA

(207) 568-3717

US & Canada:
1 800 929-9108
www.centerpointlargeprint.com